To Caroline

1

Typical, William Dougal thought. *How bloody inconvenient.*

He was standing just inside the door of his supervisor's room in the History Department. Three yards away, a corpulent, tweed-covered shape sprawled on the oatmeal carpet, to the right of the desk. The eyes and the tongue protruded from its bloated face towards Dougal in the doorway.

No doubt about it: the life had been sucked out of Doctor Gumper. Its absence left a chilly vacuum in the overheated atmosphere.

Dougal felt lightheaded and detached. *Don't panic.* It must have been a heart attack, he told himself; Gumper had always been pink with comfortable living and irritation.

The angle-poise lamp on the desk was switched on, spilling a puddle of light over the body. Did that mean that Gumper had died recently? Probably not – the lamp would have been on for hours, for the room was badly lit and the dull February day outside had been drab and overcast.

Suddenly Dougal caught sight of a detail he had missed before. The light was glinting on a filament of nylon which dangled from Gumper's neck, to the left of his Adam's apple, down to the floor. Dougal's mind clouded with the monstrous necessity of believing what he was seeing.

Not a heart attack: murder. He grappled with the idea, but it refused to succumb. Why should Gumper be killed – a dogmatic lecturer in paleography, whose only distinction was a belief that the proper study of mankind was a medieval script called Caroline Minuscule? And why did he, Dougal, have to be the one to find the body?

The nylon dug deep into the flesh of the neck. Dougal could trace the line of its passage. A garotte made the whole business so much stranger, he thought, as shivers shot through him. It suggested a degree of professionalism or premeditation on the part of the killer, which didn't tie in with a domestic crime of passion committed by a jealous wife, a disgruntled student or a competitive colleague.

A killer was the natural corollary to Gumper's corpse; he had forgotten that until now. Fear took over, and his mouth went dry, as if the moisture there had been scooped up by a powerful vacuum cleaner. The symptom was almost reassuring in the familiarity of what it portended. He kicked the door open – it was still ajar, as it had been when he came in – and stumbled across the linoleum of the passage to the lavatory opposite. He knelt like a supplicant before the bowl – he noticed gratefully that it was clean – closed his eyes and lost his lunch.

He pulled the chain and washed his hands, scalding them with the hot water in his nervousness. He dried them on the roller towel, feeling faintly surprised that routine should assert itself at such a time: toilet training must go deep.

The future stretched uninvitingly before him. What the hell was he going to do? Decision making was not his forte and he had a horror of situations which forced him to make them rapidly. He looked at the pale face in the mirror and it stared back at him, blank with uncertainty.

The police? He imagined how it would go – walking down to the Departmental secretary's office; trying to explain what had happened, which would take time because at first she would be more interested in doing her nails and then she would think he was trying to make a fool of her; the typist would gawp; they would ring the police and wait uncomfortably together before and after they came; there would be pots of tea, awkward silences, questions and statements, all of which would probably drag on into tomorrow.

Dougal swerved away from this unpleasant scenario. With his hand on the doorknob of the lavatory, he considered the alternative – a discreet withdrawal, which would inconvenience no one (certainly not Gumper) and save him a ruined evening. It could hardly affect the police's investigations. Nobody had seen him slipping away. And Doctor Gumper's desk diary would support the innocent deception, for it contained no record of an appointment with Dougal today – the arrangement had been vague: that he should drop in at some point before Friday with the transcription he should have done last week, prepared to discuss the general progress of his work. To go now would be like seeing someone shoplifting and doing nothing about it. It wasn't important.

The thought of Amanda hardened his resolve. She was doing the cooking tonight – beef Stroganoff at Dougal's request and under protest. Missing dinner could prove worse than tactless, whatever the reason.

His briefcase, though – that was still in Gumper's room. The thought of having to go back tempted him to change his mind and face the lesser evils of the secretary and the police. And what about fingerprints? . . . But no, he'd only touched the door on the outside. Anyway, he had been there perfectly legitimately last week. *(Well, Mr Dougal, your contribution to . . . um . . . scholarship this term hardly constitutes an auspicious beginning to the New Year's . . . um . . . labour.)* But perhaps the police could estimate the age of fingerprints by the degree of clarity they had, or the presence of others overlying them.

Some part of his mind, which had nothing to do with the semirational assessment of pros and cons, made its judgment: go, while it was still possible. He hadn't touched the doorknob . . . thank God the door had been left ajar . . . by the murderer.

Another factor supported his decision to retreat: he hadn't liked Doctor Gumper, a balloon-shaped man with colourless eyes behind sandy eyelashes, inflated to bursting point with the unstable gas of his own pomposity. Gumper's book-lined study reflected the man he had been − it was a cocoon of stale air where it was impossible to imagine anyone laughing or crying. It was on the first floor of the History Department, but Dougal had always thought of it as the concrete bunker beneath the ivory tower. Doctor Gumper, revelling in his status as an expert, had not been content to patronize kindly those with inferior intellectual attainments. His sarcasm had been gratuitously unpleasant; he had used his complacency as a weapon of offense. His muted spite hinted at failed ambition − a professorship, perhaps, or even a CBE for services to scholarship.

Dougal realized with a slight jolt, as old assumptions cracked like ice in the sudden thaw of new certainties, that he was really rather grateful to the person who had killed Doctor Gumper, despite the problems he had caused. It would be a relief to have to find a less abrasive supervisor.

One thought nagged him, though − what if someone *had* seen him in the building this evening? It was unlikely, he knew, but he decided to forestall the possibility of suspicion by going up to the Graduate Common-Room on the second floor before leaving the college.

He slid back the bolt on the lavatory door and braced himself for the regrettable necessity of going back to Gumper's room. In the corridor, he stood listening for a second, holding his breath. A typewriter was clattering somewhere below – from the secretary's office? – like hail-stones in slow motion on a tin roof. He heard a laugh which he recognized upstairs – it grated on his ears: Philip Primrose must be making the Common-Room unfit for human habitation again. Too bad.

Dougal shouldered open Gumper's door and stepped quietly into the room.

His briefcase lay on the chair between the desk and the door. He looked at it for an instant as if he had never seen it before, noticing its brown shabbiness, the stitching in an advanced stage of dissolution and the leather torn and scuffed.

He looked involuntarily past it and realized for the first time that Gumper's body was surrounded by a sea of scattered papers. He bent closer – most of them were photographs or photostats of manuscripts, mainly written in Caroline Minuscule. Prospective plates for Gumper's forthcoming book? All periods of the script seemed to be represented, from its blotchy origins in Merovingian cursive to the intimations of angularity in Protogothica. Better not touch anything.

Dougal shrugged. It was none of his business and it was stupid to stay here. He picked up the briefcase and edged back towards the door. He was glad to discover that, while the sight of Gumper was hardly attractive, it no longer made him retch. Progress of a sort.

He pulled the door to behind him, but didn't close it; everything must be as he had found it. Moving softly and swiftly, he headed for the stairs. The clock on the half-landing said a quarter past five – shit, the whole thing could only have taken two or three minutes.

The passage on the second floor was identical to the one below – a bare expanse of linoleum with half a dozen dirty cream doors opening off it; like the one below, it was also empty. Dougal slipped into the Graduate Common-Room – the door at the end. It was large and shabbily furnished; scuffed armchairs stood in clusters, flanked by severely rectangular coffee tables on the resiliently grey carpet. A hot drinks machine loomed uninvitingly in the corner by the window. It produced hot water for its clients, offering a generous choice of six shades of brown. On good days it provided plastic cups as well. The walls, painted with the regulation pastel green of the college, had been partially covered with glowing travel posters depicting the sort of places which were generally better in two dimensions than in three or four.

The room was not full. Philip Primrose, who seemed to live in the Department, was effortlessly dominating a little group in the corner by the hot water machine. A few individuals sat elsewhere, sheltering behind newspapers – protective screens, thought Dougal, and counted two *Guardians*, one *Times* and one defiant *Daily Mirror*.

Primrose glanced up in mid-sentence, as if scenting fresh prey, but no one else even looked at him.

Dougal walked casually to the notice board, his muscles feeling as taut as piano wires. It was so tempting to give way to the urge to confide: oh, by the way, someone's gone and strangled Gumper downstairs. He pretended to read the small ads on the board instead. Usually they fascinated him: they were peepshows on other people's lives, glimpses of alien mythologies – 'Vegetarian (Vegan) nonsmoking Feminist seeks flat share with similar . . .'; 'Will the person who stole my briefcase from the library PLEASE act like a rational & responsible adult . . .'

Today, though, while his eyes were on the board, his attention was elsewhere. Had the killer been looking for something among that jumble of papers on Gumper's floor? Had he found it? Did its presence (or absence) provide the reason for Gumper's death? Perhaps Gumper had lived a double life.

Dougal forced his mind away from the problems downstairs. With luck, they wouldn't be his. But he wasn't safe yet and he couldn't afford to ignore his surroundings.

Philip Primrose was telling an anecdote about Oxford, his favourite subject (apart from himself), which involved much slapping of his plumply tubular thighs. Dougal had no need to listen or to look. He knew the story and could visualize the way it was being told and received – Primrose's audience (a good one: four people) was like habitual television viewers, watching and hearing without concentration, almost without interest: a vacuum was being filled, and that was sufficient.

Dougal turned away from the notice board and sat heavily down in a nearby armchair, which a previous occupant had angled away from the rest of the room. He found himself facing a poster showing sunset over the Atlas Mountains – a surreal landscape with a romantically clothed Arab perched on a camel in the foreground, brandishing a musket invitingly at the camera. Underneath, the caption read, MOROCCO: REALM OF TIMELESS BEAUTY; someone had added a comma with a red felt-tip pen, and the words BAKSHEESH & BUGGERY. He wished he could be there, away from that disgusting object downstairs which had forced its way into his life.

He opened his briefcase on the assumption that it was better to look as if he was doing something. It contained a green envelope file with his notes, an eight-by-ten photograph of a page of manuscript, which he should have returned, together with his transcription, to Doctor Gumper last Thursday, a library book – Sandys' *History of Classical Scholarship in the Middle Ages*, volume I, and a green-jacketed Penguin crime novel.

Without hesitation, he chose the latter. His place was marked by a photograph of Amanda. He tried to read, but Gumper in memory and Primrose in actuality kept intervening. Dougal glanced at his watch: seventeen minutes past five; in five minutes he would start walking to the Marlborough and get there for opening time. He wanted a pint of beer in the padded security of the pub more than he could ever remember wanting anything; he hoped to God that no one discovered Gumper before he had time to leave the building and anaesthetize the nightmare with alcohol.

The rambunctious bellow of Primrose's laughter rolled over the Common-Room – he had evidently reached the climax of his anecdote. Dougal had a sudden craving to leap up and hit Primrose over the head with a coffee table. Or, more subtly, to whisper in his ear that everyone in the Department called him Madame Pee-Pee behind his back (which wasn't true – only Dougal did).

Oh, God, Primrose was starting up his seduction routine, prefacing it with a story from Cambridge, where his parents lived. Dougal had watched the routine in action several times during the last few months. It never varied, though its object altered, usually for the worse, every week or so. Primrose had started in October with the prettiest postgraduate female in the Department. The technique involved the closest physical proximity (without any breach of decorum), cups of coffee from the hot drinks machine, a breathless résumé, or rather extended exposition, of Pee-Pee's academic career to date and The Invitation. The intended victim would make her excuses – husbands, boyfriends, previous engagements and, on one glorious occasion just before a seminar, a blunt dismissal from a student from Texas: 'Ah, piss off, prune-face, you make me wanna puke.' Primrose had reached the spots and spectacles at the plainer end of the spectrum, but his ardour was undiminished.

Dougal stared at his book and monitored the conversation behind him; it was preferable to listening to his own thoughts, after all. At present Primrose's affections seemed to be directed towards a fat girl with lank black hair and a pendulous lower lip. Dougal thought she was called Muriel. Pee-Pee was sympathizing with her, at great length, on the misfortune she had suffered – getting her first degree at a red-brick university. 'Of course,' Primrose consoled, 'while Oxbridge undoubtedly marks a chap for life, it doesn't mean that the quality of the academic experience is any less valid elsewhere.' Big of you, thought Dougal.

He saw with relief that his five minutes were up. He closed the book, returned it to his briefcase and struggled out of the low-slung armchair. Primrose looked across the room at him, his gold-rimmed spectacles twinkling with sociability. Dougal avoided his eye and sidled out of the Common-Room into the corridor. He began to run down the stairs, three at a time, in his relief, but slowed to a more decorous pace as the thought occurred that it might look as if he was running away from something. He resisted the temptation to glance at Gumper's door on the first-floor landing. It wasn't difficult. As he went down the last flight of stairs, he realized that he had automatically pursed his eyes to thin slits. See no evil, or at least not too much evil.

His habitual optimism was returning; it didn't obliterate the events of the last few minutes, but it rearranged their contours in his mind. It was going to be all right:

no one would connect him with Gumper's death – his presence in the building was explained by his visit to the Common-Room. The worst he need expect was routine questioning by the police at some point, for presumably they would check all Gumper's students as a matter of course.

The corridor on the ground floor was empty, too. Dougal skipped out of the building, feeling like a reprieved prisoner, and turned left into the dimly lit alley which led to the college's side entrance. There was no one in sight.

He set out briskly, swinging his briefcase. He was only ten yards away from the Department when a burly shape slid out of a darkened doorway into his path.

'Hullo. I've been waiting for you.' The stranger moved a little closer. 'I'd like to have a chat.'

2

The second shock of the evening was worse than the first. Dougal stood like a statue, rigid with fear. It couldn't be the police already, and knowing who the man must be, he wanted to run. But the weight of his knowledge was like a physical impediment to movement.

'Please,' the stranger said.

The monosyllable changed everything. The man might have been asking him for a light. Dougal looked up at the man's face – he was several inches taller – faintly illuminated by the light over the doorway. It told him nothing.

'What do you want?' Dougal heard himself saying. He was rather surprised that he was able to say anything at all.

'To talk to you. Wouldn't take a moment. We could have a drink?'

Damn it, thought Dougal, why was the man being so polite? You don't expect probable murderers to specialize in old-fashioned courtesy. It was unsettling. It was also reassuring – he was in a position to refuse (he hoped) and rush off home by way of a crowded, well-lit tube train. Perversely, this drove him to accept. Afterwards he wondered why he had done so, but at the time it seemed natural – frighteningly automatic, almost – to prefer the stranger's company to his own.

The man suggested going to the Lamb. 'It's a bit of a walk, I know, but I imagine we'd both be more comfortable away from all this.' He waved his hand vaguely in the direction of the History Department. Dougal nodded.

The stranger led the way down the alley and they walked without obvious haste out of the college. In the street they walked side by side, a yard apart, down to Russell Square. It had begun to drizzle; the garden in the middle of the square looked dank and uninviting. Dougal's companion put up his umbrella and sheltered them both.

Neither of them spoke – Dougal had the uncanny sensation that they were both too busy sizing up each other's physical presences, like strange dogs uncertain whether to sniff or snarl.

Lambs Conduit Street appeared on the right. They crossed it diagonally and walked into the crowded warmth of the pub.

'What can I get you?'

'Special Bitter, please.' Dougal changed his mind. 'No, better make it Ordinary.' There were two empty high stools by the window ledge just inside the door. Dougal put his briefcase on one of them and straddled the other. 'I'll keep these for us.'

'Standing and drinking is so uncomfortable,' the man said. 'I've never been able to understand why some people actually prefer it. Shan't be a moment.'

The stranger nudged his way skillfully into the ebb and flow of drinkers popping in for a quick one or two after work. The atmosphere was smoky and loud with conversation. Dougal watched the back view of his companion as far as intervening bodies allowed him to do so. It was the first time he had been able to see even part of him clearly. The first impression was one of size – he was comfortably over six foot and the navy-blue raglan overcoat he wore made him look broad to match. Dougal caught a glimpse of dark blue pinstripe trousers beneath it, and gleaming black shoes.

The man turned and weaved carefully through the crowd. He put down the drinks – a pint and a double whisky – on the window ledge. Dougal felt envious of the way his hands were steady.

He sat down, raised his glass and drank. He looked with frank curiosity at Dougal, who felt he might as well do the same. If the man's back view had suggested a prosperous professional of some sort, the front view amply confirmed it. His hair, flecked with grey and thinning at the temples, was neatly cut; the face radiated a well-fed, anonymous respectability – the man looked distinguished, thought Dougal, though it was odd that he had so few lines. He was wearing a silk shirt, a pair of plain gold cuff links, and the sort of tie which has school or regimental associations.

His companion noticed the direction of Dougal's glance and, surprisingly, chuckled. 'I'm from Charterhouse today.'

Dougal laughed.

'My name's Hanbury – James Hanbury.'

'William Dougal.' They shook hands solemnly. Dougal wondered where the hell this was all leading. Had he been stupid to give his own name?

Hanbury ran his finger round the rim of his glass. 'I was in that . . . seminar room, is it? – the room next to Gumper's – half an hour ago. The door was open, so I could hear very well.' He took a long sip of his whisky.

The pause gave Dougal time to think of the implications – as he suspected Hanbury had intended. Hanbury must have heard him go in and out, twice, of Gumper's room; if he had been able to see as well, he would have noticed Dougal's indecision – possibly seen him wiping the door handle. But it didn't make sense: if Hanbury was the murderer, why should he go out of his way to meet Dougal? Supposing Dougal's arrival had prevented him leaving the building, why hadn't he slipped away while Dougal was in the Common-Room?

'You knew Dr Gumper?' enquired Hanbury blandly.

Knew. So Hanbury probably had killed Gumper. Dougal fought an instinct to recoil physically; this was the first killer he had met and he was surprised that the urge to recoil was so weak. In fact, he realized, the only thing which really concerned him was the worry about his own safety: where and why does a killer stop killing?

'He was my tutor,' he said at last, because there seemed no reason not to.

'Really? What's your subject?'

Dougal felt suddenly oppressed by the unreality of the situation – this could be an interview with a prospective employer, or a heavy-going chat with an elderly relative.

'The influence of the Carolingian court on the transmission of pagan Latin literary texts in the early Middle Ages.' The words rolled out mechanically: so many people asked this question, and most of them changed the subject when they heard the answer.

'Dr Gumper was an expert on the period?'

'Yes, I suppose so. He thought so, and I suppose he was. He knew most about the script, of course.'

'Would I be right in thinking' – Hanbury took another long swallow of his whisky – 'that you yourself have a . . . working knowledge of the subject?'

Dougal suspected the conversation had reached a crossroads of some sort – Hanbury had spoken like a chess player making a gambit which might prove crucial. He hesitated before replying, choosing his words with care.

'I've an overall grasp of it, you could say. Nothing like Gumper's, though. I know a fair amount about the script – Caroline Minuscule. I know where to look for information.' On impulse he added, 'One of the reasons I chose the subject was its obscurity. The less work that's been done on something, the easier it is to produce adequate research without too much effort. You don't have to bother with so many secondary sources. Big fish and little ponds.'

Hanbury looked at Dougal reflectively. 'That's very interesting. Have a cigarette.' He pulled out a packet of tipped Caporals.

They both had one. Dougal inhaled the pungent tobacco with relief; he hadn't noticed how much he wanted a cigarette. The conversation lapsed: the second round will start in ninety seconds, thought Dougal. What was going through Hanbury's mind? He was probably a murderer and knowing that made him, Dougal, some kind of an accessory after the fact. If Hanbury was trying to incriminate him, he was taking a great many unthinkable risks in order to – what? – how did this conversation groom Dougal for the role of culprit? The simple answer was that it didn't. The only conclusion that Dougal could see, not that it seemed a plausible one, lay in the one common link between himself and Gumper – knowledge of the Carolingian period. But it was unbelievable that someone should be killed for that knowledge – and that the killer should risk discovery by immediately approaching another source.

His own reactions puzzled him, too – he should be running for the police, or at least away from here, instead of having an amicable drink with a person who he had every reason to suspect was a murderer. He was scared, yes, but the fear was of the vicarious sort induced by a good horror film – no, it was more real than that. In a way, he supposed, the most frightening thing was the absence of any revulsion towards the act or the man who had done it. If he was going to be honest with himself, his predominant emotions were curiosity and a muted but noticeably euphoric sensation of excitement; the latter, no doubt, was not entirely unconnected with a pint of Young's on a recently emptied stomach.

Hanbury was massaging his fingers, Dougal noticed, as if the process gave him pleasure. He had well-kept hands – long and graceful, with none of the wrinkles or brown spots of age; the nails were large, square and obviously carefully manicured. He stroked his hands as if they were a cat on his lap – Dougal found it vaguely disturbing.

Hanbury spoke again, almost apologetically: 'You look rather older than the average student.'

It took Dougal a second or two to catch the question mark which dangled unobtrusively from this remark; Hanbury wanted some background information, but was trying not to be too blunt about it.

'I'm twenty-nine. I was left a little money by an aunt last year and decided to do another degree. Or do some work towards one, anyway.'

'No grant? How very self-sacrificing!'

Five years ago Dougal would have blushed; now he just blushed internally. 'Not really. I'd been away from education for seven years and I thought it would make a change.'

'What had you done before then?' Hanbury was openly curious and it surprised Dougal: why should it matter? It was, in any case, a question he disliked answering.

'Oh, this and that. The sort of things which don't make up a nice curriculum vitae. I travelled abroad quite a lot; worked in a library; drove a minicab.' All true, if misleadingly selective.

It was time to take the offensive. 'How about you? What do you do for a living?'

'Jack of all trades,' said Hanbury with a smile. Something told Dougal that he disliked the question as well. 'At present I suppose you could say I'm in the lost and found business. Gumper was helping me look for something, but he backed out at the last moment . . . between you and me it caused a great deal of inconvenience. My employers were paying him very adequately for a small service – all quite above board, though perhaps not the sort of thing one need mention to the Inland Revenue – and he had accepted their terms, and they his. Mutually beneficial. Then he started being difficult. He was a greedy man, you know.'

Dougal did know; he could imagine cupidity blinding Gumper to all other considerations. It wouldn't have been greed alone, though – Gumper had liked to make himself felt, to stamp the world around him with his image.

'Really very silly,' Hanbury continued. 'I don't think he realized the sort of people my employers are. They tend to react rather sharply to threats of any kind.'

React with a well-dressed executioner, thought Dougal; *when in doubt, garotte*. He would be finding it increasingly difficult to take the conversation seriously, were it not for the silent witness of its seriousness which lay in a first floor room less than a mile away.

'Of course' – Hanbury pulled his right earlobe reflectively – 'it is rather awkward for my employers. Gumper was doing a small but important piece of work for them. And, as you say, the literary aspect of the Carolingian era is a relatively obscure field. Which brings me to the reason that I asked you for a drink. I wonder if you would be interested in doing it in his place?'

Silence fell between them again. Dougal appreciated the leisurely pace at which Hanbury was conducting the conversation. The man was staring into his glass, now, as if he found its contents absorbing. He wasn't rushing it, despite the urgency which the events of the past hour predicated. Dougal's mind grappled with the choice: it was an impossible one – how much of a security risk would Hanbury consider him to be if he refused? Would acceptance lead to something more dangerous than being an accidental accessory to murder? He blurted out, 'Look, what's all this about? I can't decide without knowing a little more.'

'My employers had asked Gumper to transcribe a page of a medieval manuscript. He was to have done a translation as well, and to have assessed its date and provenance and so forth. He had already said that the script was Caroline Minuscule. A very straightforward job for someone in your line of country. Not so easy if you don't know a serif from an ampersand and haven't the time to find out.'

'I presume the reason for all this is none of my business?' Dougal was talking to himself as much as to Hanbury, but the latter nodded. Well, it was easy enough to think of reasons, after all – maybe Hanbury worked for a fence who had been offered a valuable stolen manuscript and wanted a discreet expert opinion on it, though Dougal hardly felt he had reached that status. It was odd, nevertheless – surely there couldn't be much of a market for stolen medieval manuscripts, unless of course the hypothetical fence had a private buyer already in mind, one who wasn't overscrupulous.

Hanbury said, slowly and quietly, 'You have my word that there's no risk here at all – for yourself or anyone else. And, in return for quick, reliable work, my employers are willing to pay very generously. In cash. Ten-pound notes.' He was looking at Dougal's tatty leather jacket as he spoke and it was as if he had added, 'And you look as though you need some money too.'

It was the detail of ten-pound notes which decided Dougal. It made the whole thing possible, no longer an academic speculation. He asked what sort of amount Hanbury's employers might have in mind (to have merely asked 'How much?' would have jarred in the circumstances).

'Twelve hundred,' replied Hanbury. 'Cash on delivery with a small retainer in advance – plus a bonus for speed, perhaps. Would you be able to drop everything and concentrate on this for a day or two?'

Dougal nodded. He hardly heard the question. The idea of getting 1,200 pounds for a couple of days' work swam like a seductive mirage in his mind. He owed his landlady two months' rent. His aunt's money had somehow reduced itself to double figures. His credit cards were on the verge of changing from flexible friends to implacable usurers. Amanda was an expensive luxury.

His thoughts swerved away from the question of Hanbury's motives, from the lengths his employers were willing to go in order to get what they wanted; it was none of his business and, if it was, it lay in the province of his conscience which he had always found to be an obliging, biddable organ. It would help no one to bring the spectre of morality into this.

Despite what Hanbury had said, there must be a risk, but he couldn't for the life of him see where it was; a reasonable degree of caution should prevent the police from linking him with Hanbury, even supposing they succeeded in identifying the latter as Gumper's killer; Hanbury's employers were obviously dangerous – but surely they would only get unpleasant if, like Gumper had done, he started trying to cheat them. If he did an efficient job, why should there be any danger?

He looked across at Hanbury. 'Okay, I'm interested. What would I be working on – the original or a photograph?'

'A photograph, I'm afraid. We don't have the original.'

Yet, thought Dougal. Aloud, he said, 'That shouldn't matter too much if it's a reasonable reproduction.' A question which had been troubling him all the time they had been in the pub, worrying him somewhere below the level of conscious thought, suddenly found words which insisted on being spoken. 'Look, why did you take the chance? I know I didn't rush off to the nearest phone when I . . . when I saw it, so you might trust me from that point of view, but I don't see why you took the gamble that I had the same sort of skills as Gumper. Wasn't it a hell of a risk?'

Hanbury smiled and Dougal realized that the man was actually enjoying himself, and boggled at the thought that someone could extract pleasure from juggling with dangers. Hanbury only slightly dispelled the illusion by saying, rather in the manner of Holmes to Watson: 'The risk was minimal, in fact. Gumper and I had a little scene, you see, during which he was unusually informative. Towards the end anyway. He told me that he had given the photograph to one of his students, who should be returning it this week. He mentioned your name. One imagines he would have checked what you had done – presumably he wanted to avoid the donkey work. The very fact that you went to see Gumper suggested you knew something about the subject – paleography is hardly a popular option, I thought. Then, as you came out of his room the second time, you were carrying your briefcase – I could see through the crack of the door of the seminar room – and the initials WD were clearly visible on it. It seemed reasonable to assume that you were you, as it were.'

Dougal laughed. 'Gumperish to the very end,' he said and then realized that he must sound flippant; but perhaps it didn't matter for surely the ordinary etiquette of death would be inappropriate here.

3

Dougal went west with rush hour crowds, his mind preoccupied with the necessity of establishing an equilibrium between the memory of Gumper and the reassuring presence of 200 pounds in his wallet. Like an automaton, he changed on to the District Line at Hammersmith and got off at Turnham Green. With his eyes half-closed he walked down to Chiswick High Road, where habit drove him into an off-licence. He bought a bottle of Veuve Clicquot – might as well do things properly – half a bottle of brandy and some angosturas. The Scot who managed the place with a grim disregard for the convenience of his customers scratched his red beard, leant his great belly against the counter and said: 'Having a party, are we? If you're going to mix those, you'd be far better off with sparkling wine.' Dougal was too tired to think of an answer. He took the clanking carrier bag and left the shop, banging his thigh on a monolith constructed of beer cans on the way out. A dry Scottish chuckle followed him out into the night.

Amanda lived on the other side of the High Road, the side nearer the river. You could sense its great grey presence a quarter of a mile away, and even see a tiny square of water, framed by buildings, from the window of Amanda's room. It was a room with a view, she said, which presumably explained why the Polish landlord felt obliged to charge so much rent for it.

The house was semidetached and had seen far better days. Amanda had a large room at the back of the house on the first floor. The door was open and he went in. Amanda wasn't there, which sent a wave of desolation over him. He felt an infantile urge to scream, 'It's not fair!' But the room was as welcoming as ever. It was large, dimly lit and cavernous; there were plants everywhere – they hung from the ceiling, crouched on the floor and occupied most of the available surfaces between the two. A gas fire – of the old-fashioned type where, if you stared long enough, it was easy to see glowing Oriental palaces – hissed light and warmth. Dougal liked the carpet best of all – it was Persian, comfortably shabby, with a dark blue pattern on a red background.

There was a step behind him. He swung round to see Amanda standing in the doorway looking simultaneously cross and beautiful; she was one of the few people he knew who could combine the two.

'Hullo, love,' he said, aware of relief oozing out of him like sweat. 'Where have you been?'

'In the loo. Some bugger's gone and blocked it again. With the *Daily Telegraph*.'

The other tenants of the house were a source of endless irritation and interest to her, according to their sex. Amanda was generally on terms of mute hostility towards the women, which occasionally burst into sporadic verbal warfare when Amanda's record player was thought to be too loud, or when old Mrs Middle, to whom the sweet and sickly smell of death had clung for years, had allowed her portly marmalade pussy to defecate in the bath once more. The male inhabitants of the house, however, venerated Amanda and she returned the compliment by sending them to the doctor when they were ill and disentangling their emotional problems with the clinical competence of a heart surgeon.

On the whole, Dougal reckoned that Mrs Middle was the most likely culprit for the lavatory, but he wisely held his tongue and changed the subject by letting his carrier bag clink suggestively.

He left his own news until they were sitting on two large cushions in front of the fire. Amanda made champagne cocktails with swift efficiency, talking of what she had done today. She did freelance work for publishers – her father was managing director of a firm – and had read a couple of tedious manuscripts.

Dougal found her words almost as reassuring as the alcohol. A part of him had been secretly afraid that the whole world had shifted away from normality at five o'clock this evening, that the earthquake within his own life was merely an insignificant tremor emanating from a more general cataclysm; it was pleasant to find the fear groundless, even if it was the kind of fear which he couldn't admit to himself.

When Amanda, her long black hair swinging like a protective shield in front of her face, asked him what sort of day he had had, he told her the truth: 'Gumper got garotted and I've been offered one thousand two hundred pounds for a couple of days' work.' He had to tell someone, and she was the only person he wanted to know, in any case. If she found the whole business distasteful – and he wasn't entirely sure that he didn't himself – then the sooner he knew the better. As Amanda had been talking, a certainty had emerged unobtrusively from his mind: he cared enough for her to do what she wanted – even if it meant turning down Hanbury's offer and going through the hideously embarrassing process of talking frankly to the police. It was strange, the way that the events of the evening had clarified, almost crystallized, his feelings – about Amanda and also, to a lesser extent, about dying. Other people dying.

But Amanda's reaction, after she had been convinced that she had heard him correctly and that he wasn't mounting an elaborate hoax, came as a surprise to him: she was exhilarated by it all and pumped him for details. She made him go through everything which had happened, even down to Primrose's presence in the Common-Room. Dougal found himself wondering if she was one of those people to whom the ordinary routines of daily life were fundamentally boring – whether, had she been born thirty years earlier, she would have looked back on the war as the only time in her life when she had been properly alive. It was an uncomfortable thought and he put it away from him.

She brought to the surface many of the questions which had been in his own mind.

'Why was that old photograph worth killing Gumper? What do you think it's all about?'

'God knows,' said Dougal. 'I've not really looked at it yet. It looks like the first page of some religious book – it's in Latin. Very pretty, really, if you like that sort of thing. There's a squiggle in the top left-hand corner – *liber* something – which might tell us who owned the book at one time. By the look of the script it's lateish – and maybe written in this country.'

'Lateish?' asked Amanda.

'I should have said, it's written in Caroline Minuscule, the script I'm meant to know about. Lateish could mean it was written in the eleventh century rather than the ninth.' He was rather enjoying being able to parade his knowledge, superficial thought he knew it was. It was the first time it had actually been useful to him, he realized, and he wondered if it would be the last.

They talked aimlessly for an hour about what might possibly lie behind it all. It was like being in heavy fog in a city, Dougal said – a few square yards of clear vision and that awful feeling of limitless, hidden activity around it. Amanda said, bring on the fog lamps, and mixed another cocktail.

They were up by ten next morning, rather to Dougal's surprise; he had expected the stresses and strains of yesterday to keep him asleep for much longer; quite apart from that, he rarely got up before eleven in term-time.

Dougal made a pot of coffee and sat by the fire. Amanda wriggled into a torn silk kimono, a battlefield for faded yellow dragons, and perched cross-legged on a cushion beside him. She had forgotten to remove her makeup last night (or had they been too drunk to bother with that sort of detail?); her eyes were ringed with blue and swollen with sleep. She looked like a battered inno-cent and Dougal found the sight so pleasurable that he wondered if he was a latent sadist.

He had two clear days in front of him. Hanbury had arranged to telephone him at the pay phone outside the Graduate Common-Room the day after tomorrow, Thursday. He decided to go to the University Library today – with luck he might get the whole of it out of the way by this evening. Amanda was in a flippant mood and tried to persuade him to dress for the part by going in disguise. It irritated him, this levity, though he tried to conceal it. To her, last night's events were only one degree more real than a crime series on the television – more exciting, because it was happening to him, but still remote enough to make jokes about it. But she hadn't seen Gumper.

He switched the radio on, wondering if the murder had reached Capital Radio by now. It hadn't – perhaps Gumper's death was too insignificant for the media to take any notice. Or perhaps – a less comfortable thought – the police had their reasons for biding their time before releasing the news of it.

Two hours later, Dougal was back in Russell Square. He walked through the car park towards the back entrance of Senate House. The great tower which contained floor after floor of the library dwarfed him; Dougal felt that its architect must have designed it as a perpetual reminder that the way of learning was austere and serious; it made him want to daub slogans all over it with a red paint spray – even WEST HAM RULES would have a humanizing effect on it.

The lift took him up to the entrance of the library on the fourth floor. He flashed his plastic membership card at the porter, who ignored it, and passed through the turnstile like a sheep into a pen. Turning right he weaved his way through the crowd round the issue desk and walked through the cataloguing hall to the swing doors leading to the northern section of the library. He quickened his pace in the next room, because he caught a glimpse of a thickset back covered with a mustard-yellow tweed jacket going into the Middlesex North reading room. He really couldn't face a conversation with Primrose at this point.

The Paleography Room was at the far end of the building. Dougal was glad to see that it was nearly empty.

A couple of female archive students were muttering gloomily to one another at the table nearest the door, their heads close together over a photostat. He heard the one with glasses saying with hushed passion, 'But the ascenders are beginning to *fork*. And Bastard Anglicana would never be so scruffy . . .'

Dougal sat down at the table diagonally opposite, close to a window. He took from his pockets a small notebook, a fountain pen and the photograph. The latter was slightly dog-eared after the journey, but fortunately it was a good print. He began by transcribing the first few lines:

Aurelii Augustini doctoris de pastoribus sermo incipit. Spes tota nostra quia in Christo est et quia omnis . . . 'Here begins the sermon of the teacher Aurelius Augustine concerning shepherds. Our entire hope is in Christ . . .'

It didn't take a doctorate in divinity to recognize one of Augustine's sermons when it was so clearly announced. The capital S in *Spes* was either decorated or ornamented: on a black-and-white reproduction it was impossible to tell whether the arabesques which writhed around the letter had been done with ink or paint.

Still, the script was easy to transcribe. The abbreviations were the standard ones for the period and in any case it would be easy to find a printed text to illuminate any difficulties. But none of this made it any easier to answer the central question – why a medieval sermon should be worth 1,200 pounds and at least one death.

Although the work was relatively simple, it took well

over an hour to jot down the contents of the page; he decided to leave the translation until later. The last line ended abruptly in mid-sentence. On rather an ominous note, too: *veniet enim dies* – 'for the day will come.'

Dougal stretched and wondered which particular day St Augustine had in mind. His neck was aching and he was thirsty; he recognized the familiar signs of boredom which working in a library tended to induce in him. He needed a change of scene, he realized, and picked up the notebook and photograph and went downstairs to the refectory.

He bought a cup of coffee at the counter and took it to an empty table near the exit. The coffee tasted of mud. Peering into its murky depths, Dougal wondered why the British put up with such an awful travesty.

He pulled out the photograph and looked at it again. The hardest part was yet to come – getting an idea of the date and provenance of the manuscript. He worked out a few rough guidelines.

For a start, it was definitely written in Caroline Minuscule, rather than the only other possibility – the deliberately anachronistic Humanistica of the fifteenth century. It was easy to confuse the two. Dougal could remember Gumper being particularly unpleasant to someone (was it Primrose?) who had failed to notice the dotted 'i's and the 't's with vertical strokes reaching above their crossbars, which distinguished the later script.

Caroline Minuscule, then: anywhere between A.D. 800 and A.D. 1200. But probably later – the characters of this script were relatively tall and spiky, the ascenders of some of the letters were wedge-shaped – which might imply it had been written in Britain.

In the corner of his eye he caught a flash of mustard-yellow cruising determinedly in his direction. Oh, God, Primrose. Dougal flipped over the photograph and looked up with a smile on his face and a feeling akin to hatred in his heart. Primrose was smiling in greeting, too – a toothy grin of satisfaction. His wiry, carrot-coloured hair was smoothed down with Brilliantine and he wore a shield-encrusted tie: he was obviously dolled up for someone.

'Hullo, Bill. Mind if I join you? Don't see you here often.'

He chuckled throatily and sat down. Dougal noticed that he had another pimple beginning to erupt on his nose. He hated people calling him Bill; it was only slightly better than Willy. And he hated himself for the way he was pleasant to people he didn't like.

'Have you heard the news? About Gumper, I mean. Terrible, isn't it?'

Dougal's head jerked up. 'No. What's happened?' Very good, he told himself: just the right note of gossipy curiosity.

'He's dead. Someone murdered him.' Pee-Pee waited for Dougal to react suitably.

'Christ . . . you're joking. When? What happened?'

Primrose bent forward confidentially. 'When I got to the Department this morning, the place was swarming

35

with police. The secretary was having hysterics on the doorstep – no one was allowed in, of course. I had a word with the chap on the door, though, and it seemed someone strangled Gumper yesterday afternoon. Just walked in, bold as brass, and did it.'

Dougal offered Primrose a cigarette, took one himself and lit them both. 'Have the police any idea who did it – and the motive?'

'They weren't giving anything away. I knew better than to try to pump them. But as a matter of fact I was able to be rather useful to them.'

'You didn't see the murderer?' Dougal spoke more sharply than he had intended and wondered if Primrose had noticed.

'No, not exactly.' Primrose sounded regretful. He was absorbed in his story. 'But the police wanted to know everyone who had been in the building yesterday after lunch. I was able to help – I'd been up in the Common-Room from about two to five-thirty. This plainclothes sergeant questioned me for ages in the incident-van – they've got one parked outside the main entrance. I had to mention your name, of course.'

I bet you did, thought Dougal. 'Yes, I popped in for a few minutes to kill time before the pubs opened.' Rather an unfortunate choice of verb.

'Just after five, wasn't it?' Dougal nodded. 'I don't suppose you saw anything?'

'No, I just came straight up. There was no one around that I can remember. Oh, I think I could hear typing

from the secretary's office.' Primrose was looking a little
disappointed, so Dougal stimulated him with a question.
'Does anyone know more details?'

'Well, there's lots of rumours flying around. We all
went for a cup of coffee afterwards – me, Monica, Judith
and a few others – and pooled our information.' *You do
surprise me*, thought Dougal with elephantine sarcasm,
for once a truly sensational carcass for the scandal
vultures. 'Judith had heard he'd been garotted – you
know, when they put a thin cord round your neck like
one of those cheese slicers they use in shops.'

'Where did she get that from?' Dougal injected a touch
of incredulity into his voice: a certain spur to Primrose's
inclination to confide.

'From one of the cleaners. She's married to Bert –
that porter who doesn't believe in consonants – he was
the one who actually found the body last night, when
he was locking up.'

They talked for a few minutes more, but Dougal could
get nothing else out of him besides a predictable spate
of speculation and the forthcoming motion the Students'
Union were planning for the next meeting, deploring
violence within the college.

But as Dougal went back up the stairs to the
Paleography Room, he had to admit to himself that he
was worried. The business had seemed manageable while
knowledge of it was confined to himself and Hanbury –
and possibly Gumper, of course. But now it was no longer
private, he felt suddenly that anything could happen.

4

By the time he had sat down with the photograph in front of him he had argued himself into a more optimistic frame of mind. Really, things couldn't be better. Primrose would have heard any rumours, true or false: he had a genius for gossip. Everything pointed to the fact that the police were making no progress, just going through the routines of homicide.

While he was thinking, his eyes were resting idly on the words scribbled on the top left-hand corner of the page – *liber*... His mind, occupied with the police, executed a swift change of direction, one of those sideways strides which make puzzle solving a pleasurable activity. The words were in a later hand than the rest of the manuscript, a crabbed cursive. Suddenly they made sense; the letters and the contractions which confused them unscrambled themselves and became, with miraculous clarity, *liber monacborum sancti tumwulfi* – a book of the monks of St Tumwulf.

Dougal had never heard of St Tumwulf, which was a good sign. Even in the Middle Ages, few churches would have been dedicated to an obscure Anglo-Saxon saint. He got the relevant reference book – Knowles and Hadcock's *Medieval Religious Houses in England and Wales* – down from the shelf and checked the index. Only two monasteries had been dedicated to Tumwulf – a small pre-Conquest convent in Northumberland, the saint's birthplace, and the great abbey of Rosington in Huntingdonshire, where Tumwulf had his ministry and found his martyrdom.

The inscription must refer to Rosington, Dougal thought. It had been one of the great foundations of the Middle Ages, ranking in prestige with Glastonbury, Bury St Edmunds and Ely. Just the sort of place where you would expect a library with up-market manuscripts like this. And wasn't it a Benedictine monastery, too? – and the Benedictines had surely been important in the process of importing Caroline Minuscule as a book-hand from France and establishing it in England.

On impulse, Dougal tried the catalogue – the small one on the way out of the Paleography Room – for Rosington. His luck held – POOTERKIN, B.W., had privately published the Ph.D. thesis which he had presented to the Eric Ehrlinger Memorial University, Alabama, three years ago and had given a copy to the University of London Library: *The Abbey Library of St Tumwulf's, Rosington: a Critical Handlist of its Actual & Putative Contents in the Middle Ages, Together with a*

Summary of the Arguments for & against the Existence of a Scriptorium.

He jotted down the class number on his wrist and wandered round the shelves until he found the right place. The book was there; it was a glossy production, bound in green imitation leather with gilt lettering on the spine. Dr Pooterkin evidently had a high opinion of the value of his contribution to scholarship. Dougal leafed through it and was gratified to find that the Augustine manuscript was listed. It was still in the library there, surviving the Reformation and the upgrading of Rosington to the status of a cathedral.

The lassitude which afflicted him in libraries (it had made being a library assistant a particularly hazardous occupation) surged over him as he stood there with the book in his hand. Oh, God, he wanted to go home and collapse in an armchair with a cup of tea. And talk to Amanda. It was only three o'clock. Perhaps if he took the book out he could work at home as efficiently as here. Besides the question of provenance, which Pooterkin could settle perfectly adequately, there was only the translation to do.

The inside cover of the book sported, for some unfathomable reason, the red Reference Only label. Dougal glanced swiftly around him. There was no one behind him and on the other three sides he was protected by shelves. With practiced ease he slipped the book into his waistband, at the back where his jacket sheltered his bottom from prying eyes. Fortunately, the book was relatively thin; the only discernible effect, he thought, was that it possibly gave him a more upright carriage than usual as it nudged against his spine.

At the entrance to the tube station he bought a *Standard*. Gumper was on page three: MAFIA-STYLE MURDER OF LECTURER; it told Dougal less than Primrose knew.

When he got back to Chiswick, Amanda was typing away with a frown on her face and a growing pile of used Tipp-Ex in the ashtray.

Dougal made a pot of tea and settled down to translating. He had finished within an hour and wished he had arranged to meet Hanbury this evening instead of tomorrow.

Next morning, Thursday, he dozed towards midday in the virtuous knowledge that there was no reason to get up. Amanda did: she went shopping and later brought him coffee and *The Times* in bed. As he leafed through the paper in the direction of the crossword, his eye caught a name he knew in the obituary column.

HANBURY, *James Edward. Suddenly on February 8 in London. Funeral private.*

Dougal felt as if a safety curtain had been lowered between him and a golden future.

He didn't try to find out more about Hanbury's death. It would have been stupid to push his luck. Perhaps Hanbury's bosses were covering their tracks. Or maybe an old grudge from Hanbury's past had caught up with him. Instead, Dougal counted his blessings: Hanbury's 200 pounds retainer and the comfort of knowing that he was clear of a dangerous business.

He intended to use the money to pay off his arrears of rent. Amanda persuaded him that they deserved a night out first. It was the sort of night which ends with breakfast at the Cafe Royal. After that, there seemed little point in using the remainder for debts.

Dougal temporarily quashed his misgivings. It was a very pleasant weekend indeed – for some reason he and Amanda were happiest when the moving parts of their relationship were oiled by money. For a while they could forget the dank seediness of London. Even the weather seemed better when you had money for taxis.

His happiness was accentuated by the absence of Gumper and Hanbury – it was something just to be alive in a world where people died with such alarming frequency.

Beneath this realization lurked a less comfortable consequence of the week's events. By Sunday morning Dougal could no longer pretend to himself that it wasn't there. He extracted Amanda's attention from the colour supplement and tried to explain it to her.

'Two murders, and I saw one of the bodies and collaborated with the killer. The funny thing was, it didn't revolt me. And it doesn't now.'

'You were sick after finding Gumper.' Amanda always preferred other people to be scrupulously honest with themselves.

'That was just . . . a physical reaction. It didn't upset my morals.' The last word embarrassed Dougal: morals were safer left in the abstract. He hurried on. 'And I didn't mind about Hanbury, except for the money. It's as if they didn't matter to me.'

'So? Does that make you some kind of superman? It might be useful if you wanted to be an undertaker.'

'Do you think it would have had the same effect on you?'

Amanda considered the question, her eyes straying back to the magazine on her lap. 'I don't know,' she said at length; and her tone said, 'I don't particularly care, either.' She put an end to the conversation by saying, 'You're potty,' amiably enough, it was true, but Dougal felt slightly cheated. He told himself that they were very different people, that this was a large part of her attraction for him.

And he thought of his father briefly, how he used to tell bedtime stories about killing Germans with his Sten gun. But that wasn't the same, of course. That was in the war.

Life returned to straitened normality with surprising rapidity; it was as if that Tuesday had been a hiccough in the usual rhythm, a day whose significance could safely be disregarded because it was so unlike everything else. Dougal did a little desultory work, wondering yet again why he had chosen such a strange subject. Barring an economic miracle, this would have to be his last term.

The thought of retiring from being a student failed to worry him unduly; the research had always been on the periphery of his life, an activity to lend occupation to spare moments, a tidy answer to supply when people at parties asked him what he did.

He asked Amanda what she felt about moving out of London altogether and ending this fiction of maintaining separate residences. She said she'd think about it.

One evening Dougal looked through Pooterkin's thesis and found that a good deal of space was devoted to the Augustine manuscript. Not only did it please Pooterkin aesthetically – his remarks on the elegance of the ampersands verged on the lyrical – but he used it as the keystone of his theory that a pre-Conquest scriptorium had existed at Rosington. He was convinced that the bows of the 'g's clearly showed the influence of a particular Continental scriptorium; he hypothesized the presence of a writing master from Cologne at Rosington in the late tenth century, and who was Dougal to disagree with him?

Pooterkin was also delighted to be able to demonstrate that the Rosington Augustine was an unusually home-loving manuscript. Unlike the majority of British medieval manuscripts, its progress through the centuries was well charted. A twelfth-century catalogue of the Abbey library mentioned it, clinching the identification by noting the person to whom it was dedicated. Four hundred years later, Leland listed it among the library's treasures. By that time it had acquired mildly miraculous powers and was associated anachronistically with St Tumwulf himself.

After the Reformation the Abbey had received a new lease of life as the centre of a newly constituted see. An antiquarian Minor Canon included the manuscript in a catalogue he made of the Cathedral library in the reign of James I. And it was still there, according to Pooterkin, on display in the Chapter House.

Dougal toyed with the idea of a day trip to Rosington. It should be possible to examine the manuscript closely – he could easily write himself an enthusiastic testimonial on headed writing paper from the secretary's office. But he regretfully abandoned the idea: there was no real point in going. He didn't know what he was looking for, or even if the original manuscript was in itself in any way relevant. If someone was planning to pinch it, there was nothing he could do – or wanted to do.

He closed Pooterkin's book and persuaded Amanda to come down to the Crown & Anchor instead.

On the Thursday after the weekend the police interviewed him. A notice at the Department had requested those who had been in the building on Tuesday afternoon and those who were students of Dr Gumper (an unfortunate phrase, Dougal thought) to arrange with the secretary a time to see the police. The mobile police headquarters and the paraphernalia of a murder investigation had been withdrawn from the college by now, but a room had been set aside for police use. Dougal qualified for interview on both counts and thought he might as well get it over with sooner rather than later.

In the event, it didn't take long. A bored, plainclothes sergeant sat behind the desk, with a constable on his right taking notes. Within three minutes it had been established that Dougal knew nothing of any use to them. The sergeant, however, was mechanically affable:

'Well, that's all most useful. Helps us eliminate some points in the afternoon and corroborates what we already know.' Dougal watched the constable with fascination: he had found an unexpectedly satisfying treasure trove picking his nose, and was rolling it to and fro between the index finger and thumb of his left hand.

'Now. Just one thing more, Mr . . . um Dougal. You last saw the late Dr Gumper the Thursday before he died. Did he seem at all odd then? Anything unusual? What sort of mood was he in?'

They must be baffled to be asking such vague questions as these. He wondered momentarily whether to introduce an appetizing red herring, as much for their sakes as his, but decided to stick to the truth. The constable carefully deposited his bogey under the seat of his chair.

'He was normal.' It sounded unhelpful, so he expanded it. 'He was a little flushed, I think – looked as though he'd had a good lunch. But that was fairly common.' He had also been pompous and had tried to bully Dougal into producing some work – the Augustine transcription, ironically enough. That too had been normal.

The sergeant thanked him and asked him to send the next one in. Dougal felt oddly disgusted with the police. The last vestige of his childhood belief in their infallibility had vanished. There was no rational basis for this, he knew: merely an infantile disappointment at the absence of a hawk-faced officer who by intuition and deduction should have known precisely what he, Dougal, had left out. Which would have been extraordinarily inconvenient.

He walked up the corridor before going home – he hadn't checked his pigeonhole for a few days and had forgotten, earlier this afternoon, to find out if a substitute for Gumper had been arranged.

There was no notice, but there were several things for him in the pigeonhole he shared with the rest of the Ds. The society circulars went straight in the wastepaper bin which the authorities had thoughtfully placed nearby, together with an invitation to become a Friend of the College in return for arranging an annual payment by banker's order. As an afterthought he threw in the envelope as well, since it was marked PLEASE REUSE. Lastly, there was a note from the secretary: would he please collect a package which had arrived for him by registered post.

Dougal found this puzzling. Had he ordered a photostat of something? But in that case, why registered post? He went to the office. The secretary, a large, rabbit-faced woman in her mid-thirties, who radiated surly inefficiency, broke off a description of her boyfriend which she was transmitting telephonically to an unknown destination and gave Dougal a large envelope. It was buff-coloured and bulky, firmly secured with Sellotape and string. Dougal thanked her, to which she replied with a sniff; he correctly interpreted this as a reproof, in a language which transcended mere words, such as 'We're not running a post office here.'

He left the room, exchanging a brief conspiratorial smile with the West Indian typist with a pert bottom, who had to suffer Miss Adlard's moods on a nine-to-five basis.

In the privacy of the passage, he examined the envelope. His name and the address of the college were written in a firm, rather elegant hand. He turned the envelope over, and was about to tear it open when he saw there was a sender's address on the back.

James Hanbury,
c/o Messrs Coutts & Co.,
10 Mount St,
London W.1.

5

The house where Dougal lived was in a turning off Finchley Road. Its front door was set in an archway which was chiefly Perpendicular in inspiration, though there was more than a trace of the glory that was Greece in the pillars which supported the porch. The hall was gloomy now, but refreshingly cool and dark in summer. Its flagstones were laid out in a black and white chequerboard which reminded Dougal of Venetian palazzi and chamber music. Today, for some reason, he found himself thinking of that Emperor of China who laid out a courtyard as a chess board and played with condemned men, suitably attired, as the pieces, their deaths delayed or hastened according to the skills and strategies of the players. And would it have been better to have been a king or a pawn? Or even the Emperor on his balcony?

Dougal took the stairs two at a time, his eyes gradually adjusting to the dim light which filtered through the stained glass windows at the half-landings.

Dougal lived in the attic, on the third floor. Originally the space had housed a gigantic billiard table and nothing else; now it supplied him with a sitting room, a bedroom and a minute kitchen. Over all three rooms ran a long skylight which projected like a small aerial greenhouse over the flat roof of the house.

He found Amanda in the sitting room. She was playing patience – a complicated two-pack version – on the rug in front of the electric fire. She didn't look up, but when he touched her shoulder said, 'Hullo, William,' to the twelve columns and eight depots of cards on the floor. 'Shan't be a moment.'

'Red nine on black ten?' said Dougal. 'I'll make some tea.'

'It won't help. All my kings have gone. There isn't any.'

'I bought some.'

Dougal squeezed into the kitchen, filled the kettle and switched it on. While he was waiting for it to boil, he decanted the tea he had bought into the caddy, washed a pair of mugs and found the tray under the rubbish bin. There was a curious smell there again, he noticed, and wondered what exotic growths were thriving in its plastic lined interior this time. The kettle boiled, relieving him of the moral obligation to search for the source of the smell. He filled the teapot, put it on the tray and took it into the sitting room.

Amanda was scraping the cards together. 'The skylight's leaking again,' she said conversationally. 'How were the police?'

'Dull. One was bored and the other picked his nose the whole time. Routine stuff.' He put the tray on the octagonal table between the two armchairs. Suddenly he couldn't preserve his facade of nonchalance any more. 'Look, I had a letter today. From Hanbury. At least I suppose it's a letter. I haven't opened it yet.'

Amanda looked at him incredulously. She wore the expression which always made Dougal feel about five and on the verge of committing some hideous misdemeanour such as putting his knife in his mouth.

'You mean you didn't open it?'

'No. It seemed better to wait. I mean, God knows what's in it. Why don't you pour the tea while I open it?'

Dougal took out his penknife, cut the string and slit open the flap of the envelope. Inside were two smaller envelopes, one containing a letter, the other a bundle of bank notes fastened with a rubber band. He looked across at Amanda who laughed and said, 'Read the letter out.'

Dougal unfolded it. It was long: six or seven sheets of hotel writing paper covered with that flamboyant script.

My Dear William,

I hope you will never read this letter. I shall send it to my bank with instructions to forward it, if I haven't told them not to within a week. It's a sort of insurance policy, I suppose.

You will be wondering what all this is about. When

*we had a drink together earlier this evening I knew
that certain people were wanting to kill me; now I think
it likely they will try much sooner than I had anticipated. I'm afraid this must sound a trifle melodramatic.
I am writing to you because I like you – perhaps I see
something of my younger self in you; also there's no one
else to write to. In any case, I owe you some money.*

*I misled you intentionally tonight on a number of
points. Gumper was working for me. I used to know
him, very slightly, at Oxford. He accepted the commission and then tried to blackmail me. He knew money
was involved somewhere, and wanted a share. He
believed his leverage was increased by the fact he knew
something of a youthful peccadillo of mine.*

*Enough of him. For you to understand the events
which led up to this, you must allow me to outline a
short story. You may have seen the obituary of Canon
Oswyth Vernon-Jones in the press last month. His work
among the criminal classes attracted a good deal of
attention in the fifties – you're probably too young to
remember the shock which his controversial reassessment
of the Crucifixion,* My God Among Thieves, *caused
at the time. He was once a chaplain at Dartmoor, and
was then intimately concerned with several rehabilita-
tion centres before he became a Canon of Rosington.*

*So far as I know, only one other person besides
myself knew of the Canon's other profession. While at
Dartmoor – with my help, I might add – he developed
a sideline to supplement his income: he became a fixer*

in a very discreet, superior way. He always operated through intermediaries.

At first his concern was to supply a few home comforts to selected prisoners; he probably saw it as an extension of the command to love thy neighbour. But he soon grew involved in the activity – not only financially, but intellectually as well. He was ideally placed for it, of course – it's incredible how easily a clergyman may move in all ranks of society (particularly if he has a legitimate pastoral interest in criminals). His organization soon extended beyond the confines of Dartmoor; when he left his chaplaincy there, he travelled widely and extended it still further (with my help, of course). He was, in the Johnsonian phrase, a clubbable man, at least externally; he could make himself equally agreeable to an archbishop or a child murderer. And frequently did.

A mission to take Christianity behind bars, a wide range of social contacts and a phenomenal memory: these three qualities were the secret of his success. At his prime – between about 1965 and 1975 – he could arrange almost anything: from a murder to a kilo of heroin; from preferential treatment by the local council to (on one occasion at least) a bishopric.

He was successful because he was moderate, I think. He never went for large, uncertain profits, always for small safe ones. He was merely a voice on the telephone, at most, to those few of his clients who had any direct contact with him. The majority went through

me or another person. On several occasions, his clients
knew him in his spiritual capacity, without realizing
that in his time he had supplied them with far more
material comforts. You see, all he did was to put
buyers, as it were, in contact with sellers (or vice
versa) and charge a commission. Breathtakingly
simple.

I handled one end of the business for him, and a
person called Michael Aloysius Lee saw to the other. In
the main I dealt with wealthy amateurs – respectable
people who suddenly found themselves needing temporary assistance in bending the law. Lee, on the other
hand, mixed with the habitual criminals – those who
found themselves in difficulties owing to a pushy rival
or a consignment which they could not deliver. Lee and
I had little contact except through the Canon, when he
would supply us with names, telephone numbers,
addresses, etc.

He trusted us for the simple reason that he held
particularly damaging information about both of us.
But to give him his due, he was a generous employer.

This secret career of his brought a comfortable
income which he used so cautiously that even his wife
never suspected he had more than his stipend (or whatever they call it) and a small private income. I believe
he had several pet charities (for animals rather than
human beings), some rather nice eighteenth-century
prints and an excellent cellar. The considerable residue
which remained he invested in jewellery – chiefly cut

diamonds, I believe. He kept it, of all places, in a strongbox at Barclays Bank in Rosington.

Very occasionally, I stayed with him at Rosington (Lee never) and was introduced as a distant cousin in stockbroking (a suitably vague profession). Vernon-Jones took pleasure in introducing me to local worthies, I used to suspect. He was like that. Which brings me to another characteristic of his which is directly relevant: he was malicious. Not in a crude way, but delicately, obliquely. I imagine that as a boy he was the sort who didn't stamp on any unfortunate insect which crossed his path, but slowly removed its limbs, one by one, or drowned it in a spoonful of honey. And he was the same way with human beings – when there was no need for him to be affable. I firmly believe his wife died, gradually, in a little domestic hell which he had painstakingly constructed. Lee and I were not so expendable. I sometimes wonder if he would have been a nicer person if he hadn't been a clergyman. He knew that Lee and I disliked one another intensely – this suited him – divide and rule. He enjoyed the tension but was too intelligent to let it reach an unbearable degree of strain.

During his life, that is. But evidently he felt that no such scruples need restrain him after death. When he died, I went down to Rosington for the funeral. I spoke with his solicitor and his bank manager, both there, paying their last respects in a cemetery like a municipal park, and then later in a local hotel. They were, perhaps, more open about their late client's affairs than they should have been, believing there to be a degree of consanguinity. Also they were sorry for me – the man's will left everything to the RSPCA, which failed to surprise me. The bank manager, after three whiskies, believed that Vernon-Jones knew his death was near, for he had removed the contents of his strongbox just after Christmas. The solicitor chimed in and said that the Canon was a man of strange quirks, which to my mind was the understated epitaph of a lifetime. He also said he had promised to forward two letters on the day of the funeral. It wasn't difficult to discover that one was addressed to me, the other to Lee.

It arrived the next morning. The envelope contained nothing but the photograph which you have and one of Vernon-Jones's cards which I enclose. It's the back of it which is important – he scribbled Matthew vii 7 *on it, which is,* Ask and it shall be given you; seek and ye shall find; knock, and it shall be opened unto you.

I know all this must seem increasingly nonsensical to you. Bear with me a little longer. You see, I am convinced that the two things he sent me are, correctly interpreted, pointers to the whereabouts of his jewellery. I also believe that he sent similar – but not the same – clues to Lee. He didn't particularly care to whom he left the diamonds – what he wanted to leave was dissension. This is hard to explain to an outsider – what you have to understand is two things: Vernon-Jones's malice and his penchant for the cryptic. For the first, he knew

Lee and I didn't get on, and it must have tickled him to think that he could intensify our enmity beyond his death – manipulate us from the grave. He told me, and I have no doubt that he told Lee as well, that the value of the stones was well into six figures. A good, substantial motive for competition! Secondly, he was a compulsive puzzle solver, a searcher for devious solutions. He was the sort of person who finished the crossword in the paper before looking at the headlines. He was also an ardent cryptographer and cryptoanalyst; in the last decade of his life, his greatest ambition was to decode the Voynich manuscript attributed to Roger Bacon. Add to this his interest in medieval manuscripts and the fact that he knew that neither Lee nor I had a natural aptitude for puzzles, and you will see where this was tending. He had set us a problem, with a fortune as the prize, and split the clues between us, secure in the knowledge that we would never join forces because one would inevitably try to double-cross the other.

We can be certain that there is a prize to be won. The Canon was cruel, malignant and cunning, but, to do him justice, he did have a code of conduct of a sort – the code of a crossword compiler: if you pose a question, there must be an answer, or it isn't fair.

Now to the present. I was followed back to my hotel tonight – I suppose it was foolish of me to take no more radical action than move from Brown's to the Bristol when I realized what Vernon-Jones was doing. Habit leads to carelessness. Lee has a man watching my window. No doubt there are more. Lee is always strong on manpower. Unfortunately, I have to go out tonight – a small but urgent piece of business, the omission of which would be personally and financially awkward in the extreme. Lee, either now or later, will try to detain or kill me: the latter, probably – he will feel, as I do, that it would be more productive in the final analysis. He will weigh the certain advantage of a dead competitor (who is, moreover, dangerously well informed about delicate episodes in his past life) against the potential, if rather risky value of my assistance under compulsion. Besides, he's the sort of person who finds the finality of having someone killed, or doing it himself, reassuring. He may well fail. I'm not on my last legs yet. Sometimes I feel I'm growing too old for this kind of career.

Well, that's the position. If you are reading this, I will be dead. And you – if you want, just as you please – can try to get rich quickly in my place. You would have a number of advantages over Lee: you are an outsider and Lee will have no idea of your existence; you are probably better equipped, mentally, than he – your background, etc., is closer to Vernon-Jones's. It's up to you, of course. But for God's sake, take no risks. Lee is not a fool and he's not too squeamish, either. My advice would be to withdraw at once if you meet him. Don't even give him time to start wondering about you.

I must seal all this up and give it to the hotel people. I had no idea I would write so long a letter. I suppose it's rather like making a will – you don't want to leave anything out, for obvious reasons.

One final point. I would burn this letter, if I were you. I know it sounds silly, but its contents shouldn't be read by the wrong people.

Yours, if you read this, regretfully,

James Hanbury.

Dougal threw the letter on the floor. His mouth was dry with the reading. He swallowed the mug of lukewarm tea and poured himself another. It was nearly dark in the quiet room. He had found it difficult to decipher the last couple of pages, but hadn't wanted to put the light on. He could hear buses rumbling below on the Finchley Road and the occasional agonized hoot of a rush hour horn. It seemed strange that London should be emptying itself as usual.

Amanda got up, switched on the lamp and drew the curtains. The curtains were old and faded; the cotton velvet was now a restful blue. Dougal looked at them.

'He sounds a bit mad,' said Amanda briskly. 'How much money is there?'

They counted half each. Dougal was glad of the activity. He noticed that his hands were behaving as if they belonged to someone else. There was nearly a thousand pounds more than the eleven hundred which Hanbury had promised.

'The trouble is,' Amanda muttered thoughtfully, 'you can't laugh off two thousand quid as a hoax. Nobody could afford jokes that cost that much.'

'Oh, it's not a joke,' Dougal snapped. Amanda looked at him in surprise and he hastily apologized. The letter had disturbed him; it had been painful to read. But he didn't want to tell Amanda that, as she would point out firmly that such feelings were stupid. Instead, Dougal remarked that the deaths of Gumper and Hanbury weren't the usual stuff of comedy and that it seemed more likely that either Hanbury was mad (whether alive or dead) or he was not only dead but also had been telling the truth. He was starting to examine the evidence in favour of and against these alternatives when Amanda said yes, he was probably right, but she did wish he wouldn't talk so pompously.

'I think he was on the level,' she continued slowly. 'I mean, no one's *that* irrational. Or not in that way.'

Dougal agreed, trying, on the whole successfully, to ignore the fact that she had called him pompous. It wasn't the first time. She often said it when he had had a few drinks and was enjoying the sound of the syllables spilling out of his mouth. Perhaps he was. His mind returned to the problem facing them. He wondered aloud whether there was any risk that he himself had been noticed by whoever had killed Hanbury – Lee or one of his employees. Amanda said no, in the voice of one thinking of something entirely different, and if he had been seen in Hanbury's company he would probably have heard from Lee by now. No doubt she was right, thought Dougal, but he wished she could have sounded a little more concerned.

'What are we going to do about it, then?' she said. Dougal was grateful for the 'we'. He looked at her and thought she looked bright with excitement; what made him apprehensive made her look more beautiful.

'Either we spend the money and forget Hanbury or – well, go to Rosington, I suppose. That's the only possible thing we can do. The whole business points there, doesn't it? The manuscript, Vernon-Jones and Hanbury's letter. We could just have a weekend there – look round, see where he lived. Maybe we'll have a stroke of luck . . . we wouldn't even know how to sell the bloody things if we got them.'

'Don't be so gloomy, William. We'll go tomorrow.' Amanda smiled at him and Dougal realized that she had got what she wanted and he was back in favour. And, thinking about it, the prospect of a day or two in a cathedral city seemed very attractive. If they were reasonably cautious there could be no actual danger. Could there?

6

The red Mini had a whimper in its engine and pieces of chewing gum clinging to the ledge beneath the dashboard. Amanda spent much of the journey to Rosington delivering a tirade against drivers who had previously hired the car; cruelty to defenseless machines brought out all her humanity.

Most of their route lay along the A1, a road which Dougal disliked intensely. It was like a tendril of the suburbs crawling northwards, an overgrown offshoot from the North Circular which carried the memory of Neasden and Edmonton up to Scotland.

Dougal wriggled uncomfortably in the passenger seat. He was wearing a new tweed suit, chosen by Amanda, and had had his hair cut. Amanda had insisted that they look respectable. Dougal found that respectability made him itch.

He tried to distract his mind by running over the facts he had learned about Vernon-Jones. They were distressingly few. He had done his research in West Hampstead Public Library, using *Crockford's Clerical Directory* and *The Times* for January 24, which contained Vernon-Jones's obituary.

Little had been added to their meager stock of information about the Canon. Born 1911, educated at St Paul's and St John's College, Cambridge. Ordained Deacon in 1933 and Priest in 1935. Prison chaplaincies led to appointments on various royal commissions connected with penal reform. Canon of Rosington in 1961 and a CBE in 1975.

The obituary concentrated on his prison work . . . *his views on this and on surrounding social issues aroused much debate both within and without the Church of England.*

Amanda turned the Mini on to the B road leading to Rosington. The dark, flat countryside lapped like a black tide towards the road. For three years at Cambridge, Dougal had lived on the rim of the Fens and failed to come to terms with the remorseless way they slid into the chilly waters of the North Sea.

Amanda started singing extracts from *The Sound of Music.*

The road began to rise. Rosington was perched on a rocky outcrop in a sea of fertile mud. The Mini's headlights picked out a sign: *Rosington Urban District Council*, it read, WELCOME TO ROSINGTON, *Twinned with Vermeuil-sur-mer.* Beneath the words was a crude picture of the west front of the cathedral, the great rose window above the door framed by a deeply recessed Norman arch with seven members.

The darkness gave way to the yellow glare of street lights. They found their hotel by the traffic lights near the cathedral. Dougal had discovered a town guide at West Hampstead library and booked a room by telephone on the strength of the Crossed Keys' advertisement: *400-year-old hostelry mellowing in the shadow of the Minster . . . medieval charm with modern comfort.*

The hotel was on the corner, with what looked like the main shopping street separating it from the cathedral on the right. To the left of its dingy Georgian facade was an archway, through which Amanda edged the Mini, leading into a courtyard which served as the hotel car park. As she killed the engine, the rain began to drum down with sullen persistence, running down the windscreen like a miniature waterfall.

Amanda shivered. 'It's spooky.'

Dougal reached over and took her hand from the steering wheel. It was an uncharacteristic remark for her to have made – Amanda thought people imagined their nightmares (which of course they did) because she herself had never had one. 'I know,' he replied, feeling unusually large and protective. 'Hammer horror. Should we wait for the phantom ostler or go and find the ghostly butler?'

'Oh, shut up. My umbrella's on the back seat, I think.'

Normality was restored. Dougal reached round and extracted the umbrella from the clutter which, even after a few hours, littered the back of the car.

He clambered out and struggled round to the boot. Amanda gathered up their belongings from the interior, turned up the collar of her coat and wrapped a head-scarf round her hair.

'We'll have to go round to the front door,' she said as she handed him the briefcase containing, among other things, Dr Pooterkin's magnum opus. 'If there's a way in from here, it's been blocked by those crates of empties.'

They ran round to the main entrance and into the light and warmth of the hall. To the left was a doorway leading to a nearly empty bar. On the right was a number of chairs and sofas, chintz-covered and elderly, grouped round a fire. Only one chair was occupied – by a large but fragile-looking clergyman in a charcoal suit, reading the *Church Times*. In front of them was the reception desk, flanked by a flight of stairs on one side and a notice board on the other. Dougal took an immediate liking to the place: it looked comfortable and was shabbily pleasant on the eyes.

A large woman – in breadth rather than height – looked up from behind the reception desk as they came in, pushing the *Daily Mirror* aside and patting her perm.

'Good evening,' she said. 'Can I be of any assistance?' Then, more naturally, 'Filthy night, innit?'

'Yes,' agreed Dougal, uncomfortably aware of a drip on the end of his nose and the puddle which the umbrella was making on the carpet. Just in time, he remembered the name he had given over the telephone. 'Our name's Massey.' He hoped it didn't sound as untrue as it felt.

'We telephoned this morning to book a room for the weekend.'

Amanda sneezed, which galvanized the receptionist into action. 'Bless you! A hot bath and a large Scotch was what my late husband used to swear by. Not that it did him much good in the end. Heart attack. Put the umbrella in the stand over there, love. Massey, you say? Room seven. Sign here, would you?'

Dougal scribbled his new signature in the book. He decided to retain his christian name; a change of surname was unexpectedly confusing, and more radical alteration would become unbearably complicated. He gave an address in Belsize Park, NW3.

'Are you eating here this evening?' enquired the receptionist. 'Dinner's between seven and nine.'

'Um,' said Dougal, looking at his watch: coming up to half-past six. 'Yes.' He looked at Amanda. 'Shall we say around seven-thirty?'

The receptionist eased her bulk from behind the desk and led the way up the stairs. 'We're thin on company, being this time of year,' she remarked over her shoulder. 'Picks up just before Easter usually. You've got a nice room, though I say it myself. Lovely view of the cathedral.'

'Oh, that's nice,' said Amanda, who was immediately behind the receptionist's plump and swaying rump. 'We're particularly interested in the history of it and so on.'

'Plenty of that here,' said the receptionist proudly.

'Why, we often get scholars and people down from college. One of them – American, he was – stayed here for *three* months to write a book about it. And nothing but the best, must have been made of money. Nice gent, though. Always regular and ever so clean and serious. Wouldn't stop telling you things, either. "Mrs Livabed" (that's me, Annie Livabed), he used to say, "there have been Livabeds in Rosington for nearly as long as that cathedral. A Livabed was deputy bailiff of the Abbey farm five hundred years ago." "You're having me on," I said, not that it was my family (I was born in Islington, matter of fact), but no, says Mr Pooterkin, it's all there in black and white in one of those documents he was studying. Just shows you, dunnit? Here we are.'

She unlocked the white-painted door of number seven and showed them in. It was a big, warm room (central heating must be one of the modern comforts, thought Dougal, and wondered where the medieval charm came in). The decor and furnishings looked as if they had been designed in 1952 by someone with conservative tastes; but they were clean. There was a large double bed with pillows enough for six people and a candlewick bedspread.

'Bathroom's in here, dears. You have to pull the chain twice if you want it to flush. Everything you need?' Mrs Livabed began to back out of the room like an ocean liner tugged backwards out of harbour. 'Just let me know if there's anything you want.'

When Mrs Livabed had left, Dougal went to the

window. They were on the first floor. Immediately below was the street of shops they had noticed from the car. The shops were closed and the pavements deserted, except for a black mongrel padding purposefully opposite. A lamp gave enough light to read the sign above the chemist's on the corner: High Street. Behind the ridges of the roofs was the great shadow of the cathedral. It was impossible to pick out any details: it was equally impossible to avoid knowing it was there. Dougal swallowed, feeling his Adam's apple bouncing in his throat. It must, he thought, do strange things to you, living in a town with that stone mountain in its middle. He drew the curtains.

'I like this,' said Amanda.

Within half an hour they were down in the bar. They had a corner table, from which they could see out into the hall and the lounge area. The elderly clergyman was still in the armchair in front of the fire, but the angle of his *Church Times* had altered; the paper covered his face and the upper part of his torso. Dougal said he represented the Church Dormant and Amanda said wasn't it touching that someone that age should take the trouble to give his shoes a polish like that, while someone of Dougal's age didn't even own a set of brushes and a tin of polish. They then debated what the old man was here for – was he a resident, a retired and widowed local vicar perhaps, or merely passing through on a tour of the cathedrals of England?

As Dougal went up to get a menu from the barman, two men came in. He didn't look up, though his mind vaguely registered an impression of bright suits and chunky gold jewellery.

'Two large whiskies,' said one of them to the barman. 'On the rocks.' Then, to his companion, 'If you've got nothing better to suggest, you're about as much use as Hanbury, and that's the truth.'

7

'Act naturally,' Dougal had said to Amanda, and they did their best to eat roast duck and chocolate mousse as if the two men, who soon followed them from the bar to the dining room, were as insignificant to them as the pattern on the wallpaper. They shared a bottle of Pouilly Fuissé over the meal and later had coffee in the lounge. The Church Dormant was nibbling at Dover sole in the dining room, so they had the fireside to themselves. Dougal had had to suppress an urge to flee upstairs. But they would never learn anything if they went back to their room, and in any case, unless either of the two men was a mind reader, there was no reason to retreat in panic. Dougal bought a histoy of the cathedral from Mrs Livabed at reception; the worst problem in the dining room had been the difficulty of finding suitably neutral subjects to talk about. It had been all too easy to lapse into a strained silence, with ears trained on the two men three tables away.

Dougal was not altogether surprised to find that the booklet had been written by the Rev Oswyth Vernon-Jones, CBE, MA, Canon of Rosington. Since they had reached the Crossed Keys, a disturbing logic had usurped control of events. First the mention of Pooterkin, then the appearance of the two men – were they staying at the hotel? – one of whom was probably Lee himself, and now Vernon-Jones's name beneath the glossy cover photograph of the west front. Dougal felt like a gambler who had transcended the statistics of probability.

Amanda and he sat on a sofa with the booklet open between them and the coffee tray on a low table in front of them. Dougal was tempted to have a drink but decided in favour of a relatively clear head instead. Amanda looked at the pictures and Dougal skimmed through the text.

Vernon-Jones concentrated on the medieval period. While it was clear that he approved of the elevation of the Abbey church to the status of a cathedral, he deplored the destructive consequences of the secession from Rome: *Puritan vandals wantonly destroyed the magnificent fifteenth-century stained glass; only a few fragments remain in St Tumwulf's chapel behind the High Altar. The interior furnishings of the church, including the earliest known example of a medieval clock in the north transept, were ruthlessly consigned to oblivion by the intolerance of the reformers. It is indeed fortunate that the last Abbot and first Dean, Gervase of Charleston, was able to preserve at least some of the priceless manuscripts of the monastic library . . .*

Amanda nudged him warningly. The two men were standing in the doorway of the dining room, to the left of the notice board and the reception desk, exchanging laboured compliments with the waitress. She was laden with a tray piled high with dirty dishes but was accepting the badinage civilly enough, in a manner which suggested she had been well tipped. With a final 'Oo, you shouldn't,' she vanished towards the kitchens and the two men came out into the hall.

Both of them were flushed and breathing heavily, as if the steaks and the litre of house red which they had consumed constituted a sort of internal assault course. Dougal thought they looked like the sort of travelling salesmen who ruled the marketing of their product over large sections of the country, and had expense accounts to match their vice-regal commercial powers.

The elder one had the appearance of a well-fed, prosperous badger. He was pear-shaped, with pepper-and-salt hair and a long, wide nose which dwarfed the other features of his face. His teeth projected from his upper jaw beyond his lips; they were crooked and yellow, and gave the illusion that they were not so much teeth as an ill-devised extension of his nose.

His companion was younger – about the same age as Dougal, probably – and taller. He gangled over his leader – there was no mistaking the pecking order here: the attitudes of the two made it immediately clear. He had thinning, golden hair, which curled over his ears in a travesty of a barrister's wig.

Both of them were wearing very new, light-coloured suits. The taller man's was double-breasted and the jacket hung loosely, flapping over the hollow between his rounded shoulders, its brass buttons twinkling in the light. The older man's was more conservative in cut. In the breast pocket of each was a neatly folded handkerchief, pink and fawn respectively, which toned tastefully with the wearers' shirts and ties.

They stood talking quietly in the middle of the hall for a moment, facing Dougal and Amanda. Then the middle-aged one turned to Mrs Livabed behind the reception desk, and said something which they couldn't catch. Her reply, however, genteel modulations to the fore, was perfectly audible by the fire:

'Well, I'm *sow* glad you enjoyed your dinner, Mr Lee. Would you care for a key if you're going out?'

'No,' said Mr Lee, more loudly than before. He had the sort of voice with the trick of carrying if he wanted it to. 'Should be back by about eleven. We're just meeting some friends for a drink.'

'Mind you don't get too wet. It's still coming down as hard as ever.'

Lee laughed and his companion fetched their raincoats from the hooks on the wall. The latter helped his leader into his, and wriggled himself into his own. His long, bony wrists dangled beneath the cuffs. They said goodnight and walked out into the rain, shoulders hunched.

The Church Dormant ambled out of the dining room,

a stately shuffle which was supported by a walking stick. He mumbled something to Mrs Livabed, looked over at Dougal and Amanda, sighed and made his way to the armchair furthest away from them, by the window. Dougal felt guilty; just, he suspected, as the old man had intended. He also felt worried. He put down his coffee cup, the spoon rattling on the saucer, and lit a cigarette.

'That settles it,' Amanda whispered. 'Hanbury was telling the truth. And there's the man who had him killed.'

Dougal nodded. He was trying to remember what Hanbury had said in his letter – something about getting out before Lee should have the slightest ground for suspicion. It would be stupid to stay here. Why risk what they had for . . .

'It simplifies things for us, doesn't it?' continued Amanda. She looked at him. 'Oh, come on, William! We can't chicken out now. It's just getting interesting.'

Before he had time to say anything, Mrs Livabed approached and asked if they wanted some more coffee. Amanda said yes and ordered two brandies as well. When she had gone, Dougal said:

'I'm a bit scared – aren't you? We're playing outside our league. I don't want us to end up dead.' It was hard to make a whisper sound convincing.

Amanda explained succinctly why they were not risking anything by staying here for a day or two and, well, being open to suggestion. She managed to make Dougal feel that to do otherwise would be a despicable course of action – not so much by her words as by her

74

eyes, which looked large and expectant, as if daring the world to disappoint her. The world might have been able to, but Dougal certainly couldn't. And, having decided to go along with her, he was about to suggest they think up an excuse for asking questions when Mrs Livabed returned.

She set the tray on their table. 'It's not stopped raining since you came. Pouring down. Mad, that's what they are – Mr Lee and Mr Tanner – going out in this weather. They'll get soaked. As if there wasn't drink enough in here.'

'Perhaps they were visiting friends who live nearby,' said Amanda sweetly. 'Or maybe they're the sort who don't enjoy their pleasures unless they make an effort for them.'

Mrs Livabed laughed, a sound which took twenty years from her age. 'You could be right there, my dear. Men are a funny lot, present company excepted, of course. And don't I know it.' Her tone hinted at a limitless reservoir of personal knowledge on the subject. 'We get all sorts here. You're from London, then?'

Her curiosity was so lacking in self-consciousness that Dougal couldn't be offended by it. Anyway, it gave him the perfect opening to show Amanda that he was perfectly capable of dealing with this business in his own way.

'Yes,' he replied. 'I'm a writer, actually.' He sipped the brandy and could feel it joining the wine and beer which had gone before it, lubricating both his imagination and his tongue. 'This is by way of a working holiday for us.'

'You don't say. I'd never have guessed. You don't look at all like Mr Pooterkin – he was the last writer we had here. Are you interested in the cathedral too?'

'Yes, but not in the same way. I'm a freelance writer for television, you see. I want to investigate the possibility of a documentary series on cathedral cities – you know the sort of thing: old and new – picturesque history, local buildings, interviews with people who live here, local industries, how the cathedral affects the city and . . . er . . . so on.'

Mrs Livabed was fascinated.

'Which channel's it going to be, dear? We get BBC of course, but otherwise you can only get Anglia properly.'

'I don't know yet. Early days. I have to write a proposal for a series and then get some company interested. It's not an easy market to break into, of course – especially nowadays.' Mrs Livabed nodded solemnly, and Dougal almost laughed aloud: it was so easy to sound convincing about something you knew nothing about. 'We're down here to soak up the atmosphere and so forth – get an idea of the potential. Which reminds me – we were reading this booklet about the cathedral by . . .' Dougal glanced down at the cover '. . . this Canon Vernon-Jones. It could be useful to have a word with him this weekend about the historical side. Can you tell us where he lives?'

'Ow, dear. You're just too late.' Mrs Livabed looked genuinely affronted by the contrariness of death. 'He passed on last month. Heart attack. Such a pity – he would have been just the man for you. He helped Mr

Pooterkin ever such a lot. There was nothing he didn't know about the cathedral. Used to live at Bleeders Hall. And such a *nice* man, too. Not all holier-than-thou and just-a-small-dry-sherry like most of the reverends round here. Liked his Scotch, he did.'

'Oh. That's a shame.' Dougal mournfully offered his cigarettes around ('Not when I'm on duty, thank you love, some of our customers are that old-fashioned, you wouldn't believe'). 'I don't suppose there's anyone else who might be able to help us there?'

'Well.' Mrs Livabed absentmindedly emptied the contents of their ashtray into the fire. 'Your best bet would be Mrs Munns in Sacristy Row. She's a widow, poor soul – her husband was Precentor here, and when he died they let her have that house because old Canon Stevens had popped off and it was empty, not that they didn't know which side their bread was buttered because she runs the flower rota and the WI and the town would fall apart without her and that's the truth. She was very friendly with Mr Vernon-Jones – helped him with his history and all that. And he made a real pet of Lina (that's Mrs Munns's little girl: shy little thing but ever so sweet), you know the way old men can be with small children, liked surprising her with presents and seeing her smile, not that he left her anything when he passed on except that dog of his . . .'

'Mrs Munns sounds a useful person to see.' Dougal rushed bravely into the flow of Mrs Livabed's conversation, directing his words at a point equidistant between her and Amanda.

'She might be called,' said Mrs Livabed with refined deliberation, as if she had thought long and hard before making the judgement, 'a pillar of society. Only the other week—' the customary speed of delivery was resumed '—she said to me at the Bring-and-Buy sale for St Withburga's central heating (that's our local parish church, the one on the other side of the green), she said, "Mrs Livabed, these functions just wouldn't happen if we weren't here to make the teas and see to the change." (We were having a quiet cuppa before clearing up after the doors closed.) And I remember saying to her, I said, where would this place be without people like us, we're like the Unknown Soldier or that man in a poem we had to learn at school, *Unwept, unhonoured and unsung.* Or was it dishonoured? It's a shame kids don't learn things like that at school these days, don't you think?'

'Women are always the real rulers,' said Amanda in the tiny pause which followed.

'Oh, that is so true. Well look at marriage. My poor husband was always talking about wearing the trousers and that shows you, doesn't it?' She winked ponderously, like an elephant lowering her eyelid, to Amanda. 'Still, mustn't give away trade secrets, must I? It wouldn't do for Mr Massey here to know too much.'

For one awful second, Dougal felt himself struggling with the urge to say, 'Who's Mr Massey?' He managed to ask where Mrs Munns lived, making a mental note to practice saying William Massey to himself in front of the mirror before going to bed.

'Sacristy Row, dear. That's up the other end of the High Street – the road that goes up by the hotel. You go past the two gateways to the close on your right and there's Sacristy Row – a little old line of houses like something out of a fairy story. It's number eight, I think. The one with the green curtains.'

The telephone at the reception desk began to ring. Mrs Livabed gathered their dirty cups and glasses on to the tray with swift, mindless efficiency. 'More trouble than it's worth, that thing,' she confided, and moved away across the hall to answer it.

Dougal looked at Amanda and grinned. The conversation with Mrs Livabed had made him feel more cheerful. Possibly the brandy had helped. In some way, hearing about Mrs Munns had given his mind something to do besides worry about the risk posed by the presence of Lee. And the more he thought about it, the more he liked the idea of visiting her. And Mrs Munns, Vernon-Jones's close friend, fitted in with the suggestion contained in Hanbury's Bible reference – the *seek and ye shall find* implied something obvious, surely. Where more obvious place to start than with a person who had known the dead man well? It was odd to think how different had been the man whom Mrs Livabed had known from the man who gave Hanbury his orders.

The other reason why his mood had changed was the glow of satisfaction caused by the tissue of lies he had told Mrs Livabed. It had been so easy, though unplanned, and seemed to have been convincing. It raised his opinion of his own powers. So much so that when Amanda said, 'William! Do you realize you'll be known all over Rosington tomorrow as that television man?' he was able to say, 'Nonsense,' without even thinking about it. His newfound fluency continued:

'We're not going to be here long enough for that. Anyway, it's the perfect cover for asking questions.'

'I must say you did it quite well,' said Amanda at length. This was unusually high praise. 'We'll have to get you one of those clipboards with a pad on and a pair of dark glasses.'

Dougal laughed. The Church Dormant levered himself to his feet and set off towards the stairs, which made Dougal think about going to bed, too, even though it was early. The thought of tomorrow excited him, and he wanted to make it happen as quickly as possible.

8

They were up early the next morning. Dougal had a weakness for cooked breakfasts, especially those cooked by somebody else. Amanda preferred to have a bath and put on her makeup, so Dougal went down alone and ordered for both of them. Having eaten his own egg, bacon and tomato, he moved on to Amanda's sausage and scrambled egg.

The dining room was empty, except for the waitress, who was listlessly sorting out the cutlery on the sideboard, and the elderly clergyman, who was making a very slow breakfast indeed – as if, Dougal thought, his metabolism was only firing on one cylinder. Seen in daylight, everything about the man – his suit, his hair, his complexion – suggested he was gradually decomposing. 'Dust to dust,' Dougal said to the last forkful of Amanda's scrambled egg and nodded politely to Mrs Livabed as she appeared in the doorway with a clutch of menus in her hand. She picked up the Church

Dormant's napkin and asked Dougal if he needed more coffee.

When Amanda came in, the room's atmosphere seemed to change subtly. The waitress straightened her spine, Mrs Livabed absently smoothed a crease from her skirt and Dougal could have sworn that the clergyman chose to drop his napkin again so he could turn to bend down, thereby getting the chance of a better look.

Amanda said 'Good morning' to nobody in particular (and Dougal thought that in an English hotel it was possibly ruder to say it to one person in particular than not to say it at all; it was one of those impossible dilemmas) and sat down. He poured her some coffee. Their table was by the window and they stared out into the High Street, passing the time talking about the weather – it had stopped raining during the night, but on the other hand the sky was not the sort you associate with a fine day. Already a good number of doleful shoppers were abroad, scurrying mournfully like people late for a funeral.

When Dougal and Amanda themselves reached the outside world, half an hour later, it was easier to understand the predominant aura of depression which had clung to the pedestrians. True, it was no longer raining, but the chief feature of the weather was now a vicious east wind which pried its way into one's clothing by the smallest crannies and treated exposed surfaces of skin with the callous indifference of fine-grained sandpaper. Amanda refused to change her elegant but light leather coat; Dougal, however, abruptly dropped his sartorial standards and dug out his elderly duffel coat from the boot of the Mini.

In the High Street they bought cigarettes and a film for Amanda's camera and then walked briskly along Minster Street, which ran south from the chemist's shop, to the west door of the cathedral. As they reached it, the clock which a nineteenth-century dean had caused to perch incongruously over the west window chimed the quarter: nine-fifteen. They had agreed at the hotel that it was obviously too early to call on Mrs Munns and the cathedral seemed the natural place to go. Dougal had an unspoken hope that the church would provide a clue of some sort.

The west door was twelve feet high and had two flaps, made of oak and covered with wrought iron foliage, interlaced with someone's initials, endlessly repeated. One of the flaps had a postern door cut into it. When Dougal opened it, he found that its weight had been augmented by a thoughtful dean and chapter: the powerful spring which held it closed nearly snapped shut on Amanda, like an ecclesiastical mousetrap.

Inside the church, Dougal's first impression was of cold and gloom; his second was of an avenue of stone tree trunks wide enough for several lines of traffic abreast. In fact the nave was filled with rows of orange plastic chairs, of the sort which bend alarmingly when you sit down in one.

'Must be expecting a big congregation,' said Dougal

in a whisper – childhood conditioning made talking at the usual level difficult.

Amanda pointed to a notice beside the door which explained the chairs: the population of Rosington was expected to attend in force a concert in aid of the World Organization Against Racism and Fascism; the programme was to be composed entirely of works by the celebrated Russian dissident Anton Petrovitch Spudovsky, and included, Dougal noted, the anticoncerto Nausea in F-sharp Minor, which had caused such a furore at its premiere in the Albert Hall last month.

A verger appeared in the north aisle, a portly person in a very large, black cassock which reached so close to the ground that it created the illusion that he was levitating rather than walking towards them. For he was certainly coming in their direction: there was no mistaking the sense of purpose on that fleshy face. Dougal saw that he wore a chain round his neck with a medallion bearing the arms of the cathedral; it swung gently as he moved, like a small, smokeless censer.

'No photography,' announced the verger, his voice a delicate blend of Fen vowels and clerical consonants, 'without permission and the payment of two pounds towards the maintenance of the cathedral.' His eyes strayed meaningfully towards Amanda's camera, which hung from her right shoulder.

'Ah. Yes,' said Dougal. 'Photographs. We hadn't actually taken any yet. But I suppose we might. Two pounds did you say?'

The verger inclined his head. Dougal wondered if the prompt acceptance of his authority had mollified him, for he volunteered the information that the permit was valid for a whole day, and you could come and go, during that day, as much as you liked.

Dougal pulled out his wallet and the verger, from some hidden pocket, produced a biro and a pad of numbered receipts. By the time the transaction had been completed, Dougal's hands were far too cold for him to want to hold a camera in them.

'The fabric,' remarked the verger, 'requires an enormous sum daily, merely for its maintenance. The shop—' he bowed slightly, in the direction of the north transept '—opens at half-past nine. Visitors are asked to remember that they are in a House of Prayer.'

The verger noiselessly retired. Dougal and Amanda looked at one another.

'I don't *want* to take any photographs here,' she hissed. 'Why did you give him the money?'

Dougal didn't know the answer, so he said it was all in a good cause and perhaps one day they would make enough money from the tourists here to be able to afford to install central heating; he also wondered aloud how one became a verger, for it was not the sort of career they advertised in job centres and employment agencies, and presumably one had to be trained up to it from an early age, like a steel welder or a butler.

Amanda, clicking her tongue against the roof of her mouth out of habit rather than genuine disapproval, wandered in to the south aisle and looked at a marble bishop reclining uncomfortably on a slab. Dougal joined her, and they set off on a leisurely stroll round the cathedral.

The church oppressed him, which was curious since he usually enjoyed churches, older ones especially. He realized that the thought of meeting Mrs Munns (assuming she hadn't gone away for the weekend and had the time and inclination to see them) was part of the reason: it was difficult to concentrate on his surroundings while various conversational ploys were revolving round his mind. Beneath the present lay unknown layers of the future; Dougal admitted to himself that there was nothing very unusual in this – but then, since he had found Gumper, he had the feeling that even the present was rushing away from his control, so God alone knew what the future was going to do. And the way information had begun to fall together last night had been disturbing in itself, as if everyone and everything were pieces in a game which an anonymous mastermind was manoeuvring towards an equally unknown end.

They walked past more bishops along the south aisle to the south transept.

The interlaced Norman arcade on the south wall was very fine, Dougal told himself, quoting Vernon-Jones on the subject. But it was no use. He couldn't make himself like this building. It felt alive to him, in a slow, bleak fashion – like a gigantic stone amoeba gradually changing its shape over the centuries.

Amanda took a photograph of the arcade. ('Might as well get some use from this bloody permit.') She took Dougal's hand and discovered it was cold. Immediately she hustled him over to a blackened stove at the bottom of the south choir aisle. It was shaped like an old-fashioned birdcage and surmounted with a mitre designed for a dwarf with a strong neck.

Her action, rather than the stove, warmed him. Dougal winked at a seventeenth-century dean nearby, whose effigy was made insignificant by the rest of the articles which cluttered his monument (three sorrowing hounds, two headless wives, a series of diminishing children, his heraldic achievement, a skull and an ornate prie-dieu).

When Dougal was slightly warmer, they strolled through the ambulatory round the east end of the cathedral. The tombs here were older; it must have been a case of first-come-first-served, Dougal thought. In St Tumwulf's chapel, nothing was left of the medieval magnificence of the shrine. The site of the saint's grave was marked with a black slab. Vernon-Jones had quoted a local legend which claimed that the last of the monks had preempted the commissioners of Henry VIII and removed the holy skeleton, bricking it up, together with some of the shrine's portable wealth, in a corner of the abbey until the True Faith returned. Unfortunately, so it was said, by the time Mary ascended the throne, those in the secret were either dead or abroad.

At the east end itself was the Lady Chapel, flanked by two chantries. Dougal and Amanda hurried past, because the Church Dormant was seated near the altar rails staring at the roof – a plain, wooden construction of the last century. It was difficult to tell whether the vacuity of his gaze was due to the intense inward concentration, which Dougal gathered was essential for communing with God, or to senility. But the last thing he wanted was that the gaze should slide down from the ceiling and entrap them into conversation.

They maintained a brisk pace until they reached the north transept, where a side chapel had been converted into an enclave of ecclesiastical commerce. The verger looked at them hard as they went in, and Amanda whispered that the authorities should buy him one of those electronic devices they have at airports; the man was obviously yearning to screen all visitors and relieve them of their submachine guns and high explosives.

Amanda bought a postcard of the kneeling dean, while Dougal looked rather despairingly at the array of tea towels, ashtrays and bookmarks which commanded grossly inflated prices owing to their status as souvenirs. He caught Amanda's arm as they left the shop and suggested that they go to see Mrs Munns right away.

She agreed at once – not so much because she was tired of the cathedral, but because walking up the nave was a large man with his shoulders thrust forwards: Michael Aloysius Lee.

Dougal and Amanda retreated through a small door in the northwest corner of the transept. There was no reason why they shouldn't meet Lee, of course – arguably he wouldn't even recognize them as fellow guests, though Dougal had noticed that people tended to remember Amanda. It was rather that his presence in the cathedral made the outside world seem far more attractive. He was surprised that Amanda shared his feelings.

They crossed the green which lay between the church and the backs of the shops which ran parallel to it, and passed through the Boneyard Gate into the High Street. Saturday shoppers were out in their hundreds by now, despite the weather. The narrow pavements were jammed with shopping baskets, pushchairs and prams, controlled with a ruthless efficiency which would have made mince-meat of the tourists in Oxford Street.

'We go right, don't we?' Amanda had to raise her voice to be heard over the squawling of a passing infant; its pushchair glided over Dougal's foot.

Dougal nodded and led the way up the pavement. They went in single file – it would have been madness to walk two abreast without special training.

After a hundred arduous yards, they came to the Sacristan's Gate, an elegant fifteenth-century entrance which would not have disgraced a college at Oxford or Cambridge. Beyond it, facing the marketplace, was a row of stone-faced cottages, a terrace which had been constructed within the shell of a long monastic building. Each cottage was divided from its neighbour by a substantial buttress which projected out into the pave-ment. The windows were small and mullioned and

Dougal said that the overall effect reminded him of Disneyland, while Amanda replied that he'd never been there, had he?

'Which is the witch's front door?' enquired Dougal. Now that they were doing something other than killing time, he felt more cheerful.

'The one with the green curtains. Mrs Livabed was right – it is number eight.'

The buttresses created little oases: the shoppers surged past only inches away, but in their stone shelter there was relative peace. The front door of number eight reinforced the impression of an island of ordered tranquillity: it was painted a soothing olive green and the letter flap and knocker had that soft sheen which brass only acquires after years of regular polishing.

Dougal rang the bell. As they waited, a poodle relieved himself against the buttress on the left, before scurrying importantly away. On the other side of the road was a little marketplace, filled with cars rather than stalls. Dougal heard the unearthly wail of an untuned violin from that direction, and eventually tracked the sound down to a small tramp with wispy grey hair, looking as perky as a sparrow in a larger bird's cast-off feathers, scraping with the aplomb of a maestro. He had a soft spot for buskers, and promised himself that he would contribute something after they had seen Mrs Munns. *If* they saw Mrs Munns. He rang the bell again.

Just as they were about to go, the letter flap was drawn up from within – an uncanny sight, as if a pump handle was rising and falling of its own volition. A voice at a level between their knees and waists said firmly, 'Go away.' As an afterthought, it added, 'Please,' with a slight question mark trailing after the word.

Dougal groaned to himself. He loathed dealing with children, especially younger ones: you never knew what they would do or say, though you could be certain that it wouldn't be decently veiled by clouds of glory.

Amanda, however, was not an only child, like Dougal, but one of a large family. She knelt down and asked the letter flap what its name was, whereupon the letter flap closed abruptly with a gasp. Three seconds later it opened again, revealing a pair of large blue eyes which stared unblinkingly into Amanda's brown ones.

'Hullo,' said Amanda.

'You've come about the Mothers' Union,' accused the voice.

'No, we haven't,' replied Amanda, quick to seize an advantage. 'We've come to see Mrs Munns.'

'You can't. Mummy's in the garden.'

Footsteps could be heard approaching on the other side of the door. The letter flap closed.

'Lina! What are you doing? Is there someone there?'

'I think there *might* be,' said Lina dubiously. 'I can see eyes.'

The door opened. A woman in her thirties smiled at them. Dougal realized that much of the impression of girth she gave was due to her clothes: faded slacks, wellington boots and a windcheater which probably covered several layers of jerseys. Amanda scrambled to her feet and Dougal failed to launch into his prepared speech, partly because of Mrs Munns's appearance. He had thought that the widow of a clergyman, a pillar of local society no less (as far as he had thought of her at all), would be an ironclad, matronly figure, with her hair in the severe control of a bun. Mrs Munns in reality had a frizzy perm, a bright red windcheater and the mobile features of an exceptionally charming monkey.

'Has Lina been keeping you there for ages? I'm so sorry. I was in the garden, you see. Not gardening – banging nails into the back gate: the local teenage Mafia rode a motorcycle into it on New Year's Eve. Not that they meant any harm – I think one of them was showing off to his mates, pretending to be that Evil Whatsisname. Lina, don't suck your thumb in public, darling, and can you go and let Rowley in, I left him in the garden trying to find something edible in the compost heap. Anyway, what can I do for you?'

Mrs Munns smiled brilliantly at them again and gently detached Lina, who was clinging to her windcheater, and propelled her towards the rear of the house.

'Well. Our name's Massey – I'm William, this is Amanda. We're staying at the Crossed Keys for a night or two. We're thinking of trying to do a television documentary on Rosington – I'm a freelance writer – and Mrs Livabed at the hotel suggested we come and see you. I hope we've not come at an inconvenient time.'

'Oh no, I've finished the gate now, at least as far as I

ever will. We really need a new one, I suppose, but that's a matter of leaning on the cathedral maintenance people, which is a bit like planting oak trees – you don't really expect to see the results in your lifetime. But do come in. Would you like some coffee? I was just about to have some myself.'

The prospect of coffee was very attractive. Dougal had nearly forgotten the reason they were there. Mrs Munns ushered them through a tiny panelled hall into a sitting room which looked out, through french windows, into the garden. Mrs Munns left them there, having taken their coats.

It was a comfortable room. The furniture suited it, from the Queen Anne bureau in the corner to the home-made bookshelves which lined the alcoves on either side of the fireplace. Dougal and Amanda sat on the sofa which adapted itself to their contours. There were several Victorian watercolours on the wall, mostly of Rosington, so far as Dougal could tell. The room seemed very quiet.

Claws clattered on the flagstones of the hall. The door gently opened and an elderly black spaniel appeared. He sniffed at each of them in turn, and, having received a scratch behind the ears from both Dougal and Amanda, evidently considered the civilities to be over, for he sat down slowly in front of the empty fireplace and blinked reproachfully at the absence of heat.

Amanda whispered, 'That must be Vernon-Jones's dog . . .' but was prevented from saying more by Mrs Munns, who came into the room with the coffee.

'You've met Rowley, I see. Disturbingly well-bred, isn't he? Probably an eighteenth-century earl in his previous incarnation.'

'He's lovely,' said Amanda. 'How old is he?' Dogs, Dougal thought, were an even safer subject of conversation than the weather.

'He's over eight years old now. Age just seems to make him more stately. The only person he unbends a little with is Lina. We've only had him for a month or so, in fact.'

'Ah, yes.' Dougal seized the opening. 'Mrs Livabed mentioned he used to belong to Canon Vernon-Jones.' Rowley raised his head a fraction above his paws. 'We were reading his guide to the cathedral last night, actually, and Mrs Livabed told us he had died recently. She suggested we come and see you – not just for the history angle but for information about Rosington as a whole.'

'You'd better tell me more about what you want to do,' said Mrs Munns calmly. 'How do you like your coffee?'

They all had their coffee black, which drew from Mrs Munns the approving remark that she couldn't understand why most people had to murder the taste of perfectly good coffee with milk and sugar. Dougal and Amanda explained the idea behind the documentary between them. Mrs Munns asked sharp questions, and Dougal found that it was impossible to be as vague as with Mrs Livabed. In the end, they presented themselves as tyros in the business – Dougal merely claimed the credit for the script of the Traditional Crofter's Breakfast Cereal advertisement, which showed a kilted Highlander quoting Burns to a bowl of oats with Loch Lomond in the background.

'You know the sort of thing,' he finished, 'a combination of predigested culture, nostalgia and the past adapting to the pressures of modern society, in the context of cathedral cities. It would be nice to have someone like the Poet Laureate introducing each programme. Have a shot of the tomb of the Jacobean Dean next to a shot of the girlie magazines in the newsagent's in the High Street. Snippets of history, lots of pretty pictures and portentously meaningful reflections on present day trends.'

For a moment Dougal wondered if he was being too flippant, if he had misjudged the character of his listener. But an impish grin flashed across Mrs Munn's face.

'The idea sounds as if it should make someone a good deal of money. But I don't really see what I can do . . . you seem to have everything pretty well worked out already.'

'Well,' said Dougal, before he was interrupted by the doorbell.

'Oh, God,' said Mrs Munns. 'Do excuse me.'

9

They agreed sometime afterwards that the moment
when Lee walked into Mrs Munns's sitting room
was the moment when they should have left Rosington
and put their involvement with Caroline Minuscule into
the mental lumber room reserved for memories one
wants to discard.

It was at this point that their belief in coincidence
became untenable. Lee in the hotel was one thing; Lee
in the cathedral was another; but Lee at Mrs Munns's
house, though explainable by the fact that he could have
discovered Vernon-Jones's connection with the widow as
easily as they had, was carrying synchronicity too far.

Hindsight later suggested that Lee must have started
thinking about them then. Not that his behaviour on the
occasion had been in any way disturbing – he introduced
himself as an old friend of the Canon's, curious to know
how he had died. (Mrs Munns had accompanied him
to the hospital after his final heart attack, and was firm

in her assertion that the dying man had never regained consciousness.) Lee recognized Amanda, and Dougal by association, and was politely interested in the projected series. He had accepted a cup of coffee – with milk and sugar.

Lee was pleasant to everyone; soft Irish charm oozed out of him, so much so that Dougal found it hard to remember that the man's eyes were narrow and cold, and that his voice had the flatness of an automaton's. Without Hanbury's letter, it would have been difficult to think badly of him.

He left before them, but Dougal and Amanda followed soon afterwards. Mrs Munns lent them the authoritative history of the cathedral – Vernon-Jones's chief source – and they arranged to return at tea time tomorrow and discuss the projected programme in more detail.

Dougal found the interlude at Mrs Munns's refreshed him, even though it got them no further. It was hard to be worried about the possibility of evil in that comfortable room with the central tower framed in the window and Lina chattering away to herself on the stairs. Lina was five, Mrs Munns told them, but small for her age; she was very imaginative – 'One's own child always is!' It was difficult to keep up with the identities of her toys, which were subject to ruthless and frequent alteration. At present she ran a bus garage in a model of the cathedral. It was necessary to be particularly deferential to her largest teddy bear who had been installed as Queen Mother on Wednesday.

'Lives in a world of her own,' said Amanda with a laugh. 'Like William.'

Afterwards, Dougal and Amanda strolled through the close arguing about Vernon-Jones. She was finding it increasingly difficult to equate the popular, septuage-narian canon with the *éminence grise* of the criminal infor-mation world.

Dougal supported Hanbury – largely on the grounds that money and murder lent an air of plausibility to his interpretation. And, if Hanbury was right about Vernon-Jones's past, he was probably right about the existence of the diamonds.

The walk through the close failed to bring them any inspiration. They saw the original of the Rosington Augustine in the Chapter House museum. In Infirmary Lane they found Bleeders Hall. The house was shuttered and deserted. The guidebook said the monastic leech had plied his trade there, which Dougal thought was an appropriate description of the house's last occupant.

If nothing else, the walk gave them an appetite for lunch.

As the only other occupant of the dining room of the Crossed Keys was the Church Dormant, slurping soup of the day in the corner, they felt able to discuss the morning's progress, such as it was. Mrs Munns had been friendly but had produced no revelations. The original of the photograph had been completely uninformative

– Dougal argued that it might well be irrelevant: 'Maybe the photo was given to Hanbury and the key to some sort of cryptogram to Lee. It could be a Cardano grill.'

'What?' Amanda looked puzzled.

'It's a sheet of paper the same size as the page with numbered, letter-size windows. You put the two together and read off the letters which aren't blocked out, in the order shown. And there's your message . . . I read about it in an annual I had for Christmas when I was ten.'

Amanda laughed. 'But if codes were Vernon-Jones's hobby, you'd expect something much cleverer. He wouldn't have wanted to make it easy.'

But none of this was helpful: they simply didn't know where to begin. Dougal was aware that Lee's presence had brought a touch of fear to the proceedings, which was sapping his enthusiasm. Secretly he admitted to himself that he wanted to leave Rosington, but found it impossible to say to Amanda: 'Look, I'm scared. We're leaving this afternoon.' Those dark, fine eyebrows would arch themselves and . . . oh, God, why was he such a coward? It made him angry and despairing at the same time. All of which led quite naturally to him resting his elbows on the table and saying quietly:

'I'm going to break into Bleeders Hall this evening.'

Dougal left the hotel at seven-thirty promptly. By this time the inhabitants of the close should be sitting down to their evening meals, watching television or listening to the concert in the cathedral.

He was well prepared physically for the expedition. He was wearing the duffel coat, jeans and a pair of boots with soles which were not only air-cushioned but virtually noiseless on hard surfaces. During the afternoon he had bought a small torch, some brown paper and glue, and a pair of fine rubber gloves. He had felt self-conscious about it, for life was imitating art, but in the absence of any other model, what else could life do? His purchases were distributed among his pockets.

With Amanda he had reconnoitered the rear approach to Bleeders Hall before doing the shopping. The house had a small garden, bounded on one side by the building itself; the second and third walls divided it from neighbours' gardens, while the fourth separated it from Canons' Meadow. This was a large, bumpy field which sloped down to the river. It was the site of the monastic fishponds: shallow, grass-covered depressions marked the spots where carp and pike had waited for the fatal Friday. The eastern border of the meadow was formed by Bridge Street, a long thoroughfare which ran parallel to the river. There were two entrances to the meadow from the close which the public could use: one was a narrow footpath which ran from the door at the southeast angle of the cloister, skirted the Canon's residence at the southwest corner of Infirmary Lane and debouched into the meadow by way of a stile; the other lay in the south part of the close, remote from the cathedral.

The occupant of Bleeders Hall had access to the meadow by a door set in the garden wall. Dougal had tried it, but found it locked. The wall itself, however, had not looked an impassible obstacle. It was perhaps seven feet high, but it sloped gently inwards with age and the mortar which held the jumble of stone and brick had in places crumbled away, leaving convenient holes for the hands and feet. Peeping surreptitiously through the keyhole, Dougal had seen the house itself – a back door on the right, and three large windows on the left. The windows were unshuttered and within easy reach of the ground.

Dougal set off down the High Street, feeling at once lonely and conspicuous, as if he were a leper wearing a placard round his neck in a crowd. It had not been a pleasant afternoon. Having announced his plan, Amanda's enthusiasm had made it impossible to change his mind. She wanted to come as well, but Dougal had opposed this, strongly and successfully. She was far too valuable to be risked and in any case he preferred to go alone. If he had to be afraid, he would rather be so without witnesses. She would dine at the hotel, keep an eye out for Lee and, if necessary, explain his absence by saying that he had succumbed to Nausea in F-sharp Minor.

He passed the marketplace – the violin-playing vagrant had gone; Dougal had dropped some change into his cap while out shopping in the afternoon. He imagined the man snug in a public bar, his overcoat open to the warmth and a pint glass in front of him. But the glow of philanthropy which this image conjured was shortlived. It left him as he walked down River Hill towards Bridge Street – the least conspicuous way of reaching the Canons' Meadow. He passed a pub; he was tempted to go in for a drink or two and then return to Amanda with the lie that Bleeders Hall had been impossible to break into.

He forced himself onwards – *how mature of you*, commented the mocking, inner voice of unreason. No, it's not, he thought, if I were mature I wouldn't be here in the first place. Maturity was a stage you were always going to reach in a couple of years. Dougal rather doubted he would ever get there. Perhaps maturity wasn't so much a state as an illusion – a condition of social beatitude which had its only reality in the minds of other people.

The wind hit him as he turned into Bridge Street. He huddled into his duffel coat and felt like a character in one of those French films whose charm resided in the fact that you never knew quite what was happening but you did know it must be extraordinarily meaningful.

The meadow was protected by a wall of roughcast stone topped with broken glass. Dougal walked along until he came to the gate – a grandiose, mock-Gothic erection which looked as if it had strayed into the Fens from a pantomime version of Robin Hood.

He plodded into the field, his pace slowing automatically as the ground began to rise and the street lighting receded. It was suddenly very dark. He knew the cathedral was up there in front of him, though he found it difficult to tell which of his senses was supplying the information. Gradually he began to pick out lights in the nave and choir windows – probably dim at the best of times and filtered through paint and a film of dirt on the glass. Several of the visible windows of the houses in the close were alight, including two in Infirmary Lane. The patch of darkness between them must be Bleeders Hall.

He tripped over a fallen branch on the ground and swore. He made himself go more slowly. It was unexpectedly eerie out here in the open, though the feeling decreased as his eyes adjusted to the lack of light.

The wall which ran along the backs of the gardens gradually unscrambled itself from the shadows. Dougal stretched out his right hand and felt the rough surface of the door in the wall; the old paint flaked beneath his touch. He congratulated himself with disproportionate fervour. It seemed very important that, although he was as scared as ever, he was still capable of finding his way in the dark.

The evening was reassuringly quiet; the only sounds were remote, emphasizing rather than punctuating the overall impression of silence. A train was clattering along the railway on the far side of the river; car engines grumbled like urban indigestion in the center of Rosington; and the wind provided a gentle background, as undefinably present as the background hiss on a record. Dougal could hear nothing, human or otherwise, which qualified as a risk for him. He told himself firmly that, if the worst came to the worst, one of the three exits from Canons' Meadow should give him an escape route.

He pulled himself slowly up to the top of the wall, the surface of the mortar crumbling slightly beneath his touch. He sat on the top for a moment, listening and peering down at the blackness on the other side. He counted three, like someone preparing to get into a cold bath, and jumped.

The pile of wet, dead leaves cushioned his fall. The heap skidded under his impact, and sent Dougal sprawling on to grass. He stood up cautiously. The lighted windows of the houses on either side were curtained; nothing to fear there – and no one could possibly have heard his fall.

A path bisected the garden, leading up to the house. Dougal walked up it, at first on tiptoe but then ordinarily, as he realized that his boots were perfectly equipped to deal with this kind of surface.

The path led to the back door, which was locked. Dougal moved to the left and came to the first window, which was set back from the door. The window refused to budge. As far as he could tell, it served the kitchen.

There were two more windows further to the left. He pushed tentatively at the lower half of the next one and, to his surprise, it moved. So brown paper and glue wouldn't be necessary after all, which was probably just as well, since it would be a messy business, especially in the dark, and would probably leave traces. He wondered briefly whether there was any significance in the fact that the window had been left open, but dismissed the thought before it had had time to take root. The people of Rosington would be less security conscious than those of London, and presumably whoever was responsible for Bleeders Hall had discounted the risk of someone wanting to burgle an empty house.

Dougal raised the window noiselessly, swung his leg over the low sill and slipped into the room beyond.

He stood up, fumbling in his pocket for the torch, and full of a strange excitement, which carried him back to childhood explorations in empty houses. Anything might be waiting for him here. He had no idea what he was looking for, but he felt a sudden, fierce gladness that he had come.

He was in a long dining room which stretched back into the house. A quick survey of its contents, using the torch where necessary with its beam shielded, showed that the executors had not yet removed the furniture. Ornaments and pictures had gone, but the carpet, curtains, sideboard, table and chairs remained. The last three were of solid mahogany resting on claw feet. Already the table had a layer of dust which Dougal carefully avoided. The dust reminded him of his gloves and he pulled them on, wiping the surfaces he might have touched with his handkerchief. He obviously had a long way to go before reaching a professional standard of housebreaking.

The door was to Dougal's right at the end furthest from the windows. He moved towards it, diligently opening drawers and cupboard doors but only being rewarded by brittle twenty-year-old copies of the *Rosington Observer*. On reflection, a dining room seemed a most unlikely place to hide things and in any case a sense of urgency was creeping up on him.

The door wasn't locked, but it creaked as it opened which made him jump. He told himself firmly that there was no one to hear it, but he couldn't help regretting having broken the specious security of silence.

On the right was a green baize door. To the left, on the same wall as the dining room's entrance, was another door. Dougal could vaguely discern further doors opposite him, and a flight of stairs going up beyond the baize door. A faint glow filtered through the fanlight above the door, an exit to the outside world which forbade the use of the torch. Dougal decided that he would move methodically round the hall, in a clockwise direction, searching each room as he came to it. He noticed unthinkingly that the floor surface had changed from carpet to stone flags.

The door on the left led to a large, square room with two shuttered windows overlooking Infirmary Lane. The sofas and armchairs made its purpose obvious. There was a grand piano, with a forlorn aspidistra on top of it, in the corner by the left-hand window. Dougal had a sudden desire to play something on it – *Ain't Misbehavin'* would be appropriate – which he murdered at birth. He made a quick circuit of the room. It was as cold and featureless as the dining room. There was a little secretaire by the other window which seemed promising, but closer inspection showed that it was completely empty. If only he had been here earlier, before the more mobile of Vernon-Jones's possessions had been moved.

He left the drawing room and crossed the hall to the door opposite. It opened into what must have been the Canon's study: it was a narrow room, rather like a corridor lined to the ceiling with book shelves denuded of books. A leather-topped desk stood near the door, a chair behind it and a long table in front of it stretching towards the window. Dougal was disappointed – he had cherished an obscure hope that the Canon's books might provide a clue – some knowledge of his interests, at least.

He returned to the hall. It was chilly and smelt like a grave. His teeth wanted to chatter. His mind lined up reasons for him to leave: there was nothing to find, even if he knew what he was looking for; he was running a pointless risk by being here; he needed the warmth and light of the hotel, not to mention Amanda's down-to-earth company . . .

Plop! The noise came from upstairs – for all the world as if someone had put a finger in his or her mouth, pressed it against the cheek, closed the lips to make the mouth airtight and sharply withdrawn the finger.

After what seemed like half an hour, the sound came again. Dougal tried to persuade himself that it must be the pipes in the house; old plumbing was notoriously unpredictable. The trouble was, he could hardly run away now. He could hear himself explaining later, 'Well, I heard

a plop, you see . . .' No, he would continue his method-
ical survey of the house, despite the plumbing.

He opened the next door and found a windowless
closet, empty except for a roll of linoleum leaning drunkenly across one corner.

The stairs were next – a wide flight with shallow treads
ascending into darkness. Dougal nerved himself.

The first floor contained four bedrooms, a bathroom
and a lavatory. Dougal contented himself with giving the
rooms the most cursory of glances. The removal process
seemed to have gone further up here than downstairs –
it was impossible even to work out the bedroom which
had belonged to Vernon-Jones. The curtains were down;
the carpets rolled up; and the mattresses lay askew on
the bare springs of the beds.

A much narrower flight of uncarpeted stairs led up
to the attics. As Dougal was about to climb them, he
heard the noise again: plop-plop-pause-plop – it
sounded like Morse code. He forced himself to go up
and found two bedrooms with sloping ceilings perched
under the eaves of the house. By the amount of dust,
they had been disused for years. Each room had a
meager, cast-iron fireplace, solid with rust. In one of
the rooms was a bedstead with broken springs and no
mattress; and in the corner was a small puddle. Even
as Dougal stood in the doorway a drop of water fell
from a sodden patch in the ceiling and sent ripples
careering across the surface of the water. The plops
were explained, and he returned to the hall in a much

more cheerful state of mind, hardly bothering to walk quietly.

There were two doors remaining to be opened before he could legitimately depart by the dining room window. The first led to another lavatory, with the pedestal raised on a regal dais. The second, the green baize door, opened into a short passage, flanked by pantries, which ended in what must be the kitchen door. Dougal's torch rapidly swept over the pantries' shelves and found a cluster of empty jam jars and a discarded fork. He turned the beam towards the kitchen door two yards away. It took a moment for his mind to accept what his eyes were seeing.

The doorknob was slowly but unmistakably revolving.

10

Dougal snapped off the torch. Sweat was breaking out under the hair on his temples. Was the door closing or opening? Fear possessed him so absolutely that movement was out of the question.

The door sighed on its hinges. A draught billowed out from the kitchen, carrying the foul smell of an unwashed body. If the owner of the smell came two paces forward, he would walk into Dougal.

Metal chinked on stone: the smell increased. The listening darkness seemed to coil itself round Dougal's mind, gripping and squeezing his thoughts like a python. The panic eliminated every other consideration except one.

The need for light.

Dougal didn't decide to switch the torch on – it seemed to happen of its own accord. There was a blur of movement in the kitchen doorway, and a frantic scuffling in the darkness beyond, as if a nocturnal animal had been disturbed in its burrow.

The light converted Dougal's panic to bravado. Without thinking, he kicked the door fully open and swept the torch beam across the kitchen. Simultaneously, his mind began to work again. Whoever was in there was more afraid of Dougal than Dougal was of him. Dougal himself must be invisible behind the light. And what was this second intruder doing in Bleeders Hall?

The beam picked out a huddle of old clothes in the space between the Aga and the right-hand wall. Dougal trained the light on the corner and moved towards it with deliberate slowness. Five feet away he stopped.

At first his eyes took in only the details: cracked and mud-stained army boots, trousers which appeared to be held together with string, the shabby black material of an overcoat, a greasy tangle of grey hair, and the top of a case of some sort.

A violin case.

The details clicked together: it must be the tramp who had been busking in the marketplace. The man's face was shielded from the light, jammed under his overcoat in a bizarre parody of the pose of a sleeping bird.

Dougal let the silence linger. The only sound was the tramp's harsh, shallow breathing. He was surprised, and rather shocked, to realize that he was enjoying the novelty of the situation. The man was demonstrably scared of him – usually it was the other way round. For the first time that evening, he felt as if he was in control.

The memory of being scared by a leaking roof seemed mercifully distant.

He took a step forward and nudged the tramp with his foot.

'Look up.' His voice sounded huskier than usual.

The bundle in the corner rustled and gave a brief panic-stricken snuffle, but no face appeared.

'Look up.' Dougal repeated the words, speaking slowly and unemotionally.

This time the tramp peered cautiously into the beam of the torch. Dougal recognized the thin, unshaven face, and wondered whether the man would be able to recognize him if his face caught the light. Better not to risk it.

'I can't see,' the violinist muttered, with the suspicion of an aggrieved whine. 'Hurts me eyes.'

'Shut up. There's no need for you to see. What's your name?' God, thought Dougal, he hadn't spoken to anyone like this since he was a probationary house prefect.

'I done nothing.'

'Name.'

'Cedric.' There was a pause. 'Mills. Everyone knows me round here. I don't do no harm. Look, mister—'

'What are you doing here?' Dougal had a sudden distracting thought that Cedric's mother might have wept happy tears over *Little Lord Fauntleroy* and named her son after the eponymous hero.

'I been kipping here. No harm, honest. Old reverend used to let me sleep in the shed in the garden sometimes. He snuffed it. Bleeding cold lately and I been sleeping here, see? Not good for a house to be left empty.'

'I don't see. How did you get in?'

'Window in there, guv.' Cedric jerked his thumb towards the dining room. 'And he said it'd be all right for me to doss down here—'

'Who did?'

There was a pause in the conversation. 'Old parson,' said Cedric, squinting up at the torch. 'He useter—'

'Liar. He couldn't have done. Not unless he talked to you from the grave. Who was it?'

'Bloke in a pub, flash bloke from London. Look, I done—'

'Oh, shut up.' Could it have been Lee or Tanner? 'Tell me about the man. Where and when you met. What he said. Anything you know.'

Gradually, by further questions and the occasional nudge with his boot, Dougal worked the whole story out of him. Or as much of it as Cedric wanted to tell.

Cedric had met someone who might well be Tanner, though it was difficult to be sure because his descriptive powers were limited, in the Black Pig, a pub down by the Nonconformist chapel near the river, a couple of nights before. The man had bought Cedric a couple of drinks and pumped him. At first the questioning had been general – about Rosington and petty crime there. Then the stranger had led the conversation to Vernon-Jones. Cedric had known the Canon as one of the less repulsive local do-gooders. Vernon-Jones had visited him once or twice at the local police station and occasionally let him sleep in his garden shed. He had given Cedric both the violin and the overcoat, and Cedric consequently felt an almost proprietorial interest in his benefactor. He had sometimes done odd jobs for the Canon in the garden.

It took further footwork and interrogation on Dougal's part to discover exactly what the stranger had wanted Cedric to do.

'Then why did he tell you to break in here?'

'Nah, he never. Slipped me a fiver, didn't he, and said there'd be another if I kept an eye on the place. Said a mate of his had been left the old bloke's furniture and thought someone would nick it . . . what's it all about, guv?'

They had reached a conversational stalemate. Dougal refused to enlighten Cedric and Cedric replied to all further questions with 'Dunno, do I,' and an expression of impenetrable stupidity.

It was perfectly possible that Cedric's store of knowledge had been exhausted. Probably Lee had set Tanner to trawl for gossip in the seedier pubs of Rosington; and Tanner, realizing that Cedric knew Bleeders Hall, had acted on his own initiative and secured the services of a watchdog for a modest outlay. Alternatively, Lee might have known that Vernon-Jones had known Cedric, though this was less likely if Hanbury had been right in believing that Lee did not come to Rosington.

Lee was certainly thorough. Dougal shivered and the torch beam wavered. Perhaps Lee had arranged to have the watcher watched. No, that was being paranoid. But he had to remember not to underestimate Lee.

He looked down at Cedric. It was bitterly cold in the stone-floored kitchen. He wanted to leave, but what the hell was he going to do with Cedric? The tramp might well get a clue to his appearance somehow – and when he reported back to Lee it would not be too hard for them to work out the identity of the evening visitor at Bleeders Hall.

Nor would Cedric hold his tongue; the trouble with threats and bribery was that Lee was far more expert in their use than he, Dougal, could hope to be. Maybe he could tie Cedric up and win time for him and Amanda to escape back to the anonymity of London . . .

The light of the torch dimmed for a moment, then brightened. That battery must be a dud if it was running down already . . . He thought quickly: best to keep Cedric moving and dispose of him while the light lasted.

'Get up, Cedric. Time for a little walk.'

'Where?' The whine had an unmistakable edge of truculence now. The man's eyes flickered from side to side.

'I want to see the rest of the house. Including the cellars.' A house like this must have cellars. Perhaps there would be somewhere to put Cedric under lock and key. He wouldn't come to any harm. An anonymous call from London to the local police – or even Lee – in twenty-four hours' time would get him out.

Cedric slowly hauled himself to his feet, using the Aga as a support. His coat chinked as he did so, and Dougal realized that there was a bottle in one of those capacious pockets.

'Where do these doors lead?' Dougal gestured with his torch towards them.

'That one' – Cedric jerked a thumb at the one at the far end of the wall behind him which contained the Aga and the window – 'goes to the back door. Little room with a sink. And a toilet.' He paused and wiped his nose with the back of his hand, an action which had a surprisingly scornful air about it. 'And that one there' – next to the dresser on the wall on Dougal's right – 'goes down to the cellars.'

'Right,' said Dougal sternly. 'We'll visit the cellar first.'

Cedric remained where he was, clasping himself with his arms like a caricature of man trying to warm himself.

Dougal grew impatient and stamped his foot angrily. 'Come on! I've not got all night. Move yourself.'

'Another door over there, guv.' Cedric pointed over Dougal's left shoulder.

'Where?' Dougal half turned. There was a blur of movement and he ducked backwards instinctively. The blow thudded down on his right shoulder, tearing a grunt of pain from the back of his throat.

The torch was now directed at the floor – fortunately the blow had not made him drop it – and by its light Dougal dimly saw that Cedric had raised his arm again. He dodged away and put the kitchen table – a large and reassuringly solid piece of furniture in the middle of the room – between himself and Cedric.

His first conscious thought was how unbelievably

stupid he had been. He had categorized Cedric as an elderly alcoholic; and had failed to realize that the man scraped a living by his wits. He had probably survived dozens of fights like this.

But Dougal still had the torch. He shone it on Cedric and was shocked by the change in him. The pert sparrow had given way to the bird of prey. The little man's head was thrust forward over the collar of his overcoat. His nose probed towards Dougal like a beak. His lips were pulled back in a soundless snarl, revealing yellow, predatory teeth. His beady, close-set eyes gleamed in the light.

In his right hand was the sherry bottle which had missed Dougal's head by inches. His left hand was in the pocket of his coat and, as Dougal watched, he pulled out a wooden handled kitchen knife, its six-inch blade honed to a glittering edge, its point masked with a cork.

Cedric gripped the cork with his teeth, pulled it from the knife and spat it on to the floor. He laid the blade on his cheek and scraped it lovingly against his stubble. Dougal could hear the rasp.

'Now, sonny. Gonna change yer tune?'

He began to move round the table, his weapons poised.

Dougal edged away from him. In a moment Cedric would be between him and his only means of escape – the green baize door and the dining room window. If he could delay Cedric—

He snapped off the torch and desperately shoved the

heavy table in the direction of the tramp. His bruised shoulder protested but he hardly felt the pain. The table skidded over the flagstones and jolted against Cedric.

Dougal leapt for the kitchen door and was through it in an instant, with Cedric scrabbling behind. There was a fleeting satisfaction to be gained from the thought that Cedric was probably even less at home in the dark than he was, after having the light in his eyes for several minutes. He groped frantically for the handle of the green baize door.

The delay was nearly fatal. Just as he realized, or rather remembered, that there was no handle – the door was designed to allow tray-laden servants to shoulder it open from either direction – Cedric cannoned into him. The bottle flailed blindly – Dougal could feel the wind of its passage – but the arc of its swing was too small to do any damage. Dougal heard the scrape of steel on stone: the knife on the wall.

He half turned towards his assailant and drove his right knee up into the darkness. It connected and Cedric screeched; it sounded as if his mouth was only inches away from Dougal's ear.

Cedric grabbed the leg as it descended, clinging to it like a lifeline. The two men fell heavily to the floor. The bottle shattered and the confined space of the passage was thick with the smell of sherry.

For several nightmarish seconds their bodies thrashed together, wriggling, clawing and elbowing. Dougal was thrust violently against the wall but managed to use the hard surface as the launching pad for a blind dive towards the jagged sound of his antagonist's breathing. By a miracle he found himself on top – Cedric, his tiny body pinned to the ground, blaspheming obscenely beneath him.

His right hand was weighing down Cedric's left arm: the arm, Dougal hoped, with the knife at the end. Dougal inched his grip towards Cedric's wrist. He could feel something twisting into the heavy material of his duffel coat. With a shock, he realized it must be the top of the broken bottle: the classic weapon of the pub brawl. He pushed out with his left elbow and Cedric's grinding stopped abruptly.

His right hand had reached Cedric's left. Dougal curled his fingers around the hand that clutched the knife and began to squeeze it. Cedric's smaller hand tightened on the handle of the knife. For a second, Dougal's pressure and Cedric's resistance achieved the strained and fragile equilibrium of Chinese wrestling.

Dougal relaxed his grip fractionally. Cedric's arm moved uncontrollably away. The man shrieked then, as if he knew what that momentary loss of muscular direction had cost him. Cedric squirmed over on to his side in a frantic effort to regain his weapon. Dougal's wrist was suddenly sandwiched between Cedric and the floor. A stab of pain seared up his arm and he lost his grip on the knife.

Cedric jerked wildly. Dougal rolled off, away from the deadly point of the knife. As he did so, Cedric shrieked:

the sound began high up the scale and trailed down in pitch and volume to a low whimper.

A faint bubbling sound came from the region of his face.

Dougal was alone in the house.

11

'Can't say I see much in this modern music, myself.' Lee bulldozed his way through the last of the Saturday night drinkers in the hotel bar and set the drinks down on their table. 'Your lady wife and me were agreeing that there's more noise than melody, if you know what I mean. I like something with a bit of a tune to it.'

'Time, ladies and gentlemen, *if* you please,' cried Mrs Livabed behind the bar.

'It was a bit boring,' Dougal admitted cautiously. 'Bloody cold. I could've done with a few more jumpers.' He wondered whether he looked as white and strained as Amanda did. A pulse was jumping erratically in his eyelid; he knew from experience it wouldn't be visible – it just felt as if it was. 'It wasn't worth missing dinner for. I kept wondering what you were having.' The memory of Bleeders Hall was trying to suck him down, like a bog.

'Carré d'Agneau.' Amanda looked at him; he could

smell the garlic on her breath. She smiled demurely. 'Thought you might be hungry so I got you some peanuts.'

She was annoyed, Dougal realized: perhaps she had been worried about him. He tore his way into the blue packet and forced himself to offer the contents to Amanda and Lee.

'How's the program coming on?' asked Lee.

Amanda answered, effortlessly embroidering their cover story, leaving Dougal marooned among the sea of unpleasant thoughts. God, he thought desperately, how he hated Lee for looking at Amanda as if he thought she was finger-lickin' good . . . the hair sprouting from the man's nostrils was really obscene . . . he mustn't think about Bleeders Hall, no, not yet . . . he felt sick with apprehension, the whisky was setting his stomach on fire . . .

He forced his mind to stop, and made it blank. He counted five, took another sip of whisky and told himself to deal with the problem on hand. What the hell was Lee doing with Amanda? How long had they been together? Dougal remembered thinking five minutes ago, as he walked at last into the foyer of the hotel, that the horrors of the evening had come to an end – or at least an intermission. At that moment, Lee had called out from the bar, 'And what can I get you, Mr Massey?' and Dougal had realized he had been fooled: the dreadful logic of the evening was pitiless.

'What do *you* do for a living, Mr Lee?' Dougal found

himself saying. He interrupted Amanda's imaginative description of the difficulties under which freelance television researchers laboured. Both she and Lee looked at him in surprise; but talking was better than thinking, and he was too tired for finesse.

Lee responded smoothly. 'I work for a firm of import wholesalers. Big sales drive in the Midlands coming up next week. I'm meant to be sorting out the details this weekend with young Tanner's help.' There was a nicely calculated pause. 'Tanner's the nephew of our MD.'

Lee droned on about his marketing campaign. Dougal knew it was as false as their own cover story, but the tone of the remark about Tanner had a hint of truth – it suggested that Lee's opinion of his subordinate was not a high one.

His opinion of Cedric would have been even lower. Dougal swallowed, the whisky suddenly tasting acrid in his mouth, at the thought of the gormless expression on Cedric's face.

For one terrible moment, he felt the weight of the little man in his arms, his head and legs trailing and scraping against walls and door jambs.

'Time, please,' said Mrs Livabed, and Dougal thought, that was just what he needed: time to work out what was happening, time to work out what he'd done in Bleeders Hall and, most of all, time to rest. He became aware that the conversation was flowing on.

'Job security's nil,' Amanda was saying. 'And TV companies tend to go for established names, not semiamateurs like us. And William's conducting a running feud with the taxman.'

'Incredible,' said Lee. For a moment, Dougal thought he meant it. 'Don't you destroy my illusions. We salesmen are so caught up on the financial roundabouts – we like to think there's some fun to be had on the swings.'

He glanced at his watch – a square monster with a broad gold bracelet and a multipurpose digital display – and pantomimed surprise. 'Getting on, isn't it?' He drained his glass and stood up. 'I'm off to bed.' His Irish accent became more pronounced. 'Och, you young things have just begun.' A roguish smile flitted across his battered features, like a kitten sprinting across an armoured car. He wished them goodnight and strolled out of the bar, turning left in the direction of the stairs.

'Whole bloody evening's been hysterical,' said Amanda. 'How about yours?'

'Let's go to bed.' Dougal was finding it hard to focus on Amanda's face.

'Hey, there's one thing I found out this evening, despite that creep Lee being around. There's an Ordnance Survey map up on the wall by the reception desk. I was looking at it after dinner. I found a village a few miles away from here. And guess what it was called. Charleston Parva.'

'Oh, no.' Despite the whisky and shock which between them maintained a delicate balance of befuddlement in his mind, Dougal saw the significance of the name immediately. That, he supposed drearily, was why Hanbury had chosen him.

One of Mrs Livabed's minions swooped to collect the empty glasses.

'Yes,' said Amanda. 'Caroline Minuscule.'

The difficulty Dougal had with the stairs forced him to realize how tired he was. On the first-floor landing, they passed the Church Dormant who was shuffling towards the lavatory at the end of the passage. Dougal averted his face and walked more quickly. Amanda looked at him sharply, but said nothing. Dougal tried to resist the flickers of paranoia; it was ridiculous to feel there might be a mark of Cain glowing on his forehead and absurd to fear that a clergyman would be particularly sensitive to its presence.

Once in the bedroom, Dougal's legs refused to work. He collapsed on the bed while Amanda stood with folded arms looking down at him.

'For God's sake, William. What have you been doing?' She had the white of the door behind her and looked dark, stern and beautiful.

'Well . . . I got into the house – one of the windows was unlocked – and searched the place from top to bottom.' His voice sounded harsh and alien in his ears: too many cigarettes, and now he wanted another one. 'It had been cleared out, except for the heavier bits of furniture.' And the damp, and the watchful darkness. 'There was nothing left to find.'

'Then why are you in such a state?'

Because I killed a man. I didn't mean to. The knife stuck in the wound like a cork in a bottle. When I touched his hair, it felt like the skin of a dead rat.

'There was a man there, in the kitchen. You remember that tramp with the violin in the marketplace? Lee had hired him. No, Tanner did the hiring, I think. Just to keep an eye on the place – see if anyone else was interested in Bleeders Hall . . .'

He'd have to tell her the truth, he realized, there was no alternative. She was too important to him. Even if it sent her scudding out of the room and down to the police. He was playing Consequences with his future: and she said . . . and the world said; but he hoped the world would never be in a position to form an opinion.

'I talked to him a little, then he attacked me. With a broken bottle and a knife. The torch went out, and we were rolling around on the floor.' No need to go into detail. 'It was all so confused . . . we were both trying to get the knife, but it got to his heart first.' Not much blood: just a slender circle round the half of the knife and a trickle from the corner of the mouth. The immobility of death hadn't ennobled Cedric's face: life and cunning had seeped away, leaving an expression of impersonal imbecility behind. 'I . . . killed him, you know.'

'Oh, Jesus.' Amanda was suddenly busy: searching for cigarettes in her handbag. Dougal lay in silence. The confession had sucked him dry. His bruised shoulder was aching. For the first time since Cedric's death, resignation filtered through the despair. There was nothing more to do – it was out of his hands. The prisoner in the dock could only wait for the jury to return. Guilty or not guilty?

'The body, William, what did you do with the body?'

Dougal stared at her with surprise and some unidentifiable feeling that was curiously close to disappointment. The jury hadn't returned. It couldn't, because it had never existed. He was facing another sort of tribunal.

'There's a cellar. Cedric – the tramp – was sleeping down there. He'd pulled a mattress down from the attics. All his stuff was there.' Cedric's parting present to the world had been a duffel bag containing a magazine named *Slinky Morsels*, a Noddy toothbrush with its bristles grey and splayed, an army surplus jersey, a pair of filthy, gaily checked, nylon socks and a half full bottle of reddish liquid which, by its smell, seemed to be a cocktail composed of red wine and methylated spirits. 'I carried him down and laid him on the mattress—' trying to keep his stomach from heaving and his heart from pounding, trying to believe that he might have been a butcher's apprentice carrying the carcass of a lamb '—and wrapped his fingers round the handle of the knife . . . it was all I could think of doing.'

He was silent, groping in a jungle of memories: the soft moaning noise he made as he crawled across the flagstones in search of the torch, dropped at some point during the struggle; that evening on the Ganges five years ago, watching the fires glowing on the ghats of

Benares, with the air hot and heavy with improbable barbecue smells; and an article he'd read somewhere which distinguished between murder, manslaughter and accidental death.

'Fingerprints,' said Amanda coldly.

'I was wearing those gloves all the time. I threw them in the river on the way back.'

'They'd float.'

'I weighted them with gravel.'

'What else did you do with him? Cedric.'

'Not much. I poured a bit of his booze over him, tried to make him seem even more pissed than he was. The bottle he attacked me with got broken, but I left the pieces where . . . it happened – he could have dropped it himself. There was no blood to clear up . . .' His voice trailed miserably away. He wished he knew what forensic scientists were capable of. 'We've got to get away from here. And I'd better destroy these clothes.'

'Did anyone see you?'

'I don't think so.' The worst moment had been leaving Bleeders Hall. A woman in the next-door garden had been calling her cat. 'There was no one in the meadow or down by the river. By the time I got back to the town itself, people were coming out of pubs. I don't see why anyone would have noticed me.'

Amanda sat down on the edge of the bed and picked up her hairbrush. Her rituals were sacrosanct, Dougal thought: even World War III wouldn't be allowed to begin until eyeliner had been applied to her satisfaction.

He began to unlace his boots – occupying his hands might occupy his mind as well. *I've killed a man . . . I've killed a man.* The words circled his mind like a blue-bottle trying to escape from a room with closed windows. It was difficult to apply them to himself – William Dougal who infuriated Amanda by rescuing spiders from the bath instead of flushing them away.

His boots thudded on the floor. Dougal flexed his toes in relief and decided that the time had come to pull himself together.

'What have *you* been doing this evening?' He spoke more loudly than intended; Amanda's head jerked up, though her brushing didn't falter.

'Damn. It's all knotted . . . got bored, mainly. I had dinner early, and then came up here and read for a bit. I wish we had a room with a television. You didn't come back, so I went down to get some more coffee and a drink. That's when I looked at the map. Do you think there's anything in this Charleston Parva business, by the way?'

'Must be, I should think. Too much of a coincidence. And, from Hanbury's letter, it's just the sort of thing which would have appealed to Vernon-Jones.' It wasn't worth mentioning, Dougal decided, that Vernon-Jones might have thought that the name of the village was a tasty red herring; the significance of Caroline Minuscule might still lie elsewhere.

'I'd just seen the village on the map when Lee came up behind me. It was horrible – as if he knew just what was in my mind, which he can't have done. He offered me a drink and I said yes, just to get him away from it. I think he's decided we're worth checking up on – he was asking where we lived, and how we knew Mrs Munns. Then you came in, looking like a ghost, which didn't help.'

'Oh, God.' With Cedric in the past and Lee looming in the future, the present was becoming increasingly unbearable. 'We've got to get away, you know.'

'We can't go now,' said Amanda firmly. 'Besides, what about Charleston Parva?'

She was right, Dougal thought. Demanding the bill at this time of night would only draw attention to themselves. And trying to slip out unobserved might be even worse.

'Early tomorrow morning, then. It's just too dangerous to hang around here now.'

Amanda nodded. 'We could go through Charleston Parva on the way – it's only a mile or two off the A1.'

Dougal looked at her. She was dabbing cold cream on her face, frowning as she smoothed it around her eyes. For her, their route home was settled. He was too tired to argue. He got to his feet. The things he had to do before sleep stretched uninvitingly before him – his teeth, washing, the lavatory and undressing, an iron routine which was justified only by its goal.

Amanda reached for the cotton wool. 'Why don't you check Pooterkin's book? He might mention Charleston Parva.'

Dougal swore. The words bounced randomly in the air between them; they weren't aimed directly at Amanda – merely at the fact that Cedric was dead and she was talking about Charleston Parva. He became aware he was being ridiculous; there were no graceful exit lines available, so he picked up his toothbrush.

Surprisingly, Amanda laughed. She tipped up her handbag and extracted the keys of the wardrobe and the briefcase from a nest of paper handkerchiefs. While Dougal concentrated on his upper molars, she found the book and tossed it on the bed beside him. It fell open at the page where Hanbury's photograph acted as a marker.

His eyes began to read automatically: . . . *after the conquest, it is possible to discern the gradual invasion of Norman script and scribal routines. The use of a more pointed quill makes its first appearance, as might be expected, in the documentary band . . .*

And then he remembered. He got up and spurted the contents of his mouth in the general direction of the basin. His mind was abruptly emptied of everything except one awkward memory.

The photograph had not been between these pages, but further on in the book – marking the passage about the Rosington Augustine.

Which meant that someone had looked at it.

'Amanda,' he said urgently. 'Have you opened the briefcase before just now?'

She shook her head. She sat in a strained silence while

Dougal examined the locks of the briefcase and the wardrobe. There were tiny scratches around them.

'It must have been Tanner.' Her voice had a taut, dry quality, which Dougal automatically put down to fear. It had been absent when he told her about Cedric. But this affected them both.

'While Lee kept us occupied downstairs . . . so now they don't just suspect us, they know.' Dougal sat down heavily on the bed.

The tic above his eye was jumping more violently than ever. His fingers groped across the bedspread and picked up Vernon-Jones's visiting card. It must have fallen out of the book. He flicked the pasteboard with his fingers. Oh, God, Tanner must have found the reference on the back – by now, Lee would know as much as they did. No, more – for he must have his own clues.

He turned the card over and stared at the pencilled reference on the back.

It should have read *Matthew vii* 7.

Nothing was that easy this evening, Dougal thought dully. Since he had last looked at the card, the reference had changed.

Proverbs xxiii 5.

12

When Dougal crept back to consciousness in the grey light of morning, he was surprised to find that it was nearly 8:30 A.M. He had expected to sleep fitfully, if at all. They had packed most of their belongings the night before, in the hope of an early start. That was now impossible – their tired bodies had seen to that.

The events of last night were fresh in his mind but they were no longer hedged in by that breathless sensation of panic; that had disappeared with the darkness. In its place had come an equally urgent feeling.

He was starving.

Leaving Amanda to slough off her morning surliness and apply her makeup, he went down to breakfast, taking the stairs two at a time. He picked up an *Observer* from the reception desk and slipped into the dining room.

The Church Dormant was there as usual – this time sheltering behind the *Sunday Telegraph*. There was no sign of Lee or Tanner. Had they already had breakfast?

Or were they going to come in after a minute or two and do their best to upset his digestive processes?

A dumpy waitress with a face like a wet sponge took his order. Amanda had generously waived her right to breakfast again, so he was able to double his allowance. While he waited, he decided to tell Mrs Livabed they were leaving.

She was sitting in her office off the hall in front of an ashtray overflowing with Silk Cut butts.

'Hullo, Mr Massey. What can I do for you?'

'Not disturbing you, am I?' Dougal pointed at the calculator beside the ashtray.

'Doesn't matter.' Her mouth drooped lugubriously. 'It's only the Value Added. Though it should be called Trouble Doubled if there was any justice in this world.'

'Drat the VAT,' suggested Dougal. She laughed. He explained that they would like their bill made up, apologizing for the short notice. Amanda had suddenly remembered it was her grandmother's birthday; they had decided to drive to Wales and pay her a surprise visit.

Mrs Livabed graciously denied any possibility that their sudden departure would inconvenience the hotel. Dougal, not to be outdone, hinted that, if the programme got off the ground, a production team could hardly ask for a better headquarters than the Crossed Keys.

It was fortunate that they were interrupted before Mrs Livabed had had time to ask too many questions about the composition, habits and requirements of production teams.

The stolid face of the waitress craned round the door. 'Yer breakfast,' it said reprovingly, and vanished.

'Oh, dear,' muttered Mrs Livabed, 'those Fen girls. I do try, Mr Massey, I really do.'

An hour later, they were out of the hotel. Dougal was full and Amanda was clean; both of them in their different ways were equipped to meet the morning.

It was sunny outside. Despite the cold, the sky was an improbable shade of Mediterranean blue. Dougal felt a mild euphoria which he sternly told himself was nothing but a reaction to last night. He was immensely relieved that neither Lee nor Tanner had put in an appearance. *See no evil . . .*

In the courtyard the Mini was waiting for them beside a grey Ford Anglia, bespattered with bird droppings, and a gleaming black Lancia with a pink fluffy object on the window ledge.

Amanda shook the car keys in the direction of the Lancia. 'Lee's?'

Dougal nodded. 'We should have checked the register.' He was annoyed with himself for missing such an obvious point. 'I bet Lee did.' It was always possible that Lee had left his car somewhere else.

The Mini gave a depressed moan when Amanda pressed the starter. They hadn't used the car since Friday evening and it evidently felt aggrieved by their neglect. Amanda patted the steering wheel and crooned to the Mini in the sort of voice people usually reserve for puppies, kittens and babies in their less revolting moments. Dougal sneered at this useless sentimentality in the privacy of his mind. The engine gave an asthmatic cough and began to roar.

'Charleston Parva,' said Amanda.

Dougal sighed. All his instincts urged him towards escape. 'We go out of town the way we came in. Then we turn off left on the B something – it should be signposted to Slungford.'

'Isn't that where they make loo paper? People got upset about one of their adverts.'

'It was the bottom that did it.' Dougal quoted: '*Sveltex from Slungford . . . the supersoft way to bring a touch of luxury to your bottom*. Charleston Parva's about four miles before Slungford, I checked on the map after breakfast. It looks as small as the name suggests.'

After a mile the outskirts of Rosington gave way to the dark monotony of the Fens. The landscape flattened them, Dougal thought, and the sky, like an immense Wedgwood bowl upturned around the horizon, reduced the Mini to a brightly coloured insect.

As they turned off towards Slungford, Dougal glanced back over his shoulder. The road was empty.

Amanda settled down to a steady forty. The road was a geometrically straight line which ran in the lee of a floodbank. Dougal lit a cigarette, whereupon Amanda said he was smoking too much, and didn't she get offered one too?

Dougal replied by passing her his cigarette, lighting

another and saying, '*Wilt thou set thine eyes on that which is not? For riches certainly make themselves wings: they fly away as an eagle towards heaven.* I don't like it, love. Too bloody devious by half – as if the whole business is a nasty series of illusions.'

'What worries me—' began Amanda.

'I know. Who put the card with the second reference in the briefcase. And why? It's all cockeyed. It made sense before we found the card – that Lee should have kept you and then us occupied while Tanner searched our room for anything suspicious. Even that Tanner should have taken our reference—'

'That was a pretty stupid thing to do, actually. One way of making sure we knew the room had been searched.'

'Well, Tanner looks stupid,' Dougal objected. 'Maybe he wanted a little hard evidence to show Lee. But what about the second card left in its place? Could it have been meant as a warning?'

Amanda nodded. 'I suppose so. But it's not really Lee's style, is it? It doesn't fit in with what Hanbury said about him, either. You'd expect a more . . . forceful reaction.'

Dougal shivered and automatically glanced behind again. Simultaneously, Amanda dabbed viciously down on the accelerator and the Mini jerked forward. They had both seen the same thing.

A black car nearly a mile behind.

There was a bitter taste in Dougal's mouth. The Mini, he knew, would have difficulty outdistancing a healthy tractor; it stood no chance whatsoever against a new Lancia.

The road saved them – or rather those forgotten engineers who had drained the Fens. The floodbank turned abruptly to the left, like a dog offered a more interesting scent. The road obediently followed. Amanda, taken by surprise, negotiated the 90-degree bend in top gear. The car's brakes shrieked as it skidded on to the other side of the road. Dougal clutched his seat belt as if it was a lifeline.

'Jesus,' he said in gratitude as the Mini picked up speed. The word was cut short by Amanda bringing the car to the sort of emergency stop that takes months from the life of a driving instructor.

'The gate,' she said tersely.

Dougal was out of the car before he understood what she meant. The road had swung gently away from the floodbank, leaving a depression running between the two. A barbed wire fence, pierced by a five-bar gate, separated the road from this dry moat.

He swung the gate open and Amanda wrenched the Mini through the gap. A notice nailed to the lefthand gate post announced GREAT OUSE RIVER AUTHORITY – TRESPASSERS WILL BE PROSECUTED. As he ducked down beside the Mini, uncomfortably aware that an observant driver would still be able to see the car from the road, he thought longingly of the relative physical security which a court of law implied.

A few seconds later, the black car swept round the

corner. Dougal felt his fear change into a sense of his own stupidity.

The car was not the Lancia. It was an elderly Morris Traveller driven by a grey-haired woman with a perm like a German helmet. A wire grill divided the front seats from a writhing mass of dogs in the back.

A few minutes later, Dougal and Amanda drove on. They were both shaken. The woman in the car was unimportant, Dougal knew; in any case she couldn't have seen them, for she drove crouched over the steering wheel with her eyes glued to the road. It was the way that an unnecessary fear had swooped out of the bright sky which was alarming.

I'm just not cut out for this sort of life, Dougal thought. Aloud he said: 'If Vernon-Jones gave Lee two clues as well, and if that quote from Proverbs was one of them (leaving aside how it came to be in our room), then we've got three of the four clues.'

He felt his pulse surreptitiously: it was returning to normal. Talking of clues was a reassuringly academic activity.

'Probably Lee's got four now,' Amanda remarked crushingly. 'If we'd hidden our two better, that wouldn't have happened.'

'Yes, well.' Dougal was annoyed with himself for rising to the oblique reproof. 'But let's see what we have got. If the photograph gives us the name of the village, the *Seek and ye shall find* quote implies the diamonds are somewhere obvious there. And the Proverbs one suggests they're hidden off the ground – riches making themselves wings and so on. The bit about flying towards heaven might mean they're in the church – up the tower, perhaps. After all, it's the only building in the village that we can be reasonably sure Vernon-Jones knew.'

'Oh, sure,' said Amanda. 'And what about the first bit of that Proverbs quote? *Wilt thou set thine eyes on that which is not?* That could be Vernon-Jones telling us that there's no pot of gold at the end of the rainbow. Or Lee warning us off.'

Dougal stared out of the window. They were passing through a featureless Fen village, an island of drab buildings in a sea of mud. CHARLESTON PARVA 2 said a signpost. 'We've covered that,' Dougal said. 'If we trust Hanbury's reading of his character, there's got to be a pot of gold. And Hanbury's reading of Lee's character suggests he'd warn us off in a much more . . . unequivocal way. And I rather doubt' – Dougal felt a touch of sarcasm creep into his voice – 'that Lee has a pile of Vernon-Jones's cards to use when he runs out of postcards.'

Amanda made a moue with her lips and then laughed, which warmed Dougal. 'Okay, William, we look at the church first.'

A few hundred yards later, Dougal realized that her concession and her laughter were equally meaningless. The glow evaporated. Amanda had gained her main point last night – the agreement that they would go home through Charleston Parva. (*Don't be so timid, William. I want to be rich even if you don't . . . that old tramp may be dead but we're still alive, for God's sake . . .)*

So were Lee and Tanner.

'We're going to be painfully obvious when we get there,' Dougal observed, 'if Charleston Parva's as empty as that last village, Mudgley whatever it was.'

'Mudgley Burnham. And nonsense, we look perfectly respectable. Lucky you're wearing those tweeds. We'll look just like the sort of tourists who always go for parish churches.'

In February? thought Dougal, but kept the thought to himself. The new tweed was prickling through his shirt and scratching his legs.

The road wiggled violently and they found themselves, without warning, in Charleston Parva. There was so little of the village that they overshot the centre and had to reverse back to the crossroads which seemed the only reason for the village's existence. Amanda turned into the forecourt of a pub which sprawled across the north-west corner of the junction.

The inn was L-shaped and called the Burnham Arms. Its roof, green with age, undulated irregularly. There were already half a dozen cars in the little car park, including the Traveller which had passed the Mini on the road. It was odd that there should be so many cars at this time of day – and even odder, Dougal thought, that there should be a coach as well.

The coach was old enough to have begun life as a char-à-banc. It had recently and inexpertly been painted

purple. Flaming yellow capitals staggered along its side:
RICHARDS OF ROSINGTON — THE ONLY WAY TO TRAVEL.
It was empty.

They climbed stiffly out of the Mini. A chorus of
barking, led by a fox terrier, greeted them from the back
of the estate car. There was a sticker on the back window,
just in front of the fox terrier's slavering jaws. VIVISECTORS
ARE MURDERERS, read Dougal, and thought that the fox
terrier probably would be if he could, as well.

Across the road was a shuttered village shop, the last
and largest of an uncoordinated terrace of cottages.
Diagonally opposite the Burnham Arms was the small,
dilapidated church. It looked as if it had grown out of
the mound on which it stood by a long and entirely
fortuitous process of organic growth; nature seemed to
have given the experiment up as a bad job several
centuries before.

The only other building of note occupied the fourth
corner of the crossroads. It was a trim Queen Anne house
guarded by blank, neatly regimented flowerbeds and
black iron railings. It reminded Dougal of a grown-up
doll's house.

Apart from the dogs, there was no sign of life. Perhaps
all the villagers lived in a council estate tucked inconveniently out of sight.

Amanda strode across the road to the lychgate. Dougal
followed, watching her hair bouncing on her shoulders
and thinking that the village was like a stage before the
actors came on.

There was a notice board to the right of the gate. They stared at a weathered poster advertising a bring-and-buy sale in July of last year, in aid of the church spire. Dougal looked up at it. The sale seemed to have failed to achieve its purpose, for the spire perched like a tattered tepee on the squat tower of the church. Several of its slates were missing and the weathercock was bent at a 45-degree angle.

The only other notice was a sheet of paper which informed them that the church was dedicated to St Tumwulf – 'D'you see?' said Dougal – and the vicar was a Reverend H. B. Black, BD, who was also Vicar of Charleston Monachorum five miles to the east and Rector of Mudgley Burnham. Services during Lent at St Tumwulf's would be held on the . . . but at this point some mischance had removed the lower half of the paper, leaving a jagged tear.

'What · a name,' said Amanda. 'The vicar's, I mean. Imagine all those jokes about putting lead in your pencil.'

The hinges of the gate squealed in agony as Dougal opened it. They began to walk up the path through the churchyard. Aging gravestones, chipped, cracked and forlorn, clustered thickly on the mound around the church. The path led to a porch on the north wall of the nave, sending out two lesser tributaries, one of which circled the church, while the other continued eastwards to an iron gate rusting in the middle of a screen of rhododendrons and pines at the end of the churchyard.

When they were still twenty yards from the porch, the

sound of an engine made them stop and turn their heads back to the crossroads. A black Lancia cruised into the forecourt of the Burnham Arms and drew up beside the Mini. Dougal felt almost glad. The waiting was over; the Sunday morning tranquillity was a fake.

The driver's door opened and Lee lumbered out. He was alone, which was something. It also showed how low he rated their potential abilities as opponents – he must have thought Tanner would be unnecessary. But how had he known they would be here?

Without noticing, Dougal and Amanda had been backing towards the porch. But they were too late. Just as they reached the shadow of it, Lee saw them. He raised his right arm in greeting. Or threateningly? His heavy body began purposefully to move across the road towards them.

Panic gripped Dougal and Amanda simultaneously. They turned and ran into the porch, losing the vestiges of their credibility as innocent bystanders. Dougal scrabbled at the heavy iron latch of the door, pushed at it with all his weight and fell into the church with Amanda at his heels.

They both gasped.

Instead of an empty building, the church was full of people, many of them sombre in gowns of purple or black. A sonorous voice was saying, '. . . Hymn number four hundred and seventy.'

A harmonium somewhere out of view wheezed the opening bars and was followed by a wave of sound which swam round the dumpy Norman pillars of the nave, ricocheted down from the grimy rafters and overwhelmed Dougal and Amanda as they stood by the door.

> *Praise my soul, the King of heaven;*
> *To his feet thy tribute bring . . .*

13

'Quite frankly,' said the Reverend H. B. Black, BD, to the plate of cheese and tomato sandwiches which he held protectively to his broad, black-fronted chest, 'I don't hold with this sort of goings-on at all. Apart from all the Romish tendencies of the service, all these middle-class trappings aren't entirely what *I* call Christianity.' He put down the plate of sandwiches and downed his glass of sherry with one defiant swallow. The mournful, Mancunian voice droned on: 'I wanted a city parish, of course – some sort of chance to open a valid dialogue with the secular lower-income bracket . . .'

Dougal and Amanda sighed sympathetically and continued to eat and drink. Mr Black represented security: he guarded them in one corner of the large, elegant dining room, while Lee was across the other side of the room, blocking the only exit.

It had been extremely embarrassing in the church, though Dougal realized that the unexpected congregation had saved them, for the moment, from Lee. During the hymn a black-gowned personage, who radiated ineffable superiority, had swept them into a pew beside the Morris Traveller woman. The latter had glared at them and said 'Shush!' before they had had time to say anything. There had been nothing for it but to fumble through the hymnals with which their guide had thoughtfully provided them. Then Lee had come crashing through the door and had been immediately deflected into another pew.

Gradually the jungle of impressions had sorted themselves out. The godlike beings in black and purple gowns were public schoolboys; one or two girls, similarly attired, were among them. They looked like sixth formers. There were several masters and mistresses, distinguishable, from the rear, by the hoods on their gowns and the greyness of their hair. In the chancel of the little church, two priests, assisted by a pair of servers in surplices, were conducting the service.

Dougal fumbled through the prayer book and discovered that they were in the middle of Matins. He calculated, with the aid of childhood memories, that they were in for Holy Eucharist after this. And probably a sermon at some point. It was a quarter to eleven and it seemed unlikely that Lee would be able to do anything until midday at least, as long as they stayed where they were.

The service lasted for an eternity. They mechanically knelt, stood and sat when appropriate. The sermon, delivered by Mr Black's colleague, a wiry, square-faced priest with flashing teeth and reptilian sibilants, explained what was happening. They were in the middle of a service in commemoration of the foundation of Rosington School.

Tradition claimed, it seemed, that the school had been founded by St Tumwulf himself at Charleston Parva, and had moved to Rosington in the twelfth century to swell the ranks of the Abbey choir school. After generations of medieval obscurity and post-Reformation sloth, the vision of a Victorian headmaster had moved the school's site outside Rosington again and turned it into the major public school it was today. (At this point Dougal thought he detected a nuance of sarcasm in the preacher's voice.) But it was only right that they should gather together to remember their roots – a tiny school in this minute village, struggling to keep alight a small and flickering torch of learning. In such a way, the clergyman concluded, his delivery increasing in speed as the end drew nigh, did God keep the light of love burning in the human soul; and it was our duty, both as members of the school and of the human race, to nourish this precious flame which had been passed down to us from generation to generation. In the name of the Father, and of the Son, and of the Holy Ghost. Amen.

The service continued. The only person who appeared to be enjoying it was the chaplain, who scurried about the chancel, occasionally muttering an instruction to Mr Black.

During the last hymn, priests and acolytes processed away to the vestry. The congregation shuffled to its feet and eased its way out of the narrow and hideously uncomfortable pews. Dougal began to panic again and to wonder what Lee was about to do; he felt helpless, incapable of decision. But the immediate future was abruptly removed from his hands when the woman beside them leaned across Amanda and asked loudly: 'Are you an Old Boy or a journalist, young man?'

'Neither, actually,' said Dougal diffidently. The old lies came out, in the absence of anything to put in their place. 'We're researching for a possible television documentary on Rosington and of course we could hardly leave out the school.'

The implied compliment was more effective than Dougal could have wished. The woman blushed with pleasure, which Dougal found oddly disconcerting. She wasn't wearing a wedding ring.

'How d'you do,' she said gruffly, as if not quite at home with the phrase. 'My name's Burnham, Molly Burnham.' She extended a large square hand, which was larger than Dougal's and considerably rougher-skinned.

Dougal and Amanda introduced themselves, and in return were invited across the road for a sandwich and a drop of something. 'Nothing fancy, you understand, but you always need something inside you after a couple of hours in this church. Too damn draughty.'

She shepherded them out of the church, pausing to pick up an elderly lady who had been sitting alone in state in a rather larger pew up by the chancel arch. Molly Burnham introduced her as her aunt, though conversation was limited, since Mrs Burnham was not only very deaf but also seemed frankly uninterested in the world around her.

There was safety in numbers. The entire congregation strolled in a body through the churchyard, crossed the road and went into the Queen Anne house opposite. Molly Burnham let out her dogs on the way. 'Would have done it earlier,' she said, as if in answer to an unspoken reproof, 'but I was already late for the service. Should have been up the front with Auntie.'

She talked nonstop to Dougal and Amanda until they reached the dining room, evidently under the impression that 'you television people – never watch it myself, except the news' required to be subjected to a constant flow of information. She was unexpectedly efficient about it too, despite the continuous demands made on her by her dogs, her aunt and her numerous acquaintances among the congregation.

The different coloured gowns denoted school prefects (black) and Queen's Scholars (purple); the fact that the service was held here rather than at the cathedral was a sop to her wealthy aunt, a granddaughter of the celebrated Victorian headmaster mentioned in the sermon who had in fact inaugurated the tradition of a founder's day service; the rector, Mr Black, disapproved of the whole business, and she, Molly, wished the living was still in the gift of the Burnham family because the bishop simply couldn't be trusted these days.

While this was going on, Dougal and Amanda were

surreptitiously looking round to see what Lee was doing. To their despair they saw him deep in conversation with Mr Black. Molly Burnham noticed the general direction of their glance, which prompted her to make a pointed comment that the only local people in his church had been herself and her aunt, and who was that man in the extraordinary raincoat to whom he was talking?

Dougal said he rather thought the man had been staying at the Crossed Keys with them that weekend; perhaps he was an Old Boy? To which Miss Burnham said, 'Certainly not,' in a very firm voice and led them into the house.

They crossed the hall and entered the dining room. The table in the centre was covered with food; one sideboard was loaded with sherry glasses, while another contained an array of coffee cups. Presiding over this was a plump woman with a lined face wearing a vast apron advertising Heinz Baked Beans. She at once came forward, took Mrs Burnham by the arm and settled her in a wing armchair by the fireplace with a glass of sherry. Mrs Burnham took one birdlike sip of her sherry and appeared to fall asleep at once.

Miss Burnham left them to fulfill her duties as surrogate hostess. The room filled with people chattering, clinking glasses, cutlery rattling on plates. Lee had now come in; he was telling a joke to a mistress with tightly controlled iron-grey hair. Dougal and Amanda swiftly attached themselves to Mr Black who was meandering around the room carrying a plate of sandwiches with the aimless and irritating vagueness of a lonely blue-bottle. He was only too glad to find someone to talk to.

It was, however, difficult to concentrate on the rector's monologue. Dougal caught fragments of it and could construct the general drift without effort. Mr Black felt obliged to justify his presence in a place which had, he said, 'no real meaning at this point in time.' He pointed out that he had gone to a grammar school and that he wished that circumstances could have permitted him to attend a comprehensive. He blamed the bishop – obviously the scapegoat for all seasons, thought Dougal – for the conservatism of the Diocese of Rosington. 'The smugness of the place kills honest emotions,' he said, his Adam's apple leaping up and down in his emotion above his broad and slightly grubby clerical collar. 'The only priest here who had some sort of concept of the sociological role of the Church was old Vernon-Jones – and he's just died, of course.' Mr Black frowned at the inept timing of the Almighty. 'You must have read his book – *My God Among Thieves*? Bit elitist naturally (his background was against him), but he was basically on the side of the People . . .' Mr Black offered to give them a tour of the depressed areas in and around Rosington – 'just the thing for truly meaningful documentary material.'

Lee was beside the only door from the dining room with a glass of sherry in one hand and a vol-au-vent in the other. If they were to leave, it would have to be with someone else; preferably with a coachload of sixth formers for maximum security. Perhaps they could say that the Mini had an oil leak or something. But there would probably be an officious amateur mechanic on hand, eager to mend it for them. And even if they could cadge a lift, Lee would only have to trail them in the Lancia until they were alone again. Mr Black's dandruff, Dougal noticed dispassionately while this was going through his mind, had left rich deposits on the black shoulders of his clerical suit.

At this point the chaplain approached, moving towards them through the intervening clusters of people with the adroit efficiency of a natural diplomat. He detached Black from Dougal and Amanda ('Herbert, could you possibly give Molly a hand with the coffee? She's rushed off her feet over there.') and smoothly introduced himself as Derek Prenderpath.

'I couldn't help noticing you in church – we get so few strangers at the Commemoration service usually. Of course, it used to be a much grander affair than it is now – between ourselves, the Head only keeps it on for the sake of the Burnhams.'

Mr Prenderpath had gathered, by the bush telegraph which operated in this small social group whose members knew one another only too well, that Dougal and Amanda were connected in some vague and potentially delightful way with television. The tip of his tongue moistened his finely moulded lips. Dougal was reminded of a well-preserved lizard.

Prenderpath's hair had originally been blond, but was

now dappled with grey; his movements were faunlike; his teeth flashed frequently with the glaring regularity of a toothpaste advertisement; and his clerical suit was dove grey with a red silk lining.

He was polite to Amanda, but concentrated his conversational efforts on Dougal. These tended towards two ends: to discover more about the proposed programme on Rosington; and to familiarize them with his opinions of the other people in the room.

'Molly Burnham's on the Board of Governors now we've gone coeducational; I sometimes wonder whether she confuses the school with her dogs and vice versa.'

Amanda was white-faced by Dougal's side. They were both smoking now, inhaling their cigarettes with furious concentration, as if tobacco could bring about a miracle. As the chaplain's waspish voice whined effortlessly on, Dougal began to wonder desperately if they could get out of this by telling the truth – by throwing themselves on the mercy, respectability and common sense which everyone here except Lee presumably possessed. The prospect of such a scene appalled him, which he recognized as mildly ironic. But the main stumbling block was one of belief. They had no proof. Lee need only deny the whole thing. Maybe he should pretend to faint; Miss Burnham would surely let him and Amanda stay for a few hours, by which time . . . but that was no use: Lee would wait.

Or they could leave like lambs to the slaughter and try to make a deal with Lee – to trade information for immunity. God knew, the diamonds now seemed insignif-icant enough; they were like something you wanted a long time ago when you were quite a different person, and now you couldn't even remember why you had wanted it. But would Lee consent to that? After having their room searched, he must already know most of what they knew. But did he know how to use it?

'Pardon me, Padre,' said a familiar voice behind them. Lee had moved into the attack.

'Just wanted to say how much I enjoyed your sermon.'

Mr Prenderpath stopped in mid-sentence and swung round. 'People always say that to priests.' His eyes raked Lee up and down, like a farmer inspecting his neigh-bour's bull and finding it wanting. 'Especially those who don't usually go to church.'

The venom, Dougal supposed, was due to the fact that Lee was a stranger who showed no outward signs of being of any use to anyone. But Lee's blunt, bland face remained unchanged. 'Och, Padre—' he was begin-ning, when an interruption occurred.

The fox terrier, who had been foraging among the eaters with unlovely persistence, had managed to seize a leg of chicken from Mr Black's unguarded plate. Judging that the size of the prize warranted a rapid retreat, the dog shot across the room with a fine disre-gard for intervening human legs, and took refuge under the armchair in which Mrs Burnham slumbered. The chair juddered under the attack. Mrs Burnham jerked awake.

'Oh, Sophie,' said Molly Burnham from the other side of the room, 'you shouldn't.' She sounded unconvinced.

'Sophie?' echoed her aunt. 'Bloody dog. I call her Oaf.' She peered towards her ankles, between which protruded Sophie's snout; the chicken leg was now no more than an undigested memory.

Mrs Burnham snorted and reached for her sherry. Ignoring the people around her, she then picked up her glasses and the *Sunday Times*. 'Mr Prenderpath!' she said to the room at large. 'Come here.'

The chaplain shrugged and obeyed. Dougal could hear Mrs Burnham saying, 'Now, my man, let's see if you're as clever as you pretend to be.' Prenderpath murmured something deferentially. 'Rubbish!' the querulous voice continued. 'It's the crossword – a prize one. Only six more clues to go, so pull up a chair and start thinking.'

Lee smiled at Dougal and Amanda, reminding Dougal of a lupine grandmother fortuitously left alone with two Little Red Riding Hoods. 'It was a grand sound, wasn't it,' he said, 'all those voices raised in the praise of God. Now, Mr and Mrs . . . Massey, we need to have a chat.'

'I don't know what you're talking about—' began Dougal.

'Yes you do. I thought I'd eliminated the competition. Then I began to wonder when I found you with the Munns woman. And last night I knew for sure. So I'll need a lot of answers, okay?' The smile broadened. 'You know what happens to people who don't give me answers.

Remember Jimmy Hanbury?' The memory seemed to give Lee pleasure.

'How did you know we were here?' asked Amanda.

'Slipped that flat-faced waitress a tenner when we got to the hotel. She heard you mention Charleston Parva this morning . . . Christ, you kids are careless.'

'The professional's opinion of amateurs?' Dougal knew it was a silly thing to say, but he had to speak, to prove he still could. It was a token gesture towards the skimpy remnants of his self-respect.

Lee gave no sign of having heard him. 'We'll leave together. We can talk in my car.'

'What if we don't?' Amanda stared at him, her chin rising.

'You won't get far in that clapped-out car of yours, even if you reach it. These people won't want to know you if you try and disturb their little party with a cock and bull story you can't prove. Face facts, can't you? We're going to do business sooner or later. The sooner it is, the less you're likely to get hurt. You're playing with the big boys now.'

And then what? Dougal wondered. You throw away the peel when you've got the juice from an orange. Especially if you don't like leaving litter around.

'Molly!' Mrs Burnham hailed her niece like a taxi. 'Dear Italian has broken nails in U.S.A.'

This gnomic observation cut through the conversations in the room and quelled them all. 'Blank – A – blank – O,' she continued, with the air of one making a necessary but unwelcome concession to the stupidity of her listeners, 'three blanks – A – blank. Well?'

'Carolinas,' said Dougal automatically. He had often noticed that, when his mind was crumbling before a crisis, it compensated by working rapidly and well in other directions.

Molly Burnham, homing towards her aunt with an anxious expression on her face, smiled warmly at him. 'Carolinas,' she echoed, bending towards Mrs Burnham, enunciating each syllable with care. 'Isn't Mr Massey clever?'

'Humph! Don't make faces at me, gel. I can hear perfectly well.' She settled her glasses more firmly on her nose and beckoned Mr Prenderpath.

Molly Burnham drew Dougal aside. 'Thank you so much. She gets so fractious after going to church. Her only real interest in life now is finishing that damn crossword. Last few clues are always sheer hell for everyone else around.'

Dougal stared at her, hearing the words with only half his mind. An idea had just come to him, a theory of such simplicity that it must be right. It increased their desperate need to get away from Lee. A wild notion of how this might be accomplished, based on the sticker on the Morris Traveller's window, occurred to him, but it was so far-fetched that he discarded it. An instant later, he realized he'd have to try it; there was no alternative. He glanced over his shoulder: Amanda and Lee were apparently deep in conversation.

'Miss Burnham,' he hissed. 'There's something I must tell you. You remember you were asking about that man with Amanda? His name's Lee. He was telling us what he does for a living.'

The gratitude on Molly Burnham's face had given way to surprise, which was itself followed by a look which seemed to suggest that she feared Dougal was on the fringe of some unforgivable *faux pas*. Sophie, as if sensing her mistress's distress, heaved herself up and waddled over.

'He works at a lab near Cambridge. Privately funded experimental biology. He enjoys his work. *He cuts up animals.*'

In the long pause, Dougal tried to calculate the odds against Miss Burnham being so fanatical an antivivisectionist that she would set at nought the laws of hospitality. Even if she threw Lee out, he thought gloomily, it would only delay their confrontation.

'Mr Lee,' she said at last. Lee looked up and smiled encouragingly at them. Dougal swore to himself. Molly looked upset, but not angry enough to cause a scene.

Then Sophie began to growl.

The fox terrier must have been alerted by some nuance in her mistress's voice. The growl became a snarl as the dog started to advance.

Lee turned pale. Sweat broke out on his forehead. He backed away.

'Sophie!' cried Molly Burnham and grabbed the dog's collar, which had little noticeable effect on her implacable progress towards Lee.

It was easy for Dougal and Amanda to slip away in the confusion. As they reached the hall, Mrs Burnham's senile treble could be heard above the hubbub: 'Go on, Oaf, sick 'im, you stupid dog.'

They ran across to the Mini. While Amanda started the engine, Dougal pulled out his penknife and began to savage the valves on the tires of the Lancia. When air was escaping from two of them, he climbed into the Mini's passenger seat.

'Back to Rosington. Quick.'

Amanda, to his surprise, obeyed. After a few miles, she broke the silence between them. 'You fool,' she said, 'talk about taking risks. What would've happened if it hadn't worked?'

'Something nasty. But it did work. What we couldn't have even hoped for was that Lee would be afraid of dogs.'

'And why Rosington? Though I suppose it's the last place Lee would expect us to go to.'

'Because it's where the diamonds are. I'm sure of it. Look, Hanbury's clue was a photo of a manuscript written in Caroline Minuscule and connected with Rosington. Especially with the cathedral. We chased over here because Charleston Parva translates Caroline Minuscule.' Twenty years of academic conditioning made him add, 'Well, more or less. But suppose the name of the village was a deliberate blind. Suppose Vernon-Jones meant the connection to be made, to confuse Lee and/or Hanbury, so they would end up thinking the name of the script was an irrelevancy.'

'All right, I suppose.' Something in Amanda's voice made Dougal look at her, made him realize they were both exhausted.

Enthusiasm returned. 'I think Vernon-Jones counted on all his silly clues, and his reputation for deviousness, to cloud the obvious. And the answer is obvious. It's right in front of us, like the Purloined Letter. *Seek and ye shall find.* Who are the people he was closest to in Rosington? Connected with the cathedral? Who has got a *model* of the cathedral? And whoever heard of someone christened *Lina*?'

14

'It sounds awful,' said Mrs Munns, who was wearing pink dungarees and lying on the hearthrug beneath Lina, 'but George, my husband, actually preferred small congregations when he was Precentor here. He used to say that a crowd ruined the acoustics in the choir. Not that there are many – that place is like a vaulted bathroom – the sound keeps bouncing back.'

Dougal stretched out his legs and settled himself deeper into the sofa. He was at last warming up. They had spent nearly two hours in the Mini, most of the time parked in a side road on the outskirts of Rosington, waiting for half-past four and congratulating themselves on having failed to cancel the arrangement to have tea with Mrs Munns.

Really, he thought lazily, no one would think she was the relict of a clergyman, with all the phrase implied. He must try not to look at her. She looked about seventeen in this light. Amanda had an almost infallible instinct for detecting when he found someone else attractive and tended to object. Which was silly, of course, because the attraction was either a purely aesthetic response or a sort of public hangover, and in neither case was it accompanied by the desire to do anything about it.

They had arrived at her house punctually, pinched with cold and the fear that Lee or Tanner might have seen them as they trekked across the town. (Taking the Mini to the door would have been much too risky.) She had told them to call her Katie because being called Mrs Munns made her feel like somebody else. She had quickly produced tea, biscuits and fruit cake in the sitting room ('We skip the bread and butter stage on Sundays because of having to go to church').

The way in which Katie Munns both expected and welcomed them came as a shock. It was as if Bleeders Hall last night and Charleston Parva today had never existed in the real world, the world of drawn curtains, a glowing coal fire and a pot of tea which might reasonably be expected to stretch to three or even four cups all round. No, Cedric and Lee belonged in limbo, unlike the second piece of fruit cake which he was lovingly consuming.

Amanda asked Katie about the recipe. 'It's the sherry that does it. And the brandy. But you can't be mean about quantities . . .'

Lina had rolled off her mother and was trying to tie Rowley's front paws together with a piece of string. The spaniel was dozing, retaining just enough consciousness

– not much was required – to frustrate her efforts when necessary.

It was time to implement the plan they had agreed on the way here. Dougal was to engage Katie Munns in conversation, while Amanda concentrated on Lina. The opposite strategy would have ended in immediate failure.

More general topics of conversation – the weather, Rowley, today's service in the cathedral and the fruit cake – had been suitably aired, so Dougal felt justified in raising a few points concerning the history of the cathedral. Katie responded at once; Dougal suspected that, since Vernon-Jones had died, she had been forced to leave her hobbyhorse in the stable, and she welcomed the chance to exercise it. They argued about the legend that the original central tower had been deliberately undermined by Abbot William of Woodbridge who was reputed to have been undermined himself by the laudable temptation to increase the terrestrial glory of God by building a new one. Then there were the ghosts, a topic which hadn't been covered in any of the books Dougal had read. They ranged across the centuries: a line of Benedictines was said to pass along the nave, or rather along the walkway of the triforium above the nave, at twilight ('Though what they think they're doing up there, I've no idea'); a transparent eighteenth-century lady occasionally strolled down the Deanery stairs, graciously inclining her head if she met anyone; and then of course there was the cat which only Rowley appeared to be able to see, but when he did he barked furiously and his hackles rose, which was most unlike him . . .

Dougal noticed that Amanda had succeeded in establishing guardedly friendly relations with Lina with the lure of cat's cradle, but then he became engrossed in what Katie was saying and the next thing he knew was that the sitting room door clicked shut, leaving them alone. Even Rowley had gone. Everything was out of his hands now. Either Amanda would find the diamonds or she wouldn't. There was nothing he could do; the realization stopped him worrying and in any case he was enjoying talking to Katie.

After twenty minutes, the conversation wound down of its own accord. The teapot yielded the last of its contents. The cathedral clock boomed once: half-past five: Dougal suddenly became conscious that they had been here for an hour and shouldn't overstay their welcome. Katie, in the friendliest possible way, showed that she agreed. Dougal's offer to help with the washing up was refused and they went out into the hall.

'I bet that brat of mine is showing Amanda her entire collection of toys,' she said. 'She's got all the instincts of a showman. I should have done something about it sooner – Amanda must be freezing up there.'

'I shouldn't worry.' Dougal grinned at her. 'Amanda likes kids.'

'Ah well, it's an acquired taste.' Katie raised her voice. 'Lina! Put those things away and come and say goodbye.'

There was a muffled squawk in reply. Shortly afterwards, Lina clattered down the stairs, announcing importantly that Amanda had gone to the loo. Dougal took the opportunity to do the same.

As he came out of the little cloakroom which opened off the hall, the upstairs cistern flushed and Amanda appeared on the stairs. She smiled quickly at Dougal, and he felt excitement jump in him, wondering if he had imagined that flicker of smugness on Amanda's face.

Saying goodbye seemed to drag on forever. Dougal had a strong urge to smack Lina, who was determined to prevent Amanda from leaving, though it was difficult to tell whether this was due to love or merely to a wish to defer her bath for as long as possible. She clung to Amanda's legs and enumerated, in considerable detail, those of her possessions which Amanda would miss seeing if she went now. But once they were out of the door, he found himself wishing they could be back inside, lapped in warmth and civilization. He was oddly moved despite himself: the three of them, dog, woman and child, were framed by the doorway against a backdrop of light from the hall; he envied their completeness.

Amanda slipped her arm through Dougal's and they set off rapidly down the High Street. The car was about a mile away on the northern outskirts of Rosington, parked in a residential side street. Amanda said: 'I've got them,' and Dougal squeezed her arm in reply; it wasn't the place to talk about them, let alone look at them. It was quite likely that Lee and Tanner were somewhere in this town, and it was impossible to relax while there were passing cars and pedestrians and dark corners. It was like having a toothache, Dougal decided, this constant, unhappy wariness. There would be no peace until something was done about it. Another source of worry was what they should do now: they were both tired and desperately needed somewhere safe to rest; at the back of his mind lurked the suspicion, which he preferred not to think about at present, that this need for safety was not going to be satisfied while Lee was around. But the priority was to find somewhere for tonight. He wondered what Amanda was thinking.

Dougal cheered up when they rounded the corner of the road and saw the Mini waiting for them. It must be the tiredness, he thought, which was making him yo-yo between despondency and optimism. Looked at rationally, they were in an excellent position: they had the jewels, the car and enough cash for the present – and, best of all, Lee had no idea where they were.

When they were in the car, Amanda rummaged in her handbag and produced what looked like, in the dim yellow glow of a streetlight a few yards along the road, a thin cylinder about six inches long. She passed it to Dougal, who nearly dropped it because it felt alive. A chamois leather had been wrapped round and round and sewn tightly together. Its hard, knobbly contents shifted under the pressure of his index finger and thumb. It was surprisingly heavy.

'The stones must be loose – unmounted,' he said, finding himself whispering.

'We'd better not open it now – they'd probably trickle out all over the place. God, it's weird to think you're holding a fortune, William. Makes me go all shivery.'

'Wouldn't it be funny if they were fake? Glass or something. Vernon-Jones's last joke . . .' His voice trailed away. The prospect was too appalling to be considered. After a pause, during which he wished he could see the expression on Amanda's face, he said, more loudly than he intended, 'Look, I've been thinking about where we should go. I don't like the idea of London tonight – it's too far and it's where Lee will expect us to go.' Hadn't he read somewhere that London was the worst place to hide if criminals were after you?

'Okay,' said Amanda calmly. 'Where?'

'How about Cambridge? It can't be more than thirty miles, if that. And I know it – maybe Lee doesn't. Give us time to sort out what to do next.' The weight of the problem oppressed him, but he tried to ignore it for the moment. He deftly changed the subject: 'How did you find the jewels?'

'Lina's got a playroom upstairs – just this big bare room like a draughty icebox with her toys in it. She didn't seem to feel the cold up there at all. She started showing me her things one by one . . . I'd forgotten how exhausting kids can be with a captive audience. I was looking round while she rattled on. The model of the cathedral which Katie mentioned was full of buses and cars and stuffed away in a corner. It was horrible – covered in dust and cobwebs – my hands are filthy (I didn't have time to wash them properly). About a yard long, I suppose, made of cardboard and hardboard and Sellotape. I asked her where she got it from, and she said, Uncle Oswyth, just before he went to heaven. It was easy enough to see what Vernon-Jones had done: the whole roof lifts off and he'd taped a false ceiling in the central tower. If you were looking for it, it was obvious – he'd used newer cardboard, and of course it was heavier than it should have been.'

'When did you get it out? Is there any risk of Lina noticing?'

'I doubt it. I got it while I was meant to be in the loo – just ripped the false ceiling out (it's in my handbag) and left the old one in place. There's no reason why she should ever know.'

Dougal sighed. He hadn't expected the search for the diamonds to end like this, leaving Cedric dead and two killers out for their blood. The diamonds weren't worth killing or dying for, he should have known that. He felt oppressed by the gross manipulations of chance which had brought him from Gumper's overheated study to the cold, uncomfortable Mini. 'One can't help wondering,' he murmured, 'what would have happened if Katie or Lina had found them . . . they probably would have done, sooner or later.'

'William! When you start calling yourself *one*, you sound so bloody pompous and boring—'

Amanda stopped suddenly and turned her head away. Dougal felt unaccountably guilty. He put his hand on her arm and they both said 'Sorry' simultaneously and began to discuss where they could find more petrol.

'Call me Oedipus,' Dougal remarked two hours later to his pink gin. They were sitting in the Blue Boar in Trinity Street waiting for the next calamity. The journey to Cambridge had been accomplished with some difficulty in the face of a squally headwind. Dougal had been forced to change a flat tyre on a muddy Fenland verge. Cambridge, when they finally reached it, had treacherously revealed itself as an alien city; it was like revisiting a dream and finding it no longer belonged to you but to someone else. Eight years ago, Cambridge had been a city of friends and welcoming homes. Now it had turned its back on him – even the one-way systems had changed.

First, they had tried Dougal's old supervisor, who proved to have emigrated to Harvard at the beginning of the academic year. They tried a bed-and-breakfast place which was full up and then two hotels. The receptionist at the Royal Cambridge explained why they were likely to be unsuccessful: not only were there always tourists in Cambridge ('Like flies round a jam pot, I'm glad to say, sir'), but a degree ceremony at Senate House on Saturday had attracted a rash of newly minted M.A.s and their partners; the noise from the bar amply confirmed this last point.

'Hubris,' said Dougal. 'We were too puffed up about getting away from Lee and finding the diamonds.'

His fingers kneaded the leather bundle in his jacket pocket. Amanda said nothing, but yawned; her eyes were red-rimmed from night driving. Hotels had been a last resort – they were too risky, being the first places Lee would try, if his search for them reached Cambridge.

If only he had relatives in Cambridge, Dougal thought. Even his father. He considered his college briefly, rejecting the idea because any spare rooms would have already gone to the M.A.s and there would be problems getting Amanda inside in any case.

He cast his mind back through friends and acquaintances. No one he knew now lived in Cambridge, no one even came here occasionally. No one except possibly—

He drained the gin at a gulp, which made him sneeze, smiled at Amanda and asked the barman where the telephone was.

15

The ancient universities drew Madame Pee-Pee like a moth to a pair of candles; he was already singed for life. The only remaining question was which one would have the privilege of roasting him for posterity.

There are few Primroses in the Cambridge telephone directory and Dougal had plenty of spare change. Tracing Philip's parents wasn't difficult – they lived on the Histon Road. Primrose spent alternate weekends at Oxford, where he had been educated, and Cambridge, where he had been bred ('One likes to keep in touch'). There was an even chance that he would be here.

At this point, Nemesis relented. Philip Primrose was not only at his parents' house, but he was there alone. His parents were in Bournemouth at the deathbed of an aunt; Philip had come down partly to be on hand when a builder came to inspect the roof on Saturday, partly to attend a concert at Caius on Sunday afternoon, and lastly to do some work at the University Library, which he expected would keep him in Cambridge until Wednesday.

Dougal dealt delicately with Madame Pee-Pee. Over the telephone, he banked on Primrose's desire for company and merely said that they were passing through Cambridge and how about meeting for a drink? They met in a pub on the Huntingdon Road, where Dougal filled Primrose with double Scotches and left Amanda to do her work. Her long, black hair, her astonishingly brown eyes, framed by lashes which had no right to be natural, and her shapely figure usually went down well with heterosexual males, particularly those whose sex lives were largely confined to their imaginations.

So, when Dougal had explained that they had nowhere to spend the night and Amanda had seconded the appeal by looking at Madame Pee-Pee as if she were thinking, 'My hero,' Philip Primrose asked them to spend it under his parental roof with an eagerness which bordered on the indecent. Dougal swiftly inserted his host into the back of the Mini and drove them to the house.

'Home, sweet home,' said Philip, so mournfully that Dougal wondered if he was regretting his invitation. He hastened to confirm it by saying how terribly nice it was of Primrose to put them up, while Amanda settled the matter by saying that she didn't know what they would have done without him.

Madame Pee-Pee ushered them into the house. Dougal suddenly understood the reason for their host's last-minute hesitation: at college, Primrose gave out that his father was in the communications industry; hanging on the coatstand in the hall was a bus conductor's cap and jacket.

They went into the sitting room on the right of the door. It was a comfortable room with a large colour television in the corner and a photograph of Philip dressed up to receive his B.A. on the mantelpiece. Primrose hovered in the doorway, evidently wondering what to do with them next.

Amanda solved the problem for him by raising the subject of food. He hadn't eaten either, so any potential awkwardness was obliterated by a communal effort, organized by Amanda, to prepare supper.

Dougal was detailed to buy wine, while Amanda and Philip set about reheating the gargantuan stew which Mrs Primrose had left for her son and laying the kitchen table.

Dougal bought a bottle of Côtes du Rhône and half a bottle of Glenfiddich: if malt whisky couldn't make the evening easier, nothing could. When he got back, Philip and Amanda were in the kitchen. Philip had removed his mustard yellow tweed jacket (hadn't he any other, Dougal wondered?) and had rolled up his shirtsleeves. His crinkly hair had escaped from its prison of Brilliantine and stuck out from his scalp in a number of directions. His face was pink with excitement; his glasses had steamed up; he had a bottle of sherry in one hand and was telling Amanda about last year's Commemoration Ball at his Oxford college. He looked very happy. Amanda was stirring the stew (which smelled excellent) and making the kitchen apron she was wearing look as if it had been designed by Dior.

They sat round the kitchen table drinking whisky while the stew heated through. Primrose was persuaded to abandon the sherry in favour of stronger liquor and became pinker, louder and jollier more rapidly than Dougal would have believed possible. He left the conversation to Amanda and Philip; he looked forward to hearing what the former thought of the latter (the contrary viewpoint was only too apparent). He could feel the effect of the whisky, and realized that he must be more tired than he thought. The whisky was followed by the wine, great bowls of stew and coffee. By the time they had returned to the whisky, all three were leaning heavily on the table.

Dougal's elbow was resting on a note from Philip's mother: *Milk bill Saturday (Should be 3.52 pounds). Laundry beside fridge – leave outside back door Monday morning . . . Take care of yourself Darling.* This was normality, a world where Monday would follow Sunday: for Dougal, the prospect seemed immensely attractive after a weekend which, on two occasions, had seemed as if it wasn't going to be followed by a Monday. It must also be nice to have a mother . . .

At this point, he realized he was on the verge of becoming maudlin. He only thought of his mother, who had died when he was eleven, when he was reaching a dangerous level of intoxication. He made an effort and managed to contribute a few remarks to the conversation Amanda and Philip were having about the Holbeins at Kenwood on Hampstead Heath. ('The self-portrait is very overrated,' said Philip, and to his surprise Dougal saw that Amanda genuinely agreed.) They were getting on perfectly well without him – no, he *wasn't* jealous; who could be jealous of Madame Pee-Pee? – so Dougal decided to try to think calmly about what they were going to do. He hoped the haze of alcohol in his mind would simplify the problem.

He tabulated the salient points, one by one. First, they had the diamonds. Second, realizing them would take time – Dougal had a vague idea that Amsterdam was the place to go, but unfortunately the only friend he had who had some acquaintance with the underworld of that city was at present in jail. Third, Lee would be after them: they were not only business rivals, but they had damaged his pride. Fourth, it seemed probable that, despite today's events, Lee would continue to regard them as amateurs – he would believe he could deal with them himself (possibly with Tanner's help, since he was already concerned). It followed, thought Dougal as he drunkenly turned a drop of spilled wine on the table beside his glass into a spiral, that Lee was the only person they had to fear.

As Dougal saw it, they had two options open to them. One was to hide from Lee: to lie low, either here or abroad, hoping to turn the diamonds into cash to live on, until they could safely assume that his interest in them had abated. The difficulty was that they would never feel secure. Never. The money would not be much compensation for a life spent under an indefinitely suspended sentence of death.

The alternative was to take the offensive. It meant the worms turning and pretending to be predators. It meant risking everything for the sake of peace of mind and a tolerable bank balance.

It meant the deliberate murder of Lee. Technically difficult, quite impractical and of course absolutely unthinkable in any case.

Dougal splashed more Glenfiddich into the three glasses and added a dash of water to his own. Primrose was looking at him like a plump and puzzled owl, as if he had forgotten that Dougal was there and now found it difficult to account for his presence.

'Philip,' said Dougal gravely, as the mad laughter welled up within him. 'You must remember to put out the laundry before we go to bed.'

The evening had passed more quickly than Dougal had thought. It was nearly midnight by the time they went up to bed. On another occasion he would have derived a great deal of innocent pleasure from the delicate and long-winded fashion in which their host, before he would let them upstairs, had approached the two difficult questions which tact forbade him to pose directly. Were Dougal and Amanda expecting to sleep together? If yes, could they be trusted in his parents' double bed without leaving unmentionable and embarrassing evidence of their presence? Having been assured, in a similarly oblique way, that the answer on both counts was yes (and was it Dougal's imagination that Philip, on hearing the first answer, looked distinctly peeved?), they stood up, deciding to leave the washing up to the morning.

Philip led the way upstairs. The change of altitude must have accelerated the effect of the alcohol, for he swayed alarmingly from side to side and, at one point, nearly fell back on Amanda. He showed them the bathroom, where he sat down heavily on the dirty linen basket and evinced a determination to talk about Spinoza. At this point, Dougal basely fled, leaving Amanda to deal with the situation, making the excuse that he had to nip downstairs and pick up their luggage from the car.

When he returned, Philip's bedroom door was closed and their host was presumably behind it. Dougal asked Amanda how she had done it, to which she replied, 'Oh, you know,' with such a complete lack of emphasis that further enquiry was obviously unwelcome. They went to the bathroom together and brushed their teeth for thirty seconds, before giving up the ritual as a bad job. Back in the parental bedroom, they pulled off their clothes and climbed into bed: Amanda didn't even remove her makeup or brush her hair.

Dougal switched out the bedside light and the darkness enveloped them. Almost at once, through the thin partition walls, they heard Philip's door open, footsteps, the slamming of the bathroom door and the distant noise of retching.

'Oh, the poor lamb,' said Amanda absentmindedly. 'God, it's nice to be in bed. William, what the hell are we going to do?'

Dougal pushed the need to sleep away from him. It couldn't be avoided any longer: he and Amanda would have to talk about it. Suddenly he remembered.

'We haven't even looked at them yet. The diamonds.'

He switched on the light again, clambered out of bed and padded over to the chair where their clothes were piled in confusion. He extricated the sausage of leather from his trouser pocket; it was an index of his tiredness, he thought, that he had noticed the bulge while undressing, without thinking anything of it. As an afterthought, he found the pair of nail scissors in Amanda's makeup bag.

Dougal sat naked on the side of the bed (there was something to be said for the Primroses' central heating system) and slit the stitching at one end of the sausage. Its contents poured out into the palms of his hands. Both he and Amanda involuntarily gasped.

Vernon-Jones's legacy consisted of unset diamonds, nothing else. All of them were cut; the light shimmered through them, creating a dazzling array of rainbows. The largest of the stones was the size of a child's marble. Amanda put her hand out and picked it up.

'If this isn't real, I don't know what is.'

'But we don't *know*.' Dougal found his scepticism

unconvincing, even to himself. 'We just have to work on the assumption that they are.'

Amanda shivered. 'Put them away. It doesn't matter if they're real or not. We've still got the same problem. Lee.'

Dougal fed the stones, one by one, back into the bag. The occupation gave him an excuse for deferring his answer. At last the stones ran out, and he tossed the package on to the bedside table.

'Pee-Pee – Philip – might be useful.'

'Why?'

'Lee doesn't know him. Suppose Lee has traced us to Cambridge. If we get Philip to do our shopping or whatever, it'll lessen the risk.'

'But what do we tell Philip? We can hardly blurt out the truth.'

'No,' agreed Dougal, 'but we'll think of something. He's pretty gullible, especially where you're concerned. The real problem' – he reached for a cigarette, deciding that he could put it off no further – 'is how we get round the fact that Lee is after us. I know he's small-time by Mafia standards, but we've got in his way and he's probably going to want to . . . well, kill us. Particularly if he finds out we've got the diamonds. He knows we daren't go to the police.' It was strange, he reflected: England had always seemed such a law-abiding country, and here they were fighting what amounted to a private civil war in the middle of it without anyone outside those directly concerned being in the least disturbed. He wondered what other manifestations of anarchy were going on around them.

Amanda said: 'The only way we can ever get free of this is by killing Lee.'

The silence between them was flat and featureless; words, thought Dougal, cross like caravans in the desert. Amanda let her hair curtain her face again, which muffled her words:

'Either we kill him, or we hide and wait till he kills us.'

'It's been one of those progressions, starting when I found Gumper, hasn't it? A sort of ratio of inverse—'

'William! You're blathering again. We're talking about—'

'Deliberate manslaughter?' Dougal stared down at his legs: they were white and covered with black hairs and looked as if they didn't belong to him. 'No, of course not. Murder.'

'Well, be realistic. Got an alternative?'

'No. It won't be easy. And I don't like it.'

'Nor do I, William. Too dangerous.'

'Too bloody everything.'

Dougal got back into bed and switched out the light. For once Amanda wanted his arms around her. She cried a little – softly, as if it was something which had to be done as a matter of form. Then her breathing grew steady and slowed to the peaceful regularity of sleep.

Dougal lay there awake. His left arm beneath her was asleep but nothing else was. He felt too hot, and perversely blamed the Primroses for their central heating. The bathroom door closed and he heard Philip going wearily into his bedroom. Despite Amanda beside him, he felt as lonely as a blind man in a cinema. With a silent movie on the screen, of course.

16

The coffee was thick and steaming: it had flecks of light brown foam on its surface.

Dougal's jersey was inside out. He was wearing yesterday's socks because they were warmer and nearer than the clean pairs in the suitcase.

'Much better this way,' he said, 'made in a jug. Any cigarettes in your bag?'

Amanda pulled out a half-full packet and a matchbook from the Crossed Keys. 'How about Philip? You taking him a cup?'

'No. Give him a bit longer. He's probably had a rough night.' The Glenfiddich bottle was empty.

Amanda refused a cigarette and waited for Dougal's morning cough to die away.

'William, I've been thinking . . .'

So this was it. It was no longer possible to forget what had to be done, if not today then soon.

'. . . as I see it, we've got four separate details to settle.'

She tapped a fingernail on the table for each point. 'One, we've got to disappear, so Lee can't trace us unless we want him to (I know he probably can't anyway, but we've got to be sure). Two, we need to think of a place and a method to kill him. Three, we have to get him there. And finally we have to do it.'

Dougal blinked. He felt almost envious of Amanda's directness. She had fully digested the implications of last night, while he had only just got to the point of forcing himself to swallow them. But it was a relief, too, to have the problem presented in the shape of a set of practical necessities. It was wonderfully simple that way, for one thing, and it gave one something to work on, for another.

'The only way Lee can trace us,' he said slowly, 'is by the car. Assuming he can throw his net of contacts wide enough, that is. And we have to assume that he can. We could leave it here, in Cambridge; put it in a long stay car park, and send the rental firm the keys and some cash.'

'Philip could do it,' Amanda said. 'And he could hire us another one in his name – just in case Lee knows who we really are.'

'How about the diamonds? Philip could take those, too – put them in a safe deposit box. We could both have a key. As a precaution.'

Amanda nodded. Neither of them added: as a precaution against Lee killing one or both of us.

'Easy enough to think of a story for Philip,' Dougal continued. 'Though the most important thing is that you look like a damsel in distress and stare into his eyes as if he was the only man in the world . . . it'll work. It'll have to – otherwise you and I will have to wander around Cambridge, changing the car and going to the bank, leaving a trail Lee could follow in his sleep.'

As he finished, Dougal wondered if he wasn't over-reacting, crediting Lee with superhuman powers, dodging away from shadows in his own mind. He had no yardstick by which to judge what was happening and felt curiously disoriented. On the other hand . . .

Amanda was talking. He shrugged the uncertainty away.

'Okay, as you want. I don't think it'll make much difference. The real problems come afterwards, anyway.' Her mind jumped suddenly forwards, with Dougal clutching for the sense of what she was saying. 'I suppose it's got to look like an accident – either that, or Lee will have to vanish entirely.' With her fingers, she was shredding one of the matches from the match-book, painstakingly splaying the slithers around the unstruck head.

It looked like a thistle in the last stage of its life, a thistle from the flora of another country, another time. Dougal tried not to notice it. He found Amanda's down-to-earth approach to murder amazing – it made his own fumblings in that direction, with the unwilling assistance of Cedric, seem humiliatingly amateurish. She was looking at him, expecting him to say something. The words, when they came to his lips, tumbled out as if somebody else was speaking them: their sense was gross and he found it curiously difficult to articulate them.

'Somewhere lonely. Get him there to make a deal. And club him over the head. Kill him.'

He thought of Malcolm: the friend who knew Amsterdam; who, if he had not been in prison, might have been able to help; for he was an expert negotiator of the trickier corners of life; who sailed away from problems whenever possible . . . whose boat was moored in a Suffolk estuary.

Shortly afterwards, Dougal climbed the stairs with a tray which held a mug of coffee, a glass of water and a couple of Alka-Seltzers. He knocked on Philip's bedroom door, pushed it open and was hit by a cloud of stale air.

Pee-Pee lay on his back, his chin in the air, breathing heavily. The bed was narrow, a child's size. The walls of the room were lined with books and photographs, chiefly of school and college groups. Primrose had prudently placed a bowl beside the bed; Dougal was glad to see it was empty.

He drew back the curtains, letting the grey February morning pick out the details – the patched teddy bear at one end of a bookcase, the tie Philip had worn yesterday dangling over the side of the wastepaper basket. Philip stirred and Dougal asked how he was.

'Uh. Thirsty. I might have a fever . . . is there any tea? There's a thermometer in the bathroom cupboard—'

'Here's some coffee,' said Dougal brutally. 'It'll be

better for you. And Alka-Seltzers, to perk up the metabolism. Can I use the phone? I'll find out how much it comes to.'

He put the tray on the bedside table, noticing as he did so that Primrose was apparently reading Milton's prose works at night. Personally, he would have considered *Areopagitica* to be an emetic rather than a soporific; but perhaps Pee-Pee kept it there for purely decorative purposes.

Their host was barely awake. He groped for his spectacles, nearly nudging the coffee off the table. Dougal found them for him and said he must be going. There were signs that Philip's need to talk was about to triumph over his need to sleep.

The telephone was downstairs in the little dining room which was sandwiched between the sitting room and the kitchen. Dougal collected the matchbook with the telephone number of the Crossed Keys, a cigarette and an ashtray. There was no point in putting it off. Amanda was piling crockery into the sink with a look of distaste on her face. She smiled at him but said nothing.

While the number was ringing, he lit the cigarette with the last match. Supposing Lee had left Rosington last night, supposing . . .

Mrs Livabed answered. She was one of the rare people whose voice retained its natural resonance on the telephone.

'Mrs Livabed? Good morning. This is William . . . um, Massey—'

'Oh, hullo, love! Was it something you left? The chambermaids are upstairs now (they don't come on Sundays, of course, but then it's not like before the war, is it?)—'

'No. Actually, I wanted a word with Mr Lee, if he's still there.'

'Oh, the Irish gentleman. You're in luck – he's leaving this morning. Having his breakfast now, him and his friend. How's Wales, by the way?'

'Where?' asked Dougal before he remembered it was where they were supposed to be. 'Oh, fine, thanks. Raining rather a lot.' That seemed a safe touch of local colour. 'The old lady was delighted to see us.' Thank God Lee hadn't left. First hurdle cleared. 'Anyway, Mr Lee . . .'

'Well, he is having his breakfast now – shall I ask him to ring you back when he's finished?' Mrs Livabed's tone implied that the bond between a man and his breakfast was not something to be broken lightly.

'It is rather urgent,' said Dougal apologetically. 'I have to go out in a moment. It's a business matter, you see.'

Mrs Livabed appeared to notice nothing incongruous in this. 'Ah, *business*,' she said knowingly, as if this explained and even excused the most blatant irregularities. 'I'll get him – he must be at the toast and coffee stage by now.'

The line went silent. Presumably Lee would take the call at the reception desk: there had been no phones in the bedrooms and Dougal couldn't remember seeing a booth with an extension for guests to use. The door of the dining room opened, and Philip's face, bleary and bristly, peered in. Dougal waved him frantically away – 'Shan't be a moment – very important call.'

'Mr Massey?'

On the telephone, Lee's voice sounded even flatter than usual, as if it came from the vocal cords of a slightly imperfect automaton. Made in Ireland, of course.

'Hullo,' said Dougal. He suddenly felt rather foolish. 'Look, we'd like to come to an arrangement with you.'

'About what?'

'After we left you yesterday, we found . . . what we were looking for.'

'The devil you did.' Lee's voice suddenly dropped in volume, as if he was looking round for potential eavesdroppers.

'It was just one of those absurd flukes – you know.' Dougal made his voice sound as apologetic as possible: it was an accident, Mr Lee, please don't hurt us.

'Where was it?'

'At the Munnses'. Vernon-Jones gave Hanbury a photo of a script called Caroline Minuscule. Well, Lina's real name is Caroline. Little Caroline, you see.'

'Well I'm damned.'

Probably, thought Dougal. 'It was in the roof of a model of the cathedral which Vernon-Jones had given her – a pouch of leather with the diamonds sewn in.'

'So that explains it.'

'What?' For a moment Dougal wondered if he had misheard.

'You got that photograph. I got a little brass paper-weight, in the shape of the cathedral. Souvenir from Rosington sort of thing. The cunning old bugger.'

'He certainly made things unnecessarily complicated. And the Munnses might have got hurt.' Dougal sounded priggish to himself, but Lee grunted in agreement.

'Do they know about it?' he asked after a pause.

'No. We managed to remove the diamonds without any fuss. There's no reason why they should ever know.' Dougal felt that he owed this at least to Katie Munns, to keep her and Lina out of the mess.

'How much was there?' Lee seemed to take his willingness to tell him anything for granted.

'I've no idea. Maybe about forty stones of varying sizes. Some of them are pretty big. Neither of us knows anything about diamonds. That's the trouble. That's what I want to talk to you about.'

'You do, do you? You know there's not a cat's chance in hell of you keeping them? I can fix anyone you could find to handle them for you. If I don't find you first. Never fear, I'll find you. Some things are too expensive.' The monotone of Lee's voice had acquired a breathy, gravelly quality, like a cat using its purr to express menace. Dougal turned the other bar of the fire on.

'Exactly, Mr Lee. That's why we'd like to come to an arrangement. Please. You see, we're out of our league in this sort of business.' And what, Dougal wondered, did Lee think was their league – part-time, shabby-genteel conmanship? Perhaps he wasn't so far wrong. 'We wouldn't even know how to go about converting the diamonds into money, let alone how to spend it safely. So it occurred to us that the best thing to do was to come to a business arrangement with you. If we held on to them, we'd lose our peace of mind—'

'At the very least.'

'—and you would have to waste money and time finding us. And there would always be the possibility that something would go wrong and we'd both lose the diamonds.'

'Come to the point. What are you proposing?'

Dougal tried to give a convincing verbal impression of a person overwhelmed by the magnitude of the matter which had embroiled him. 'Well – not to put too fine a point on it – would you care to have the diamonds in return for a cash commission for us? Assuming they are worth about a hundred thousand, how about ten per cent? Then we'd both gain. No hard feelings on either side. After all, without us, you might never have found them.'

Lee did not reply at once. Dougal became acutely aware of the sounds around him – the clatter of dishes, water trickling into the lavatory cistern and the murmur of Primrose's voice.

'Yes, that sounds possible. Simpler all round, eh? London or Rosington, then, depending where you are. This morning?'

'Well, actually —' here came the difficult bit '— I'd prefer tomorrow and Suffolk.' Surely Lee wouldn't quibble about the conditions of the transfer, not if he believed they had been terrorized into good behaviour? 'You see, we want to leave the country. Not just over this business – there are several other reasons why we'd be better out of the way at present.' Dougal hoped he sounded convincingly mysterious and harassed. 'We're hoping a friend will take us over to the Continent tomorrow. If we could meet at the mooring, fewer things could go wrong, we could make the exchange and be off on Tuesday's tide—'

'Where in Suffolk?'

'I don't know, yet. I'll have to contact this bloke first. He prefers to be discreet.'

'If you're just trying to gain time . . .'

'No. Really.' Dougal tried frantically to think of reasons why Lee should not suspect any sort of double cross. 'I wouldn't have rung you in that case, let alone told you we'd found the diamonds.'

It seemed to satisfy Lee.

'When will you let me know the details?'

'I could phone you tomorrow morning – I've got to get hold of this friend today and sort everything out.'

'Make it between nine and ten. Without fail. Got something to write with?' Dougal grabbed the pad and biro which the Primroses had thoughtfully left on top of the telephone directories. Lee gave a London telephone number – Hampstead, Dougal recognized. 'Remember, the time for playing games is over, son.'

The way Lee said 'son' made Dougal swallow. He gave the appropriate assurances. There was no need to act the terrified innocent: that was exactly how he felt. And it was vital that Lee should believe him. Their only hope of pulling this off lay in Lee underestimating them as much as possible. When he finally put the phone down, his hands were clammy with sweat. He hated Lee. It occurred to him that fear wasn't good for the character.

In the kitchen, Amanda was drying the casserole dish which had held the stew.

'It's okay,' he said, as he slumped into a chair. 'Lee agreed to everything. The bastard. Where's Philip?'

'He's upstairs now. He told me about his research while I was washing up.'

The door opened and Pee-Pee came in. He darted a curt glance at Dougal, as if he wished he wasn't there. Scraps of bloodstained lavatory paper clung wispily to parts of his neck and face: his razor liked the taste of blood.

'I must say, Bill, you were on that phone rather a long time. And it is at peak hours, too.'

Dougal forced an apologetic smile and reached for his wallet. Sometimes he wished life would pause at a request stop, so he could get off for a while.

17

'Americans, you say?' said Philip Primrose, rubbing his chin in a spasm of agitation, thereby dislodging a shred of tissue paper and causing one of his cuts to start bleeding again. 'That's bad. You simply can't trust them. Revolting colonials,' he added with an air of conscious originality.

Up to this point, he had listened warily to Dougal and Amanda as they explained what they wanted him to do. But mention of the cut-throat American rivals of Amanda's father's firm had swept away his caution.

'I applied for a research scholarship at Harvard a couple of years ago. Just after I left Oxford. And you know they turned me down flat, without even the courtesy of going through my Ph.D. proposal properly. That shows the sort of people we're dealing with. And Bill, you remember that awful American girl at college?'

Dougal did indeed: *Ah, piss off, pruneface, you make me wanna puke.*

194

'Which of course is why I ended up in London. All very well but not quite the same. I thought I'd save the Other Place until later.' Primrose glanced at Dougal to see if his reference had been taken.

Amanda murmured sympathetically. Dougal had a vision of Philip's life, each stage planned on the principle of deferred gratification, so he could say, after the event, 'When I was up at Oxford/Harvard/Cambridge . . .' according to the context. He put the thought away from him as unworthy and mostly untrue. The trouble with being with Primrose was that he encouraged the baser side of one's nature, just as with other people it was easy to appear, and in fact to feel, consistently pleasant and generous.

'You're sure there's nothing criminal about this?'

'No,' said Dougal patiently, 'that's the trouble. We know we had a car on our tail on the way to Cambridge yesterday – a black Lancia, but they've done nothing, so we can hardly ask for police protection. The police would think we were mad. Once the Americans do something, it'll be too late, of course. That's why we need your help – to get us another car and deposit the formula (there's an electronic component with it, by the way).'

'In a way, it's a matter of life and death.' Amanda stared earnestly into Philip's eyes and he looked back with his mouth slightly open, like a rabbit caught in the beam of headlights. 'Not just for Daddy – though of course he's financially committed – but because of all the jobs that depend on Britain using the idea first. The minister told him it was vital, because if we develop this, contracts should flow in from abroad . . . I don't really understand it fully – I expect you've got a better idea of how these things work than I have – but I do know how important it is.'

'But why are you and Bill involved in all this? I should have thought—'

'Because this business is too delicate to go through the usual channels,' said Dougal firmly. 'Mr Jackson – Amanda's father – insisted we have contingency plans, even so; the bank deposit idea was one of them. The component's far too delicate to go by the post. He was afraid the Americans might get on to us after all.'

'It wasn't just Daddy, actually. The minister himself said the people concerned with the transfer should be absolutely trustworthy, not just employees.' A straightening of Primrose's spine told Dougal that he had not missed the implied compliment. Amanda rushed on: 'He wanted MI5 (or is it MI6 or something completely different these days?), but there was a hitch because technically Daddy counts as private sector.'

'In fact,' Philip summed up, 'this is a case of Unorthodox Action in the Public Interest.' He said the words as if they were sacred. Dougal suddenly realized they would have to be careful about offering money. Primrose was genuinely moved by his own nobility, as if the demand they had made on him had revealed, to himself, a hitherto unsuspected spring of adventure beneath the arid surface of his life.

Dougal leant forward and lowered his voice. 'This isn't the sort of business one can publicize, you know. I doubt whether anyone besides Amanda's father and the minister will know of your involvement. Which is not to say there may not be repercussions, you understand?'

Philip nodded violently and said, 'Not at all' several times. He had turned pink again. Dougal felt rather guilty: Primrose's emotion was worthy of a better cause.

'Daddy gave us an emergency cash fund, so at least money won't be a problem. Which reminds me, we'll have to give you something for last night and everything, or he'll throw a fit. He's one of these people who insists on paying his way or else he goes all broody, poor darling, and feels guilty about getting something for nothing. You will let us, Philip, won't you?'

A genteel discussion ensued, during which Amanda was charmingly obstinate, Primrose repeated polite disclaimers of any desire to be paid, the conviction in his voice rapidly and audibly dwindling, while Dougal said, 'Come on, old chap,' in a manly voice, as if Philip was being offered a dose of castor oil which he should accept to please the lady.

Once Primrose had been brought to see that acceptance was more gentlemanly than refusal, the matter was quickly settled. Amanda schooled him in what he had to do – parking the Mini, posting its keys and a postal order to the hire firm, hiring another car in his own name and going to the bank – while Dougal went upstairs to wrap up the diamonds and count out the cash.

He begged materials from Philip and constructed a misleadingly shaped package of cardboard and brown paper, secured with string and several yards of Sellotape. It remained to write a brief covering letter to the bank. They decided to use Philip's local branch for simplicity's sake. Dougal requested two keys for the safe deposit box and enclosed specimen signatures from himself and Amanda.

Primrose left the house in a flurry of excitement. The collar of his overcoat was turned up and he insisted on wearing a muffler which obscured most of his face.

The house was secure and tranquil without Primrose in one or other of its rooms. They had some Shreddies in the kitchen, feeling too lazy to cook breakfast. Amanda questioned him about Malcolm's boat, the potential refuge which had occurred to Dougal over the first cigarette of the day.

The *Sally-Anne* was more than Malcolm's boat; it was his home and his livelihood. He lived on it for eight or nine of the warmer months of the year, financing a leisurely outdoor life for himself by importing hash from Holland. He kept clear of its distribution and relied on a few trustworthy black market contacts at either end of the operation.

Last summer, one of his most reliable Amsterdam connections had asked him, as a personal and extremely well-paid favour, to deliver half a pound of cocaine to what Malcolm described as the Fortnum and Mason of British dealers. The consignment was urgent and he flew from Amsterdam to Heathrow with it. There he was unlucky – he fell foul of a spot check by customs officers on the green, nothing to declare channel.

In October a judge, who was shocked to find that Malcolm had been an undistinguished junior member of his own Cambridge college, called him a sore on the body politic and sentenced him to twelve months' imprisonment.

Dougal had promised to keep an eye on the *Sally-Anne* in her owner's absence. The boat was moored in Suffolk, in the Alben estuary, one of five fingers of the North Sea which dig deep into the East Anglian coast, as if a large and powerful child had spread his hand and gouged the earth out in a fit of absentmindedness.

The responsibility was not an arduous one. Every month or so, Dougal would go down to pump out the bilges and turn the engine over. So far, he had kept these visits brief; he was an amateur among amateur sailors at the best of times and, though he enjoyed boats of all types, he preferred to enjoy them with people who knew what they were doing. Nor did winter encourage nautical experiments – Dougal had once accompanied Malcolm on a trip up to Lowestoft in November and had spent most of the voyage convinced he had frostbite.

But now the *Sally-Anne* seemed the most attractive object in the world. The loneliness of the mooring and its approaches was ideal. There would be few people on the river at this time of year; and even fewer would be around midweek.

There were other advantages besides privacy. If Lee had little experience of small boats, he would face all the physical difficulties of an unfamiliar element – the cramped space, the constant shifting of a small boat in water and an ignorance of what might be used against him as a weapon. If Lee tried to rush them with overwhelming force, they would have an infinitely extendable moat between them and him. You can't follow a boat in a car.

If they did succeed in getting rid of – the euphemism still came more easily to his mind – Lee, the *Sally-Anne* gave them a good chance to dispose of the corpse. A weight would take it to the bottom and an ebb tide would sweep it out into the chilly depths of the North Sea.

It was odd how trifles could be important at a time like this. In the middle of planning a murder, Dougal found himself feeling smugly virtuous at the thought that visiting the *Sally-Anne* would have the additional benefit of allowing himself to discharge his obligation to Malcolm. He hadn't been down to the boat since the week before Christmas and had been beginning to feel slightly guilty.

In theory, the one problem remaining was the method of killing Lee. It would have to be done cleanly – it would be awkward to have Lee's blood spattered over the saloon, for example. And God knew what Malcolm would say if he found his beloved home had been doubling as an abattoir in his absence.

Straightforward poisoning would be simplest. But

where would they get the poison? And how could they find a way of introducing it into Lee's system? The man could hardly be expected to ask for a cup of cocoa to keep out the cold.

Using knives was a possibility: Lee would not be able to prevent one of them getting behind him. The tidy, fairly bloodless nature of Cedric's death had impressed Dougal, but it had been due to luck alone. Sticking a knife in some nonvital part of Lee's body would only outrage him and in any case there might be an uncontrollable spurt of blood.

They could not hope to obtain a gun unobtrusively. On the whole Dougal favoured a blunt instrument. There was a tool kit aboard the *Sally-Anne* which included a monkey wrench and a large spanner. They could always buy a couple of knives in case anything went wrong. Or to use for the *coup de grâce* once Lee had been safely stunned.

Discussing the details of Lee's forthcoming death gave the entire plan a welcome unreality. Concentrating on physical details – knives, spanners and so on – blurred the outline of what they were actually planning to do. Dougal wondered if soldiers on the eve of an offensive forgot the possibility of deaths, their own included, in the mundane rituals of cleaning weapons and studying maps. His father must have done the same thing dozens of times. Once the initial decision was taken – whatever one's reason for it – the process of trying to destroy somebody acquired an irresistible momentum of its own.

Assuming it was irresistible. And that they didn't meet the immovable object.

The rest of the morning and most of the afternoon must have passed in the usual way, one after the other, but Dougal found afterwards that his memories of the period were incomplete and jumbled. It was as if a cinefilm had been reduced to a few clips and stills.

Philip came back to the house with a bright yellow Ford Escort, his various missions successfully accomplished, radiating a certain coy smugness. Amanda cut him short when he was trying to render an exact account of his stewardship, down to the last half pee. Amanda was notoriously uninterested in financial details, but Primrose didn't know this, and his mouth drooped like that of a reprimanded child.

About an hour after that – it must have been around two o'clock – Dougal and Amanda left Cambridge. Amanda pecked Philip on the cheek as she said goodbye, returning his self-esteem to him as quickly as she had removed it.

Amanda drove them down to Ipswich on the A45. Dougal dozed for most of the journey, vivid and uncomfortable dreams about nothing in particular, except they all shared the hypnotic whine of the car's engine and the rushing movement of air. His head kept dropping down on his chest and swaying painfully against the window.

Amanda parked in a side street in Ipswich. Dougal

woke up sharply when she turned the engine off. They spent half an hour rushing round shops. Neither of them had a clear idea of what they needed. Amanda thought Dougal should have been making a list in the car instead of sleeping and said so. Uncertainty about the length of their stay on the *Sally-Anne* didn't help. They acquired three carrier bags and filled them with a variety of tins and bottles. Dougal bought a bottle of brandy in the vague belief that it would be the right thing to drink during an emergency.

They passed an ironmonger's and Amanda remembered they needed knives. Their choice fell on a model with a slender blade about eight inches long. Dougal felt they should be signing a pointed instruments' equivalent to the poisons' book; the knives were purpose-built for murder. They were served by a stooping man with grey and greasy hair in a grey and greasy coat, who merely expressed surprise that they were buying the most expensive knives in the shop. He was not a natural salesman. Amanda said firmly that they were for a friend's wedding present and they wanted the very best. 'Don't say I didn't warn you,' he replied mysteriously.

Dougal grew happier and more alert as they left the anonymous outskirts of Ipswich behind them. They drove up the A12 towards Woodbridge. It was growing dark now, and when they turned right into a B road leading to Albenham, the evening closed around them with a rush. The land on either side became flatter and bleaker, the temperature seemed to drop perceptibly.

'Where the hell are we?' asked Amanda irritably.

'Somewhere south of the Deben estuary and north of the Alben. Not far now. When you get through this village, take the next right. There's no point in going through Albenham itself.'

After a mile on a lane which had evidently been designed with tanks or tractors in mind, during which they met no traffic, which was just as well as there wouldn't have been room for two vehicles abreast on the road, they reached the entrance of the drive of Havishall Place. A roofless lodge cottage marked the spot.

Amanda inched the Escort into the drive and drove slowly along its uneven surface. 'Only another half mile,' Dougal told her.

'Shit.'

The grounds of Havishall Place included the creek where Malcolm kept the *Sally-Anne*. The house itself was a substantial but plain Edwardian building which had been derelict since a fire had gutted its interior just after the war. Both house and land were owned by a prosperous builder in Albenham, who planned to turn the site into a marina when funds and planning permission were forthcoming. In the meantime he had leased the mooring to Malcolm, and the handful of fields which went with the house to a neighbouring farmer.

The stable yard had hardly been touched by the fire. The roof of the coach house was intact and Malcolm left his car there when he was on the *Sally-Anne*, and a bundle of oars, sails, rowlocks and miscellaneous essentials when he wasn't. A footpath led across a couple of fields to the creek.

They left the car in the coach house and spent an irritable ten minutes ('*Why* didn't you bring a torch?') getting Malcolm's bundle down from the rafters, collecting the shopping and extracting from their luggage anything which wouldn't be useful on the boat. Dougal realized, but decided not to mention it to Amanda, that what they had packed for a winter weekend in a country hotel might not be altogether appropriate for a few days on the *Sally-Anne*.

They would have to make two journeys. Dougal shouldered Malcolm's bundle and led the way down the path. It was muddy underfoot, and he could hear Amanda swearing softly to herself.

At the end of the second field, they had to clamber over a stile. Dougal politely went first. As he stood with one leg on each side, he caught his first sight of the graceful outlines of the *Sally-Anne*, riding at her mooring fifty yards away.

He was glad they had got there before the light had entirely faded. It looked as if the boat was floating on a sea of grey ink.

Amanda nudged him. 'Come on. I'm freezing.'

18

Dougal had always identified boats with people, usually females. Punts, for example, reminded him of the squat, black-browed bedmaker who occasionally did his room during his first year at Cambridge. The *Sally-Anne*, however, suggested a lady in reduced circumstances from the provinces; she was elderly and dowdy, but possessed an in-built individuality; she was quiet, quirky and reliable.

She was a gaff-cutter of clinker construction, dating from the thirties. White's of Brightlingsea had built her for the son of the beer baron who owned Havishall Place at that time. When he died ten years ago, the boat was put up for sale and Malcolm abused his credit to buy her.

Dougal, then sharing lodgings in Cambridge with Malcolm, had absorbed the *Sally-Anne*'s history, specifications and qualities through constant exposure to them. Sometimes he suspected he knew more about the boat than he knew about Malcolm.

Malcolm found the *Sally-Anne* ideal for his purposes. She was twenty-six feet long and held four berths: sturdy enough for the North Sea and small enough for him to handle by himself. Three years ago he had replaced the elderly Stewart-Turner petrol engine with a more reliable Volvo Penta. Dougal knew he would have to use the diesel engine if they left the mooring – he mistrusted his ability to manage the *Sally-Anne* under sail, particularly if there was any sort of wind blowing. It would also be difficult to make a quick getaway: it had taken half an hour to get up the mainsail alone the last time he had tried without Malcolm's assistance. He wished to God he'd invested more effort in learning from Malcolm. It might have been very useful to be able to leave the Alben estuary – if Lee turned up with a small army, for example – and sail away up the coast. The *Sally-Anne* was well equipped with navigational aids, including a Seafix radio direction finder which was Malcolm's especial pride, but Dougal's knowledge of the art of navigation was limited to dim memories about the constellations in the night sky.

These thoughts were chasing through his mind as he and Amanda lifted the *Sally-Anne*'s dinghy from the blocks of wood on which it lay near the stile, and staggered with it between them towards the bank of the creek.

The *Sally-Anne* was moored in the middle of a brief cul-de-sac off the main estuary. She lay with her bows towards them, for the tide was beginning to ebb.

Fortunately the water was high enough still for them to turn the dinghy and get it into the water without having first to lug it across the grey and greedy mud of the bed of the creek. Dougal, it was true, managed to get his boots and the bottoms of his trousers soaked with the icy water, but Amanda remained reasonably dry-shod. He clambered in and, holding the boat to the bank, told Amanda what to pass to him. They spoke in whispers, which was strange: the twilight and the empti-ness of land and water somehow forced them to lower their voices.

At the last moment Amanda said she would go back to the car for the rest of their luggage. 'I'm cold enough as it is, without going out of my way to get colder before it's absolutely necessary.'

Dougal let go of the bank and pushed off with one of the oars. Their belongings in the boat left no room for his feet: he was forced to spend a moment reorgan-izing them, during which one of the carrier bags disgorged the tins it contained. Dougal ignored them; it was less arduous than swearing at them. He was worried about Amanda, a feeling which overlay the deeper worry of what was going to happen with Lee. He tried not to resent the fact that she was obviously uncomfortable here but only succeeded in feeling bewildered.

He began rowing, using short experimental strokes with pauses between them; rowing was like riding a bicycle – once learned, never forgotten – but it took a little time to get used to the process again. His hands felt raw and blazing – chafed on one side by the oars, and on the other by the breeze which was springing up.

The *Sally-Anne*'s bulk loomed up behind him. He paddled round to the stern. The delicate but cumbersome business of transferring himself and their belongings to the cockpit took longer than he had expected (he remembered belatedly that everything does on a boat). By the time he got back to Amanda it was fully dark. He wished they had come in daylight.

For the next two hours they tried to keep moving. The cold and the damp were in everything, constant goads to activity. It was difficult to disagree with Amanda when she remarked bitterly, 'Words like *freezing* and *cold* have a completely different meaning on a boat.'

The first thing they did was to raid the oilskin locker, where Malcolm kept a collection of clothing, including sea-boots of various sizes.

Amanda lit the small, solid-fuel heater in the saloon, using three fire lighters in her haste. Dougal, knowing the electric lights they were using were draining the battery, lit the gimballed oil lamps and drew the blinds down over the portholes. He then pumped out the bilges; the exercise warmed him as the pumped water, running over his hands, chilled him.

The next necessity was to turn the engine over. Just in case Lee came out of the night like a bogeyman to get them. It wasn't likely, true, but things had stopped being likely for some time now. He used a blowtorch to warm the cylinder head. He turned on the fuel, lifted the compression switches and cranked the engine violently. With a silent prayer, he pushed down the compression and, miraculously, the engine mumbled into life.

Amanda, meanwhile, had been unpacking and boiling water.

'If you've finished playing, there's some tea here. Where's the loo?'

'The heads,' Dougal began, some pedagogic instinct surfacing even now, only to be rapidly suppressed, 'I mean it's opposite the oilskin locker. Just before you get to the berths in the bows.'

The tea improved everything. They had two mugs each, destroying its flavour with sugar and brandy. The heating was beginning to take effect, and the soft yellow radiance of the oil lamps added to the illusion of warmth. By tacit agreement, they ignored the things they should have been doing – making a meal and deciding how to kill Lee, for example – and were exaggeratedly gentle with one another. They were sitting on either side of the collapsible table in the saloon, halfway through the second mug, when Amanda suddenly suggested playing cards.

The absurdity of the idea appealed to them both. Dougal found a greasy pack – his oily hands soon made them greasier – and they played a couple of hands of picquet, choosing the game because it seemed more out of place than any other.

When Amanda started dropping her cards and Dougal knocked over his brandy, they decided to go to bed, despite the fact it was only eight o'clock. One berth held a large American down sleeping bag. They pulled off their boots and struggled into it together, fully clothed. Dougal had to extract himself to turn off the oil lamps.

Cramped in the single berth, they cuddled together for warmth. He could feel the stubble on his chin tangling with the dark, sweet-smelling mass of Amanda's hair. As they drifted through the no-man's-land between waking and sleeping, they made love in a gentle, detached way. As if, Dougal thought sleepily, they were absentmindedly pandering to a whim on the part of their bodies.

With the ghost light which preceded the dawn came fear. It nibbled its way into Dougal's mind. At first it was merely a sense of something wrong, a malaise which had nothing to do with physical discomfort. Each time he awoke, a detail of it became clearer, as if a pencil in his mind was joining up the dots which marked the outline of the picture. It hardened into a savage headache.

Today was the day they had to try to kill Lee.

Today, it occurred to him, was the first day in his life that he knew might not be followed by tomorrow. Panic hovered over him: I don't want to die, he screamed in the silence of his thoughts, I'm too young, there are so many things I want to do. It's unfair, all these things left undone. The word, undone, had an echo of memory attached, and he suddenly remembered the service at Charleston Parva on Sunday morning: *We have left undone those things which we ought to have done; And we have done those things which we ought not to have done; And there is no health in us* . . . The words seemed appropriate – not that he was in tune with the sentiments of the general confession as a whole (quite the reverse), but because they expressed the feeling that he was stupid to have got himself in such a position as this; it was unhealthy to be in this particular here and now . . . Malcolm would have shaken his head over the business and delivered his most severe verdict: 'Un*cool*, William, it's just un*cool*.'

He had to stop this; the best way was to get up and do something. It was fully light, now. He could make out the condensation which had collected overnight on the glass of the portholes. The saloon must be full of stale air, but his nostrils were still blocked from sleeping.

He levered himself out of the sleeping bag. Amanda groaned and spread herself more comfortably. His socks, thick though they were, were no protection against the cold which crept up from the deck to the soles of his feet. The act of standing up made his headache worse: it savaged the middle of his forehead at the spot traditionally reserved for the third eye. His tongue felt twice its normal size and rasped against the roof of his mouth. It must have been the brandy, he thought. Always a mistake to buy cheap stuff. Rémy Martin wouldn't have had this effect.

He edged round the table to the tiny galley in the corner by the companionway up to the cockpit. There was enough water in the kettle, but he had to try four matches before finding one which was sufficiently free from damp to light. The little stove beside the galley was still alight; he rested his hands gratefully close to its warm top.

A tin which had once held Oxo Cubes contained Malcolm's supply of medicines. There were paracetamol among them; Dougal took three and followed up this shock to his system by brushing his teeth as gently as he could. While waiting for the water to boil, he fed a few lumps of coke into the heater, noticing with distaste that his fingers were grubby and his nails were rimmed with black. He considered washing, but decided he couldn't face it yet. In any case the water had boiled, and coffee was infinitely more important.

After a few mouthfuls of coffee, his outlook on life improved. He felt relatively clearheaded and considerably less fragile than he had half an hour before.

Twenty minutes later, just after 8:30, he took the dinghy ashore to telephone Lee. The morning was cold and overcast, but seemed unexpectedly spacious after the saloon of the *Sally-Anne*. He walked up to the stable block, his feet crunching on the frosty grass. Nothing was stirring. The desolate, smoke-blackened facade of Havishall Place heightened the sense of isolation; it was a landscape that was fundamentally indifferent to humans – it couldn't even be bothered to be hostile to them.

The car, an emissary from another civilization, took him in efficiently padded comfort to Albenham, two miles up the road. He found a telephone box outside the post office. It seemed to be a local forum of debate. IPSWICH RULES had been scrawled in heavy-duty black felt-tip over the glass protecting the list of local exchanges. IPSHIT ARE WANKERS had been scratched on the grey metal above the coin slots.

Dougal dialled Lee's number. It was answered at the second ring. He fed in a coin and the pips gave way to silence.

'Mr Lee? Massey here.'

'Good. Where do we meet?' Lee sounded brusque, almost surly, as if he too had had a bad night but, unlike Dougal, had not been up long enough for its effects to have receded.

Dougal gave him detailed instructions about how to reach the boat, advising him to leave his car in the stables. 'When you reach the mooring, I'll row you over to the boat.'

'No.' Lee's voice was unemphatic but final. 'There's no need for that. I'll come to the river bank and we'll make the exchange there. I'll be there at three.'

There was a click as the line went dead. Dougal was left clutching the phone and feeling foolish. More than foolish – scared. He went back to the car and sat watching his knuckles whiten on the steering wheel.

Any planning they had done had rested on the assumption that Lee would come to the boat itself, which would ensure, at one stroke, a degree of privacy, Lee in an unfamiliar element and both Dougal and Amanda being physically close to him.

On land they would lose these advantages. Lee would be wary if they were both on the bank; he would be armed, and would probably insist they kept their distance. The usefulness of their weapons depended on being close to him. There would now be no chance of catching him with both arms occupied. It would have been so easy to hit him as he levered himself in or out of the *Sally-Anne*.

The only consolation was that Lee had implied he was coming alone – he had said *I*, not *we*. Dougal shied away from the possibility that he would not be alone. They had to rely on Lee believing them to be even more insignificant than in fact they were.

For a moment he toyed with the idea of backing out. They could take the car and vanish – the world was large enough, surely? The trouble was, nowhere was large enough to get away from the idea of Lee: they would carry his avenging image in their minds always; it would be a life on guard against the potential threat of every unexplained shadow.

There was still time, of course, to drive to Cambridge, collect the diamonds and fulfil their side of the bargain. Dougal seriously considered this idea before rejecting it. In this case, there was no honour among thieves. He knew, with a cold, hard certainty, that Lee had no intention of honouring his side of the deal. Why should he? Why should he waste his money on people he not only hated for tricking him, but also despised? Everything they knew about the Irishman, from Hanbury onwards, argued that he had as little respect for the rights of other people as a hungry bedbug. Or a man-eating tiger. If they gave him the diamonds, he would laugh in their faces; the only thing he was likely to give them was a bullet.

Another point: if Lee did get them under his control at Havishall, their one chance of staying alive would be if they didn't have the diamonds. Not much of a chance, admittedly, but he would hardly kill them if that destroyed his access to Vernon-Jones's legacy.

Dougal lit a cigarette and sucked on it with mindless fervour. He felt feverish, as if he existed in a wholly private universe of febrile conjecture. Out of which, somehow, he had to make a decision. If he was thinking rationally, and he had to pretend he was, there was only one solution, the same one as before. Lee had to be killed. They would have to rethink their methodology, that was all. There was no alternative.

When he got back to the *Sally-Anne*, Amanda was cutting the rind from rashers of bacon with one of the knives from Ipswich. Dougal told her what Lee had said.

'Well we'll just have to do something else, won't we?' she said in a tone of voice which decided Dougal not to tell her of the pros and cons which had been swirling through his head like the particles of a sandstorm. Sometimes the directness of her responses, the way she cut effortlessly through to what, for her, were the essentials of a decision, made him feel like a prehistoric animal – a survivor from an era when choices took more time to evolve.

'The best place to do something,' said Dougal hesitantly, 'would be the stables. Lee's bound to go there either when he arrives or when he finds we're not down here at the mooring. He'll be looking for the car.'

'Okay, we'll fix up an ambush there,' said Amanda, as if she was deciding that, since the butcher hadn't any joints of beef left, they would make do with a leg of pork. 'Come on. We've not got all day.'

No, they hadn't, thought Dougal. It was the rest of their lives he was worried about.

19

The Lancia was too distant, and moving too swiftly, to be much more than an element in a rapidly changing pattern of black and shades of grey. It had just reached the junction of the road from Ipswich with the road from Albenham. Staring through Malcolm's powerful Zeiss field glasses, while sweeping them in a slow arc to keep the car in view, was like looking into a kaleidoscope from which all the colour had been drained. The stunted trees and neglected hedges which lined the lane from the junction to the entrance of the drive of Havishall Place made it impossible to get a clear view of the vehicle – let alone to see how many people were in it. The branches and twigs which blocked the view formed a chaotic winter tracery. Behind it lay the strip of tarmac along which the Lancia moved with jerky spurts of speed, implying an aggressive driver on a narrow, unknown road.

Lee.

It was two thirty-six.

He was early, perhaps trying to catch them off-balance. In a way, Dougal was glad. He had already been here for nearly half an hour, perched uncomfortably on what had once been a window seat in a bay window on the first floor of Havishall Place. The house was built on a low knoll which, by virtue of the flatness of the surrounding land, was the best vantage point for miles. At the back, you could see down to the estuary, even from the terrace. Here at the front, if you climbed to the level of the first floor, it was possible to command the approach roads. And Lee – fortunately enough – was the kind of man whom it was impossible to imagine divorced from his car.

But it had not been a pleasant wait. The sky, the colour of dirty pewter, pressed down on the roofless shell of the house, enclosing Dougal with the charred beams, broken bricks and decayed vegetation. Previously, he had been able to keep at bay with activity the tension of the day. He and Amanda had spent most of it in the coach house and the stables, first examining, with the help of two large torches from the *Sally-Anne,* the rubbish that had accumulated there over the last seventy years, and then devising a reception for Lee.

Up here in the house, however, there had been nothing to do except chain-smoke with a third of his attention and watch the road. And worry. His mind was discordant with fears, like somebody playing an untuned piano very badly and very loudly. He now understood the phrase 'gritting one's teeth', except his teeth seemed to grit themselves of their own accord; his jaws ached.

Curiously enough, the tension was only partly linked to the image of Lee. Amanda was tied up in it too – not the fear of her dying, but the feeling that this sharing of complicity in murder, robbery and deception had prized them apart rather than pushed them together. They were business partners; some unspoken decision had made them put the firm before themselves. Gumper's death had started the process which changed them from lovers to associates. It was another reason to kill Lee, of course, although the probability that he would otherwise destroy them was motive enough. But his death, Dougal hoped, would also bring this episode, this aberration, to an end. He and Amanda would be able to go back to where they were before, richer, of course, and wiser in a sense, too. At this moment, watching the Lancia blur behind a hedgerow, he would have happily exchanged the largest fortune in the world, and divine omniscience as well, for the chance of stepping back. If he had not gone to Gumper's room, if he had done something else, like go back to Amanda, he would be an entirely different person now. And so would she.

Dougal shouted to Amanda, who was waiting between the house and the stable block, and began to clamber down to the ground. The forefront of his mind was occupied with the difficulties of the descent – the rusted nail that caught his jacket, tearing a triangular hole, the way the brickwork scraped his right hand (he had removed the glove to smoke and forgotten to put it on again) and the jar that went through him as he hit the ground. The back of his mind was heavy with the possibility of failure.

He ran out of the front doorway, turned to his right and sprinted towards the stables. As he moved, the field glasses, slung round his neck, bounced awkwardly against his body. Veering right, left and left again, he was in the stable yard. Amanda was waiting by the double door of the coach house. She waved him on as he appeared, and then vanished into its interior.

One leaf was open: the other was bolted. Dougal hurtled through the gap and whispered, 'Good luck,' to the scrambling noise which was Amanda over on the left. He himself went right, into a small and musty harness room, now empty of harness, and pulled the door to. A crack remained, through which he could see the door of the coach house and the pool of light which the open leaf admitted. He rummaged feverishly in his pockets, suddenly convinced that his weapons must have fallen out at some point. No, they were there; he glanced down at them: the heavy monkey wrench in his right hand and the kitchen knife in his left.

Lee would take at least a minute to get to the stables – probably longer. Dougal eased the door open. He could just make out the outlines of the Escort in the corner of the coach house, immediately on his right. In the other corner, furthest away from the door, was Amanda, crouching up among the beams which still supported the tiled roof.

'Get back, you fool,' she whispered, and Dougal obediently withdrew. She was right, of course, but he hoped that those were not going to be the last words she spoke to him.

The seconds stretched themselves indefinitely. The windows of the harness room were shuttered, and Dougal couldn't see the face of his watch. His mouth was dry. Suddenly, he remembered to remove the field glasses. He set them, with infinite care, on the windowsill. It was out of his hands, he told himself. It was all up to a coil of nylon rope from the *Sally-Anne,* a heavy, circular stone with a hole in it, which had once been used for grinding knives, and the rusted blade of a scythe.

As his ears strained to hear the first sound of the engine on the drive, his mind inexplicably emptied itself of fear. Dougal found that he was cataloguing their preparations; the details calmed him. The trap was set; the other leaf of the coach house door was bolted down; other doors in the stable block were bolted or locked; except for the patch just inside the door, the coach house was in varying shades of darkness; the hinges of the harness room door were oiled; the knife was . . .

He could hear the snarl of the car outside. An image out of a nightmare sprung briefly into his mind – of some snouted monster, snuffling remorselessly towards its prey. The engine slowed: Lee must have reached the open space at the front of the house, where the drive described a circle and went back the way it had come, sending a narrow offshoot between the house and the outer wall of the coach house which led to the stable yard. The engine revved again – a lower note, which must mean that Lee had chosen first gear for the rutted track round to the stables. The sound was magnified by the canyon between the buildings; the snarling was angrier and more vicious.

Dougal poised himself by the harness room door. One quick flick of his wrist and it would fly open. The car negotiated the 180-degree turn into the yard with painful slowness. The engine died abruptly, as if someone had knifed it. The silence stretched into an eternity of menace. The beast was preparing to spring.

The sound of a car door slamming shut was sudden and shocking. Dougal shifted his grip on the cold steel of the monkey wrench; it was slightly clammy with his sweat.

Then came another noise: the other door of the Lancia closed with a soft click, as if the person doing it wanted to be polite to the car.

Lee had not come alone.

Dougal took an instinctive, fear-propelled step backwards. His thoughts accelerated into manic overdrive, as if someone had pumped a vast dose of amphetamines into his bloodstream.

It was no longer two to one: Lee had evened the odds. And there was no way that Dougal could alter the programme they had prepared for him. It all depended on Amanda. He swore at himself for his wishful thinking – for believing, because he wanted to, that Lee would come alone, trusting in their naiveté.

Lee was a professional: of course he had brought someone to cover his back. For a second, Dougal fought an urge to run, anywhere, anywhere out of this world. But he couldn't. The exit was barred by Lee and his companion.

There were footsteps outside – town shoes on the cobbled yard. The light which filtered through the doorway darkened by a fraction. He saw Lee first, followed by the stooping figure of Tanner.

Lee hesitated, trying to accustom his eyes to the gloom.

'There's their car.' He spoke quietly, but Dougal, only five yards away, had the brief illusion that Lee was talking to him. 'Distributor cap. And anything else.'

So Lee wanted to cut off their retreat. Which meant, of course, that he had never had any intention of keeping faith either. The two men moved slowly into the coach house, Tanner on Lee's left, the side furthest from Dougal.

And closest to Amanda.

There was a sound like someone trying to whistle – a rush of displaced air. From the shadowed rafters in the far corner something swooped down on the men in the doorway, its shape blurred by the speed it was travelling at.

For a frozen instant, Dougal saw the faces of Lee and Tanner, pasty in the half-light, jerk upwards to the left, their mouths yawning like men waking after a long sleep.

Dougal's infernal engine was on the move. His fear was swamped by pride.

It was, in fact, a lethal pendulum. One end of the rope

was knotted round a beam halfway between Amanda's perch and the spot just inside the entrance. On the other end of its carefully calculated length was the grindstone, which had taken the combined efforts of Dougal and Amanda to lift; the rope passed through its center, where a square hole had been chiselled to hold the crank handle which must once have powered it. To the grindstone was lashed the blade of the scythe. It had been poised beside Amanda, restrained by a loop of rope. All she had needed to do had been to loose the rope and simultaneously thrust the stone as forcefully as she could, to increase the momentum of the missile.

Its trajectory came to an abrupt halt as the point of the blade took Tanner in the chest, between his collarbone and his heart. Dougal watched, aghast; he had never really expected his invention to work. Tanner was lifted backwards off his feet by the blow, showing his yellow teeth in a rictus of astonishment.

The pendulum, impeded by this dragging weight, came to the end of its arc and swung back. Tanner drooped from the blade of the scythe, his disproportionately long limbs dangling like those of a puppet whose master had suddenly abandoned the strings. His overcoat hung open, flapping gently in the breeze from the door. Tanner's feet trailed behind him; their friction halted the return swing of the pendulum.

Before the blade of the scythe had reached Tanner, Dougal had left the shelter of the harness room door. While his mind was responding to Tanner's meeting with the pendulum with a welter of brightly coloured images, his body was rushing blindly towards the two figures in the doorway.

Lee's attention was on Tanner; he did not notice Dougal's approach until it was too late. He had just begun to turn, his arm in the automatic act of rising to ward off a blow, when the monkey wrench thudded down on his uncovered head. He fell to his knees, swaying there for a soundless second. Then his body crumpled forwards on to the stone flags of the floor. There was the gleam of blood on his scalp.

Dougal felt a superstitious shiver running through him. Why was killing so easy?

Amanda made a sound without words. He swung round as she dropped from the rafters and stumbled towards him. They clung to one another, a few yards away from the bodies. There was no feeling of release, Dougal noticed. Perhaps that would come later. He felt slightly sick.

'We'll have to get them down to the boat,' said Amanda, drawing back a little.

Dougal looked at her as if she was talking in a foreign language. Then the sense caught up with the words. He nodded. 'Later. It'll be safer in the dark. Transport's going to be difficult. Dragging them all the way down to the mooring would be sheer murder—'

He stared at Amanda, aghast at the way in which the words had rolled unheeded from his mouth. But she laughed, and he joined her. The absurd was comforting.

She broke off. 'There's an old wheelbarrow at the other end of the stables, isn't there? How about that?'

'Let's try it. If the wheel still turns, it would be usable. We could do it in two journeys.'

Dougal slipped back into the harness room and picked up the larger of the two torches. Amanda followed him – a second door led through to the rest of the stables. They walked past empty loose-boxes on a floor grey with generations of bird droppings. At the end was the wheelbarrow, flanked by a stone garden roller and a huge, pictureless frame of grimy gilt. Behind, the unplastered wall glinted with damp.

Dougal passed the torch to Amanda and pulled out the wheelbarrow. The frame was still sound, though there was rust on every available surface and a couple of holes in the bottom of the barrow. The wheel was shod with iron.

When he pushed it over the uneven surface of the floor, the axle of the barrow screeched against its supports and began to turn.

'It'll be okay,' he said.

'There may be blood,' Amanda suggested hesitantly. 'It could drip anywhere out of those holes. It'll be hard to see in the torchlight.'

'We'll just have to spend the night here on the *Sally-Anne*. It'll be easier to do the final tidying up by daylight.'

Amanda agreed with a marked lack of enthusiasm.

'It'll work out, love,' Dougal said. 'Let's go out to dinner tonight. Somewhere warm. And dry.'

He wheeled the barrow back through the stables, Amanda guiding him with the torch. In the coach house, he glanced involuntarily at the figures by the door, grotesquely deep-frozen by death. The touch of nausea returned and he looked away.

Suddenly he stopped, just as Amanda came out of the harness room. He noticed her eyes widening with shock in the same instant as he remembered: Lee had fallen flat on his face, his arms outstretched.

But the arms of the body on the ground had moved.

As he looked round, Lee changed his position, his bulky limbs moving with swift, fluid precision, as if he had rehearsed the movement many times. His right hand emerged from the pocket of his blue, quilted anorak, holding a black automatic pistol. Simultaneously, he levered his head and shoulders from the ground with his left elbow and slapped his left hand against his right wrist. The muzzle of the gun pointed unwaveringly at Dougal, Lee's eye bulbous with concentration behind the V-shaped rear sight. With both his elbows supporting him, the man was immobile again – but now his stillness effortlessly dominated the coach house.

Lee broke the silence with a sound which made Dougal bite his lip to the sudden, shocking taste of blood.

Lee tittered.

20

The titter moved gradually down the vocal register, changing its character until it became a flow of obscenities. The words were terrifying not for themselves, but for the manner in which they were spoken. Lee's face was twitching. His hand squeezed the butt of the pistol. Dougal recognized the make of the gun, now – the knowledge was another legacy from his father, who had a small library on the subject of firearms – a 9-mm. Walther PPK. He couldn't remember how many bullets the magazine held – probably eight. More than enough, in any case.

Lee's voice was as low-pitched and monotonous as usual, but his words seemed to have the cutting edge of madness. Dougal's fear petrified his body, but his mind, fuelled with panic, ran swiftly: Lee had been humiliated and had gone temporarily berserk as a result; so far it had only affected his vocabulary . . .

Suddenly the flow stopped. There was no diminution

beforehand – it was as if a switch had been flicked which cut off the current of words as quickly and completely as an electric light. When Lee spoke again, he sounded hoarse.

'Put your hands on your heads. *Slowly*. Turn around. Hands on that wall to the left of the door you came through. Feet apart. Lean against it.'

It was difficult to tell which came first: the thought that one of them was about to die, the smack of the shot, or the shower of brick and mortar fragments which spurted from the wall between Dougal and Amanda.

'Too close. Move a yard away from her, Massey.'

Dougal obeyed. His insides churned; he hoped desperately he would not lose physical control of himself. He retained a shred of detachment which allowed him to recognize, but gain no comfort from, the absurdity of worrying about breaking that taboo now. Stiff upper lippery was as obsolete as the Empire which had inspired it. He would have cried if it would have done any good. *Oh God*, he prayed with soundless despair, *if you get us out of this, I swear* . . . hoping beyond reason and belief that some deity would be listening.

His devotions were curtailed by the sound of painful breathing and scrabbling behind him. Lee must be getting to his feet. There was a scrape of metal on stone and a clatter, as the monkey wrench, which Dougal had dropped after hitting Lee, was kicked out of the way. Footsteps came towards them; the sound had a slow, conscious precision which reminded Dougal of a drunk proving he could still walk in a straight line.

'I'm going to search you. Stand very still. Frisking stiffs is just as easy.'

Dougal felt the pressure of the pistol in the small of his back. Lee's hand methodically emptied the contents of his pockets on to the ground. He found the knife and threw it across the coach house. His fingers wandered over Dougal's clothes in search of concealed objects. Always, Lee's other hand held the gun rigid.

He subjected Amanda to the same process, which made Dougal feel angry and more impotent than he could ever remember feeling. At least Lee wouldn't find the keys of the safe deposit box. Not yet, anyway. They were safe on the *Sally-Anne* – or rather in the water, attached to a length of transparent nylon fishing line, the other end of which was looped unobtrusively round a cleat at the bows.

'Okay, what have you done with them? The diamonds?' Lee's voice sounded muzzy and venomous.

'They're down on the boat.' He couldn't think of anything else to say. It must sound plausible enough. He was gambling on the possibility that Lee would need their help to get the diamonds in his present state – that he would defer killing them, and prolong the chance that a miracle might arrive, until he knew that they could be of no further service to him. It was unlikely, surely, that he would send one of them to get the diamonds while he held the other hostage; Lee was on unfamiliar ground, and could not be sure that the one he sent would not fetch outside help. Nor, for that matter, he realized, could Lee be sure that the one he sent wouldn't consider the diamonds well worth the life of the one who stayed. Amateur status might have this small advantage: a professional criminal would automatically assume the worst motives in others. Not that Lee's cynicism was likely to help them in the long run. Nevertheless, Dougal wanted to stay with Amanda.

Lee's footsteps retreated slowly. Dougal's hypotheses vanished, together with the tenuous reassurance they carried. Was Lee going to shoot them now after all? Lee couldn't be entirely sane.

That unnerving titter.

At last Lee began to talk.

'You're going to help me down to that bloody boat.' The words came slowly, as if each one had to be forced through a screen of treacle. 'One on each side. And a bullet for each of you, if either of you starts playing heroes.'

'Right,' said Dougal. He had to say it again, because the first time it came out without any sound attached. Someone had to say something. Out of the corner of his eye he could see Amanda, but she seemed to be staring down at the ground, not at him.

'Turn round slowly, and come over here. No sudden movements.'

Dougal and Amanda let their hands fall to their sides and moved round to face Lee. He was at the doorway to the yard, leaning heavily against the jamb. His face was grey and lined. In his left hand was a bloodstained handkerchief, with which he must have dabbed the wound on his scalp. He looked almost pathetic; Dougal had the fleeting impression that he had palpably shrunk. But the Walther in his other hand was still levelled steadily in their direction.

Lee gestured to them with the gun and they obediently came over and stood, one on either side of him. He swayed slightly. 'Take my arms.' He crossed them over his front. Dougal was on Lee's right. The muzzle of the Walther dug into Amanda's side. 'Now. We walk slowly down to the boat.' Behind them, Tanner's body shifted fractionally as a sudden gust of wind swirled up from the estuary.

They moved forward with united deliberation, like nurses accompanying a geriatric patient on an outing to the television room. With maddening slowness, they crossed the cobbled stable yard and the lane beyond and reached the first field. The exercise seemed to revive Lee: he began to need less of their support. A bad sign. He prodded the gun viciously into Amanda. Dougal saw her wince.

As they followed the footpath, their speed increased. Dougal surreptitiously glanced around him. On one side the field was empty: no help there. On his right was the hedge, a formidable barrier six feet high, which winter had failed to make any less impassable. Dougal's mind shot off on a tangent: the hedge must be old, to be so thick. Couldn't you tell a hedge's age by the number of plants it contained? . . . Anyone on the other side was effectively in another world. Not that there would be anyone.

The line of the hedge altered in the second field, and the estuary swung into view. It looked murky and secretive. Its surface was empty of moving boats, its waters moved in their own unalterable rhythms, oblivious of humans. The picture froze in Dougal's mind – not because he liked it at present, but because this might be the last time he ever saw it.

Dougal tried to think calmly. Lee would probably kill them as soon as he felt it practicable. Would he do it as soon as he knew that they had cheated him over the diamonds? Perhaps, if he found out where the stones really were, he would force them to extend the nightmare into tomorrow and go with them to Cambridge. Equally possibly, his rage – and the intrinsic pleasure of the action – would lead to him killing them on the spot. Which he would have done anyway, if the diamonds had been there. That was the trouble. Lee wanted the diamonds, but he also wanted to kill them. That was the difference between him and Hanbury; the latter, Dougal suspected, had only killed when he felt it to be necessary, not because he enjoyed it.

If they were going to die anyway, Dougal realized that he might as well take any chance, however slim, to overcome Lee. He almost wished there had been no chance left at all – it would have been simpler.

They reached the stile. Lee's face was expressionless as he stared out to the *Sally-Anne*. He climbed over almost unaided. There was a tree stump a few yards away. He lumbered over to it and sat down heavily. The walk might have increased his strength, but it had done nothing to improve his temper.

'You,' Lee spat at Amanda. 'You're going to get the diamonds. Your boyfriend stays with me and gets his head blown apart if you try any funny business. And remember, this little toy of mine can reach you too, my love. And will, if necessary.' Rubbish, thought Dougal. The *Sally-Anne* was at least fifty yards away, probably further, and if Lee could make the Walther shoot accurately at that distance he was a bloody genius. 'Go on. Off you go.'

'Shall I push her off?' asked Dougal politely. 'She's not very good with oars and things.'

Lee thought for a moment. It was cold, out here on the estuary, and it suddenly occurred to Dougal that Lee wasn't enjoying waiting around here, either, though not for the same reasons. Lee huddled on the tree stump in his anorak, measuring the distance from where he sat to the dinghy. Dougal glanced at Amanda and felt deluged with helpless tenderness: she looked so pale standing there – not like herself at all, but some poor quality imitation. Dougal shifted his weight from one foot to the other, wondering if he looked as ghostly as she did.

'All right,' said Lee at last. 'Walk slowly, though, and no talking. When it's done, you' – the gun barrel swung towards Dougal – 'come and sit in front of me. You' – the Walther turned on Amanda – 'don't you waste any time, or pop goes lover boy here. Got it?'

Silently they nodded. Dougal was swearing to himself. Lee must have the constitution of an elephant – his voice sounded almost normal now. If only he had had the sense to follow up the blow on the head with a quick thrust of the knife.

Dougal unlooped the dinghy's painter from the stake which served as a bollard. Amanda clambered in and awkwardly set the oars in the rowlocks. As Dougal swung the boat round by the stern, the muddy water splashing greedily up at his hands, he mouthed, 'Lie on the deck in the saloon. Don't move until you hear me shout *Caroline*. If not, wait till it's dark, and row up with the tide to Albenham, police.'

She looked up, not at him but over her shoulder. Two spots of startling red had appeared in her cheeks. It was impossible to tell if she had understood.

Dougal pushed off the dinghy. Amanda began to row inexpertly towards the *Sally-Anne* by a zigzag route. Dougal turned away. Lee stared impassively at him, and then waved the gun at a spot a couple of yards in front of him. Dougal walked over and sat down, facing the *Sally-Anne*. The damp seeped through the seat of his jeans. No need to worry about rheumatism now. He stared at the diminishing figure of Amanda, as if he was trying to fix her image in his mind forever. His awareness of Lee's presence behind him was like a weight on his shoulders.

Amanda scrambled over the stern of the *Sally-Anne,* leaving the dinghy rocking violently behind. She looked briefly back towards the shore; the distance was too great for Dougal to catch the expression on her face. She vanished down the companionway to the saloon.

Dougal let thirty seconds crawl by to the end of the world. He and Lee were like passengers waiting for a train – terrified to move in case it passed through the station without them noticing. Only the river had motion: the water rubbed and slapped against the mud, its surface movement rocking the boats deserted at their winter moorings in the estuary.

Water.

'Mr Lee.' Dougal half-turned his head. 'I've got to piss. May I stand up?'

There was a chuckle behind him, with an undertone of derision, as if the weakness of Dougal's bladder confirmed Lee's overall opinion of him. 'Yes. Do it where you are. Where I can see you.'

Dougal slowly got to his feet. The muscles in his legs, especially around the knees, shrieked at the change of position. The cold seemed to have permeated every cell of his body. He flexed his fingers and made as if to fumble with his flies. His shoulders were tensed – hunched of their own accord. Would Lee notice?

Three – two – one—

He spun round and flung himself in a dive which was almost horizontal at Lee's right hand. Before impact, he noticed several things so quickly that they blurred into

237

one another in his brain: Lee wasn't even looking at him – he was staring blankly at the *Sally-Anne* as if she was the promised land; the gun dangled from his hand, barrel downwards; and the patch of drying blood on his head glowed somberly against the dull winter background.

Dougal's body hit the frozen ground with a jolt; simultaneously, he grabbed Lee's gun arm with both hands. His momentum toppled Lee from the tree stump. Dougal used his right hand to club the wound on Lee's head – not once but again and again, until his clenched first was smeared with warm blood.

Lee's body went limp, giving Dougal the chance to scoop away the Walther and knee his adversary in the crotch. Then, as before with Cedric, all element of calculation deserted his actions. Dougal found himself on his feet, sobbing helplessly and kicking Lee again and again, anywhere and everywhere. His boots thudded against Lee's torso, deflected to batter that bulbous, badgerlike nose and elicited squeals of pain from lucky shots in the solar plexus and the kidneys. The only coherent thought Dougal was aware of was regret that he wasn't shod with steel.

It was weariness that stopped him. He gave Lee's groin a final kick, but it lacked the frenzied conviction of its predecessors. He found himself shaking uncontrollably as he stood there staring down at Lee and at the mud and the blood which covered him. *Oh, you bastard*, he mouthed at the squirming shape on the ground, *why did you make me do this?* His vision dissolved out of focus.

He realized his cheeks were wet with tears. *How long ago since I cried?*

He supposed he should look for the pistol – mustn't repeat the mistake of last time. A bullet in Lee's head and the business would be settled. It would be like a mercy killing, though he wasn't sure to whom the mercy was going to be shown.

Wiping his face with the back of his hand, Dougal turned and stared along the bank of the creek. He saw the Walther, its butt in the air and its barrel buried in a clump of grass; he had thrown it further than he realized – it must be a good ten yards away.

A brawny blue arm flashed out and flicked his feet from under him. For the second time that day, the coarse grass and iron-hard ground of the river bank rushed up to meet him. Before he had had time to absorb the first agony of impact, Lee crashed down on top of him. Dougal shrieked with pain and fear, a high, mindless keening which lost itself in the grey dome of the sky.

When his perceptions cleared, Dougal realized that Lee was sitting astride him, crushing his rib cage with his weight and driving his back into the unyielding ground. Lee's thumbs were locked into position underneath Dougal's jaw. He could see the stile out of the corner of his eye, the beginning of the path to comfort and normality. Which was now forever impassable.

Lee's thumbs relaxed their pressure fractionally, and hope leapt unreasonably within Dougal.

'Now,' said Lee calmly, in a voice which murdered

hope, 'that's it, you tricky little bugger.' The softness of the brogue was even more at odds than usual with the slablike face. Lee's nose was bleeding; the drops showered down on Dougal like crimson rain.

'That snotty girlfriend of yours has left you in the lurch, hasn't she? Stupid of her, in the long run. And you've tried to pull one too many fast ones on me. Don't you know who you're dealing with? God I hate you poncey-faced English with your snotty little accents and your mean little minds. I'm going to squeeze the life out of you, slowly, so you know just what's happening to you. With pauses, so you can beg me to stop. I'll maybe make it slightly easier, that little bit quicker, if you tell me what you've done with the diamonds.'

Lee's thumbs dug viciously into Dougal's neck, and then withdrew to give him the chance to speak.

As the unbearable choking sensation eased, a movement in the field beyond the stile pulled Dougal's eyes away from Lee's face. There was a man standing by the stile, his features weatherbeaten and partially obscured by a patriarchal beard. He wore a battered pork-pie hat and a voluminous waterproof. His left hand held a stout stick, his right was in the pocket of his coat. He radiated the surly, unassuming arrogance of a farmer on his own land – though Dougal knew this certainly wasn't old Spencer from Havishall village who rented the fields around here.

Dougal's teeth were chattering, but he forced the words out.

'There's a man behind you.'

The feeble whisper enraged Lee. His thumbs began to tighten.

'Oh, crap. That's the oldest . . .'

'What the hell are you doing on my land?' shouted the stranger. 'Here, boy,' he added over his shoulder and Dougal had a vision of a gigantic avenging hound rushing down the field to savage these trespassers on his master's territory.

Lee turned angrily. 'What the f—'

There was a crack, initially sharp but sending dull echoes bouncing over the estuary. Lee seemed to rise slightly, as if caught in the grip of a gust of wind. Then he slumped heavily down. Dougal became aware that there was something warm and sticky on his face. It was dark, lying here under Lee.

'Something along the lines of *Doctor Livingstone, I presume* would be appropriate at this juncture, wouldn't it?'

Dougal went rigid – not with mere physical fear this time, but with a terror which had more eerie origins. The newcomer's voice had replaced its flat East Anglian twang with the fruity vowels of middle-class English. That wasn't the trouble.

The voice belonged to James Hanbury.

21

A black tide of terror flooded over Dougal, engulfing his fragile certainties and suspending him in its oily slime, as helpless as a foetus in its amniotic fluid. Then, just as suddenly, the fear ebbed, sucked back into those hidden recesses of his mind where nightmares lay embalmed. In its place came words which shaped themselves and clustered in comforting, protective sentences.

The dead, they said, don't walk in the afternoon. Their methods of killing people are subtle and blood-less: they don't use bullets. Hanbury must be alive. And I am lying here under Lee, with the taste of his blood in my mouth.

Light and air returned to Dougal simultaneously, as Lee's body was rolled off him. The farmer stood over him, looking down with Hanbury's large, pale eyes and holding a brilliantly white handkerchief in his left hand.

'Here,' said James Hanbury. 'Take this. I expect you'd like to wipe your face.'

'How thoughtful,' said Dougal, because it was. 'How did you—?'

'Explanations later. Suffice it to say, you can't keep the good man down. But first, how had you planned to get rid of the debris?'

Dougal outlined the scheme that he had never really believed they would be in a position to implement. If they could get the bodies to the *Sally-Anne*, it would be possible, under the first cover of darkness, to ferry them just beyond the sandbank which partially blocked the mouth of the Alben estuary and drop them, suitably weighted, over the side. 'The tide will be ebbing fast by then and they will just be washed out into the North Sea.' In fact, Dougal knew, the tide would tug them north, up the coast, rather than east. He had worked out the details earlier today, picking his way with some difficulty through *Reed's Almanac* and the *Admiralty Tide Tables*.

'Very neat,' approved Hanbury. 'I suppose there's no chance of them being washed ashore inconveniently soon?'

Dougal shook his head. 'Not if they're weighted down. And it's a spring tide this evening, which should help.'

With sudden remorse he remembered Amanda, waiting cold and fearful on the *Sally-Anne*; he should have called her earlier. He shouted *Caroline* across the water. Hanbury stood there with his hands in his pockets, watching everything with bright interest.

When Amanda reached them, Hanbury allowed no

time for conversation or for coming to terms with the fact they were still alive and likely to remain that way for the forseeable future. Probably, Dougal reflected, the physical activity required was not only expedient but therapeutic.

The three of them laboured like a team of professional undertakers for nearly two hours. The light faded into darkness as they did so. First, two trips with the wheelbarrow were necessary – one for Tanner and the other for the contrivance which had killed him.

Hanbury surveyed the pendulum with amusement.

'I didn't really have time to see it properly on my way down. It's really very ingenious. Reminds me of Heath Robinson.'

Transporting Tanner to the estuary was extremely difficult, largely because of his length. His limbs, as yet unconfined by rigor mortis, flopped over the sides of the wheelbarrow, impeding their progress whenever they could.

Hanbury went through the pockets of both corpses on the river bank, putting what he found in a green plastic carrier bag which had come from Harrods. He straightened up and remarked that at least there was no need to go through their clothing and snip out the labels. It was all chain-store stuff. It usually was, these days.

The worst part of the operation was getting the cargo from the shore on to the *Sally-Anne*. Three trips in the dinghy were called for. Dougal didn't mind the rowing – it was transferring each load into the cockpit that was the difficulty. It was odd, too, how a part of Hanbury's assurance dropped away from him as he left the land. Dougal found that he was giving the orders during this stage, an experience he failed to relish.

Just before six, Dougal started the engine, slipped the mooring and set off towards the mouth of the estuary. Beside him in the cockpit, Hanbury was weighting Lee and Tanner with scrap iron from the stables. Dougal gave him a length of nylon rope and the CQR thirty-pound anchor to help him in his task; Malcolm would be furious. Amanda stood on the companionway, lighting Hanbury with a shaded torch.

Dougal kept their speed low, lit no navigation lights and hoped for the best. The sandbank and the sea lay one and a half miles downstream. Navigation wasn't a problem – he'd done this trip with Malcolm several times in darkness. If he kept the *Sally-Anne* on the north side of the estuary and steered steadily south-southeast, they would be all right. There were two farms on the north bank and one to the south – their lights were useful as a check. Lastly, as Dougal's eyes adjusted to the lack of light, he found he could make out the dim outlines of the bank on either side.

They crossed the sandbank at the mouth of the estuary and tipped the bodies into the shifting surface of the sea. Lee and Tanner slid soundlessly into the watery anonymity of their graves.

As they returned to the mooring, Hanbury and Amanda went below to boil a kettle and try to get warm.

Dougal could hear a murmur of voices from the saloon and, occasionally, the gurgle of Amanda's laughter. He lit a cigarette and stared at its glowing tip. It must be the hottest thing for miles around. Pity it wasn't rather larger.

When the *Sally-Anne* was back at her mooring, they sat around the table in the saloon with mugs of tea. Dougal and Amanda sat on one berth and Hanbury on the other. It was rather like an interview, Dougal decided, though he wasn't sure who was interviewing whom. He noticed, with a flicker of surliness which he tried to suppress, that his hands were bluer and his clothes were wetter than the others'.

Hanbury had removed his beard on the way back to the creek and borrowed some face cream from Amanda to expunge his weather-beaten complexion. His plump, unlined face beamed across the table at them, looking as prosperous and as vaguely distinguished as it had done when Dougal had last seen it, in Lambs Conduit Street.

'Well,' he said. 'I think that just about wraps up this phase of the operations. Certainly there's nothing else to worry about – Lee was as close as Delhi in the hot season. Only Tanner knew something of what he was after, and of course he's no longer a problem. Jolly good.'

Hanbury's tone, Dougal thought, was that of a commanding officer commending the actions of two promising subalterns at the close of a tricky campaign. The gentlemanly Machiavelli of the Lamb had changed into the equally well-bred colonel on active service. Or, to be more precise, the actor had changed roles. Hanbury wasn't like a real colonel, but like the public image of one, as publicized by hundreds of war films.

The clipped voice continued.

'We've got some mopping up to do, but we can safely leave that till later. We should take the Lancia up to London, I think, rather than have it found down in Suffolk. And we'll have to wait until daylight to tidy up the last traces of this afternoon's fracas.'

Dougal nodded. 'Yes. We'd anticipated that.'

'Now—' Hanbury glanced down at the table, as if he expected to find a neatly typed agenda awaiting his eyes '—your story or mine?'

'Yours,' said Amanda firmly. 'We're more in the dark than you are. Besides, you're dying to tell it to us.'

Hanbury chuckled and inclined his head towards Amanda, acknowledging the hit. Dougal suddenly wondered if women found him sexually attractive. He had the assurance and charm of a well-preserved chameleon which managed to imply, rightly or wrongly, a mysterious inner identity. Perhaps Hanbury appealed only to curious women.

'It has been something of a coup, I suppose. Though I can only claim part of the credit. Some of it must go to you two. And we've all been very lucky. Can I assume that Miss Jackson—'

'Amanda. Please.' They smiled at one another in the yellow lamp light.

'—Amanda knows the details of our previous meeting and my letter to you, William?'

'Yes. She knew everything from the beginning, actually.'

'Good. Well, I wrote that letter in perfect good faith. I left the hotel that evening in a taxi, but I must have been followed. They caught up with me when I was on foot – Tanner and another one of Lee's creatures whose name I don't know. It was the old technique – make it look like a mugging – the work of amateurs who went too far. They damaged me rather severely, rifled my pockets and left me for dead. I suspect they must have heard somebody coming – Lee's subordinates didn't make that sort of mistake usually. I was merely concussed and rather picturesquely damaged.' The skin around Hanbury's left eye was still slightly discoloured, Dougal noticed.

'Some good Samaritan called an ambulance and in the morning I woke up with a severe headache, swaddled in bandages.

'I lay in hospital for most of the day. I gave a false name and discharged myself in the evening. The hospital authorities weren't terribly happy about it – for one thing I hadn't been seen by the police, quite apart from my physical condition. But of course there was nothing they could do.

'That day in hospital was very valuable – it gave me

time to assess my position. The important thing was that Lee must assume me to be dead. His two hooligans were probably pretty sure they'd killed me, and they certainly wouldn't have allowed Lee to think there was a chance they might have failed.'

'How could you be so sure?' Amanda asked.

'I wasn't, at the time. It was just a reasonable assumption based on what I knew of the people concerned. And it happened to be right.

'Anyway, I decided to vanish. I have a little *pied-à-terre* in Acton – rather a squalid little bedsitter, as a matter of fact – which I maintain for just such emergencies as this. From there, I inserted a notice of my death in *The Times* and the *Telegraph*. (Did you know Lee took the *Telegraph?* One would have expected the *Sun* or the *Cork Examiner*. It just shows how complicated people's characters can be, doesn't it?) I must confess, I rather enjoyed seeing my name there. If Lee had any lingering doubts about my death, that must have settled it. Printing something makes it sound so authoritative, doesn't it?'

'It does,' said Dougal wryly. 'It certainly came as a shock to me.'

'I'm sure it did.' Hanbury was as bland as a glass of hot milk. 'Whereas it merely confirmed what Lee was disposed to believe already. I was gambling on that – that he wouldn't investigate any further.

'I knew Lee would try to trace Vernon-Jones's . . . bequests more openly than before, and I calculated it would be safe to follow him. He wouldn't be expecting me, for obvious reasons. Also—' for a moment Hanbury looked almost embarrassed, like a man caught playing with his son's toy soldiers '—I knew I could disguise myself quite competently – when I was at Oxford I was a member of O.U.D.S. and became fascinated by the art.' He coughed modestly. 'I was the elderly clergyman at the Crossed Keys.'

Dougal and Amanda gawked at him for a second, and then laughed. Hanbury looked mildly affronted. 'I don't see why—'

Dougal interrupted. 'You were perfect. We never had any idea . . . we called you the Church Dormant as a matter of fact.' He fell silent, trying to trace, in Hanbury's solid and regular features, the benign vacuity and shabby antiquity which had characterized their fellow guest.

'It's a matter of thinking oneself into the part,' explained Hanbury. 'Crockford's supplied me with a real name and a past, just in case anyone became inquisitive. The uniform helped, of course – the clerical suit and dog collar. People tend to notice a uniform rather than the person inside it, whether you're dressed as a traffic warden or wearing a white coat in a hospital. You slot into a category immediately, you see, which satisfies most people's curiosity at first glance.

'I came to Rosington on Thursday, the day before you did. As I expected, Lee was there already. I thought you would probably turn up that weekend, if you came at all.'

'Why didn't you contact me before? To let me know you were alive. We could have all worked together.'

Hanbury delicately answered the unspoken question which Dougal had asked. 'It wasn't because I didn't trust you – simply that I didn't know you well enough. I couldn't be sure how you would react to that letter. Also, to be candid, it was safest for me that no one should have the faintest suspicion that I was alive.' Hanbury's face suddenly crumpled into an expression of mischief; in an instant his features had rearranged themselves into the mask which they usually wore. When he spoke, he might have been talking to himself: 'It was a wonderful position, really. Lee believing he was the only contender left in the field; you two, my unwitting agents, able to operate without him knowing; and myself on the sidelines, an anonymous spectator with the ability to intervene when necessary. There are so many advantages in being technically nonexistent . . .'

Dougal felt a stillness creeping over him. He and Amanda had been fooled, right from the beginning. The entire painful charade had been set up for the benefit – and the amusement – of James Hanbury. And where did that leave them? He remembered the Emperor of China who played chess with condemned men as the pieces. What happened to those who were left on the board, in the courtyard, at the end of the game – were they shunted into a place of darkness until the next time that an imperial whim suggested a little intellectual diversion?

Dougal was aware that Hanbury was looking at him.

He shivered, for he knew with irrational certainty that the older man would realize the general trend of his thoughts. That, after all, was the central characteristic of the man – the power to insinuate himself into the workings of other people's minds. And to adapt himself to what he found there.

'Look,' said Hanbury, his face alive with intelligent concern, 'I know it must seem strange to you both – you probably think I was being criminally callous.' He paused and looked steadily at them. 'And, of course, I was – I won't deny it. But it paid off. You've had a few upsets and excitements, and so have I. We also have the happy ending: we're all richer than before and no bones broken. Dammit, it *worked*.'

Dougal stared into his empty mug, rotating it gently on the table. The last few drops of tea ran sluggishly among a black archipelago of bloated tea leaves. *No bones broken*: true enough. Gumper garotted, Cedric decomposing in a cellar; Tanner impaled with a rusty scythe; and Lee with a bullet in his head. Four people who had every right to be angry.

But there were other reasons why he was angry with Hanbury. First, he blamed him, irrationally perhaps, for the shocks and fears of the last few days – for the fact that he, Dougal, had been transported to the ultimate boundary of life, the frontier between living and dying. He had been forced to understand that he wasn't immortal.

Secondly, he had been made to discover that he was

capable of killing people himself. He couldn't go back to being the Dougal of two weeks ago; he was stuck with this uncomfortably new, unwanted self.

Instead of saying: You've turned me into someone else, you bastard, Dougal remarked in a level voice that he was upset because he and Amanda had nearly been killed. It was just a temporary reaction. Silly, wasn't it?

Hanbury bowed his head. 'I accept that.' Dougal suspected that he accepted a good deal more. 'And, as I like you both, I apologize.' There was silence in the little saloon, except for the slap of water against the hull of the *Sally-Anne*.

Dougal's anger evaporated, leaving the dregs of tiredness behind. Amanda put her hand on his and smiled at them both.

'James is right, William. No bones broken.'

Dougal was aware that they were soothing him like a fraught child. Suddenly, he laughed. Anger was a luxury he couldn't at present afford.

'Okay, tantrum over. Let's get on with your story, James. You'd reached Rosington.'

'Ah. Yes.' Hanbury pulled out his cigarettes and offered them round. The action seemed to jolt his memory. 'I ran into a series of problems which I should have foreseen. Superannuated clergymen don't smoke Gauloises. In fact, they don't do very much at all, which made it difficult for me to monitor what you two and Lee and Tanner were doing. I couldn't allow myself to walk rapidly or go into pubs and so forth. Mrs Livabed was unbearably solicitous – she would keep offering me cups of tea and hot-water bottles at the most inconvenient times.

'In some ways, it was a blessing in disguise – inaction on my part was essential. I could only hope to intervene once. I had to trust to your intelligence and Lee's cupidity. My faith in both was amply justified.'

Amanda frowned. 'Surely you must have found some way to know what we were all doing. Otherwise—'

'Only partially, I'm afraid. I overheard a certain amount. All of you were astonishingly careless in that respect.'

'There must be more to it than that,' said Dougal firmly. 'How did you know where to come this afternoon, let alone the right time?'

Hanbury deposited the coil of ash from the end of his cigarette on to the precise centre of the saucer which served as an ashtray.

'You may find it a little strange, but, as a matter of fact, that unfortunate man Tanner was for the last few days of his life working for me.'

22

'It was all rather unfortunate.' Hanbury stopped, leaving his mouth wide open. Sweat gleamed on his forehead. Dougal was momentarily reminded of a large, surprised fish. The man was genuinely embarrassed: events had slipped out of his control for an instant; the immaculate surface of his authority had received a minor dent.

Most unfortunate.

Amanda was the first to speak. 'That's ridiculous, James. Do you mean we needn't have killed him?' Her voice was sharp with strain.

'In theory, no; in practice, yes.' Hanbury smoothly regained the initiative. 'Let me explain.

'By Saturday evening I was getting desperate for information, so I took the rather drastic step of visiting your room . . . I assure you, I don't like prying into people's private lives, but I could think of no safe alternative.

'I slipped the lock while you were in the bar after dinner. To my consternation, I found Tanner there, conducting a rather inefficient search of your belongings. Not an easy situation to handle. I realized at once that my cover was exploded – and Tanner, once he started actually looking at me rather than my clothes, might conceivably recognize me. It was a simple choice, really – either he had to be silenced or persuaded to change his allegiance. The former would have been inconvenient – it wasn't the time or the place for stray bodies – so I decided to convert him instead.'

'It must have been one hell of a risk. How could you be sure that Tanner wouldn't change his mind?' Dougal was beginning to feel dazed. The gap between Hanbury's actions and the laws of probability was increasing. His left shoulder, which had been severely wrenched at some point during the tussle with Lee, was aching with dull persistence.

Hanbury solemnly waggled his index finger. 'The point you haven't grasped is Tanner's state of mind. He was a person of low intelligence – Lee used him because he was reliably vicious – and he was totally confused. First, he had been sent to search your room, which must have upset him. It wasn't his kind of job at all – I presume Lee thought he couldn't be trusted to keep you downstairs. Then he was interrupted by the last person he expected to see. And then he discovered that the old clergyman was someone he thought he had killed. It would have worried a greater mind than his.

'He became more distressed – and more biddable – as I pointed out the implications to him. Tanner wasn't so much scared of me, as terrified of what Lee would do to him when he found out that I wasn't dead. Lee was not a forgiving man. He controlled his subordinates by fear and they of course repaid him with hate. So all I had to do was persuade Tanner that working for me would be pleasanter and much more profitable. And it gave me a vital source of information.

'For one thing, he had the reference which Vernon-Jones had given Lee. Lee had thrown the card away after looking up the verse. Tanner grabbed it – he knew it was important in some way, that was all. When he produced it, I decided to swap it for your card – partly to alert you to the fact your room had been searched, and partly to – um, pool our knowledge.

'I knew at the time that the alliance with Tanner was a stopgap measure. If he had survived this afternoon, we should have had to kill him, you know. Don't look so shocked – he couldn't have been trusted to keep his mouth shut and, once the crisis was over, he would have become greedy. We wouldn't have been safe and nor would our profits. I *do* dislike not being able to trust people, but in this case it would have been rather like expecting Attila the Hun to join the Salvation Army.'

'Do you think Lee had any suspicion of this?' Dougal was rapidly reshuffling his memories.

'No. Definitely not. If that had been the case, Lee would have killed Tanner and come down here in a far less casual frame of mind. He would have believed we were knowingly working together, and taken a great many more

precautions. All along, he thought you two were insignificant – he felt he didn't have to concentrate as much as
usual. He categorized people too rigidly, which is fatal.
One should be ready to recognize new talent when it
appears.' He smiled at Amanda. 'I knew right away when
I met William that he had potential, and so have you. One
needs to chip away a couple of layers – inexperience and
outmoded, secondhand morality – before one can fully
realize it. But I think you've both done that.'

Oh, God, thought Dougal, I think we have.

Amanda steered Hanbury gently away from the
delights of generalizations. 'What happened after that on
Saturday?'

'Not much.' Hanbury had left Tanner on the landing,
on guard, and had searched their possessions without
finding anything of interest – 'Except, of course, confir-
mation that the manuscript pointed to Rosington.' Then
Tanner had warned him that the three of them downstairs were moving; he had hardly had enough time to
get safely away from the room.

'Sunday was undoubtedly my worst day. Tanner told
me that you and Lee had vanished and that he'd been
left here to look for some tramp or other who was acting
as an informer and keeping an eye on Bleeders Hall.
The man hadn't reported back on Saturday night – I
don't suppose you had anything to do with that?'

Dougal looked modest and said, 'Later. Do go on.'
He wasn't certain whether it would be wise to mention
the Cedric episode to Hanbury.

Hanbury, compelled to be inactive by his geriatric appearance and lack of information, had spent most of the day (apart from a necessary interval at divine service in the cathedral) in the hotel lounge. 'At last, in the evening, Lee turned up and I could tell at once that he was in a foul temper. When he was really angry, he didn't walk, he prowled. I can't tell you how relieved I was – I'd been imagining all sorts of unpleasant scenarios. Later on, Tanner told me what little he knew – that you'd pulled a fast one on Lee in a village somewhere south of Rosington and vanished. At this point I had no idea whether or not you'd got the diamonds – I rather thought not, I must confess.

'I spent Sunday night in the belief I'd lost control over the whole business – frankly, I'd no idea what to do next.'

But on Monday morning, Hanbury's luck had changed. Mrs Livabed had told everyone in the dining room that Mr Massey had telephoned Mr Lee, and Tanner had reported the substance of the call soon after breakfast.

'After that, it was plain sailing. I didn't know, of course, whether your offer of a deal with Lee was sincere or not – it didn't matter, because I knew he would cheat you in any case. I'm certain that he had no doubts of *your* sincerity – he wanted to believe you meant it, if only because it reinstated himself in his own eyes after Sunday's fiasco. And naturally, he would want to kill you both: he liked killing people and disliked loose ends – in your case, his interests coincided . . . I am going on, aren't I? I feel positively garrulous after living like a Trappist for the past week or so. Could I have a splash of brandy, d'you think . . .?

'Where was I? Your telephone call . . . I had to work on the assumption that Lee would continue to use Tanner – I was reasonably sure he would, because killing you and disposing of your bodies – forgive my bluntness, my dear – would be far easier physically with his support, and Lee wouldn't have wanted to bring in an outsider at this stage. I may be casting aspersions on Lee's memory (though that wouldn't be an easy thing to do), but I suspect he may have intended to get rid of Tanner as well, once you two were out of the way . . .

'After lunch, on Monday, I left Rosington and my clerical persona behind and nipped back to town. I picked up a car and these agricultural clothes and booked myself into a pub on the main road between Chelmsford and Colchester. Tanner rang me this morning with the rendezvous details. I followed him and Lee at a discreet distance this afternoon. The rest you know.'

Hanbury sat back and poked a well-manicured finger around the inside of his crumpled Gauloises packet. He extracted the last battered cigarette it held with a grunt of satisfaction. Dougal's eyes involuntarily followed Hanbury's hand as he raised it to his mouth. The man's lips were fleshy, but smugly compressed, like those of a child with a secret.

It was Amanda who put into words the question which was awkwardly shaping itself in Dougal's mind.

'James, why didn't you come here as soon as you knew where we were? We could have planned Lee's reception together. It would have been far less dangerous.'

'I'm not surprised you asked that question,' said Hanbury in a guarded voice which implied that he rather wished she hadn't. 'Of course, I would have liked to, but I had to take account of the possibility that Lee would change his plans – and the only way Tanner could have warned me of that was by phoning the pub. So obviously I had to stay there as long as possible.'

It was a reasonable explanation, Dougal thought, but then Hanbury was adept at making things sound reasonable.

Dougal jerked his attention away from increasingly gloomy speculations. Remember, he told himself, we still hold the ace – access to the diamonds. No point in panicking. He brought himself back to the lamp-lit saloon, a gently rocking cradle, blue with cigarette smoke. The wind must be blowing up a bit. Hanbury was watching him curiously. Again, Dougal had the uneasy feeling that Hanbury was watching his mind as much as his face.

'Ah, yes, one thing more.' Hanbury stubbed out his cigarette with the graceful economy of effort of the leading man in a drawing room comedy. 'Both of you are probably wondering why I didn't intervene sooner. I was about a mile behind the Lancia, navigating with the help of an Ordnance Survey map. Lee was far too old a hand for me to risk getting closer. When I reached

the lodge gates, I couldn't come roaring up the drive –
I had to park the car up the lane and then walk up to
the house. By the time I got to the stables, only Tanner
was left. I came down to the river as quickly as I could
– I got there just as Lee was describing how he would
kill you . . . his imagination and vocabulary seemed
equally trite. *I* thought it was rather well timed, all things
considered.'

Dougal nodded. Surprisingly well? Amanda yawned,
as if this grubbing about on the border between detail
and speculation was tedious to her. She apologized and
stretched herself as unselfconsciously as a cat when
waking up.

'Now,' she said briskly, 'you'll want our side of the
story.'

Amanda did most of the talking. She seemed unusually
vivacious – Dougal thought that their moods at present
were like people facing one another at opposite ends of
a seesaw; he was filled with a great longing to annihi-
late himself with alcohol, but put the kettle on for more
tea instead.

By tacit agreement, they left out one or two episodes
– or rather Dougal did, for he purposely took over the
story at times. For example, he said he had seen Cedric
at Bleeders Hall, and the tramp had run off into the
night. He was deliberately vague about their stay in
Cambridge – he could see no reason to bring Philip
Primrose to Hanbury's attention.

Hanbury was flatteringly complimentary. Dougal was unwillingly aware that the older man's approval gave him pleasure. He asked several questions about the stones, which Dougal did his best to answer, and laughed aloud when he heard where they had been hidden.

'I sometimes wondered whether Vernon-Jones nurtured a senile passion for Katie Munns. Though one imagines his lust would have been entirely cerebral. She's quite attractive, isn't she?' Amanda nodded mechanically and Hanbury continued, 'in terms of Rosington, anyway. Not much competition.'

Malcolm engaged Hanbury's interest as well. 'Such a pity he should have run into difficulties. Perhaps we can help him when he comes out.'

Dougal had expected the conversation to move to their plans for the immediate future, once everyone had been brought up to date with the present. Hanbury, however, began to talk of himself, as if he suddenly felt the subject needed an airing.

'One seems to have this strange yearning to be one respectable person, settled in one particular place. It must be a symptom of middle age, I suppose.' He thought he might buy an apartment in a small town within easy reach of Paris and hang up his collection of old school ties for a while. Dougal had a vivid picture of the nomadic life – in terms of identity as well as geography – which Hanbury accepted as normal. Hanbury? The name had only an algebraic reality: a convenient symbol for an unknown quantity.

Dougal's mind wandered from what Hanbury was saying to how he was saying it. He visualized it set up in type, printed on a page. He counted the semi-colons and the places where split infinitives were conspicuous by their absence.

While Hanbury enthused about Gallic civilization, Dougal's attention feverishly flitted over the doubts and difficulties ahead. He felt smothered by exhaustion, and past the stage where he could think rationally. It's balanced, he thought vaguely, between the keys in my pocket and the weapons in the Harrods bag on the bunk beside Hanbury. Both parties had some right – in a context where 'right' was little more than an acknowledgement of shared interests – to a share of the diamonds. Would Hanbury be content to divide them fairly?

Hanbury's air of being an honourable privateer on the high seas of public morality was assumed. It was one more mask, its expression moulded to reassure Dougal and Amanda. Dougal was certain of this: he used the same technique himself – the difference between him and Hanbury was only one of degree. He must bear in mind that Hanbury was wooing them now – not their affections but their confidence.

'Look,' said Amanda. 'Isn't it time we talked about what we're going to do next? We've got these diamonds to turn into money, and after we've decided how to do that, I'd like to go and have dinner somewhere. I'm starving.'

'You're quite right, Amanda,' said Hanbury. 'On both

counts. Assuming we're all in favour of a quick, easy sale, our best bet's Amsterdam. I know the city quite well, so arranging the details wouldn't be a problem. They're unmounted stones, which helps . . . come to think of it, as they haven't actually been stolen, we should get a better price than I'd anticipated. Of course, it's impossible to have an idea of the size of our profit until their value has been fixed.

'As to the method of payment, one can usually take it either in cash (American dollars are the most popular) or a cheque on a Swiss bank . . . the latter method would in fact be more profitable: otherwise the, um, cash discount would operate against us. Do either of you have Swiss accounts?'

Dougal and Amanda shook their heads with becoming gravity.

'Then you should. Very convenient in every way, particularly as you may wish to use its facilities again one day.'

'And how should we divide the money?' asked Dougal.

Hanbury grinned, which made him look young and endearing (he probably wasn't more than forty anyway, thought Dougal, that impression of maturity is just another mask). 'That's an awkward one, isn't it? You two probably think straight thirds all round would be equitable. Naturally enough, I feel my claim is greater, and that I should get at least half. We should deduct all our expenses from the total beforehand, of course.'

'Let's compromise,' said Amanda suddenly. 'It's stupid

to quibble at this point. Why don't you take forty per cent and we take thirty per cent each? Or you take fifty per cent. I really don't care that much. I'd much rather argue about the division of these notional thousands over a real dinner.'

'How splendidly pragmatic,' said Hanbury. Dougal laughed.

'The diamonds are in Cambridge,' she went on, 'and one of us has to be there to collect them. I think it'd be best if we did it tomorrow morning. One of us – you'd be best, William – could stay here and tidy up.' Dougal had a vision of him hoovering bloodstains from the coach house floor. 'Two of us will have to go to Cambridge, because the Escort has to go back there. If James and I sorted things out there, we could be back to collect you by mid-afternoon.'

'And then to Amsterdam?' asked Hanbury.

'Why not? We'd have to collect our passports in London, of course.'

'Fine,' said Hanbury, stroking his chin. 'We could drop the Lancia there, too. We could fix the air tickets at Cambridge and pick them up at the airport.'

Amanda turned to Dougal. The excitement in her face made her astonishingly pretty. 'We'll do that, shall we?' She squeezed his hand.

Dougal said, 'Yes,' because he couldn't think of anything else to say. His earlier doubts about Hanbury seemed absurd, cobwebs spun from insubstantial fears in the privacy of his own mind through which Amanda crashed without even knowing of their existence. The last few days had made him overanxious, he decided. She trusted Hanbury enough to go with him to Cambridge. It was a matter of assessing feelings, in the end, feelings about Hanbury. And Amanda was good at making that sort of judgement, where the opposite sex was concerned, at any rate. She did it naturally, too, without any of those tortuous and frequently ineffectual inquisitions which so often muddied his own feelings about other people. If she trusted Hanbury, then he should trust her intuition.

'Good.' Hanbury looked relieved. 'Now we can enjoy ourselves. I booked myself a room by phone at the Crimford Hall Hotel this morning—'

'That place near Albenham?' asked Dougal.

'That's the one. It's got quite a reasonable restaurant. You could probably spend the night there, if you wanted to. It's hardly likely to be crowded at this time of year.'

'No, I don't think so.' Dougal spoke quickly and without thinking. To leave the *Sally-Anne* at this point would be desertion of a kind. He noticed that Amanda had opened her mouth to say something, but closed it as he got in first. Damn, he thought, I should have asked her first. But it was too late. Hanbury was saying he would change in his car and pick them up in the stable yard in half an hour, if that suited them.

'I've got *nothing* to wear,' said Amanda. By the sound of her voice, this realization brought her closer to panic than anything else in the last five days had managed.

23

'Good cleaning,' said Hanbury with a grin. 'We'll bring you a present from Cambridge.'

He looked resplendent in the early morning sunlight, Dougal thought. He was wearing the raglan overcoat and pinstripe suit, the same outfit in which he had garotted Gumper. Confidence and cleanliness shone from his face in equal proportions. Not unlike a middle-aged Apollo, dressed for a day's work at the family firm in the city. Amanda, in a black suit, cream silk blouse and high-heeled black leather boots, lived up to this vision of urban magnificence.

Dougal, on the other hand, in jeans, reefer jacket and Wellington boots, felt seedy and out of place: the ugly duckling or (to put a more hopeful construction on it) Cinderella.

Hanbury climbed into his dark green Rover and started the engine. Amanda kissed Dougal lightly on the cheek and turned towards the Escort, which was parked beside the other car in front of the pockmarked facade of Havishall Place.

He closed the door for her and bent as she rolled down the window.

'Take care,' they said simultaneously. 'I will,' continued Amanda. 'Back about four, probably. I expect we'll have lunch somewhere. Don't worry. We're over the hill, now.'

Dougal smiled. 'Yes, I know. See you.' Hurry back, I love you, he wanted to add, as the window slid back into its rubber lining at the top of the frame. But the words wouldn't come.

The cars moved in procession down the drive, slowly because of the ruts and potholes. Dougal wriggled his toes in his boots, to remind himself of their existence, and stared at the place where the drive curved out of sight, until the sound of the engines had merged with the morning silence.

Tidying up took less time than he had anticipated, largely because Lee and Tanner had been laudably moderate in the quantities of their blood which they had allowed to be spilled.

Once it was done, he found that tidying had become an obsession. He spent an hour pottering around the *Sally-Anne,* washing up, coiling ropes and pumping the bilges.

At eleven, his energy began to falter. He had put the kettle on to boil some time ago, with the plan of scrubbing the decks. Now it seemed much wiser to use the water for a pot of coffee.

The Harrods bag was still on the starboard berth. Dougal examined its contents; Hanbury had glanced through them last night, but he had taken nothing.

First, he looked at the guns. Lee's *was* a Walther PPK. Tanner had toted heavier metal – a short-barrelled Smith and Wesson Magnum which was nearly twice the weight of the Walther. It couldn't have been comfortable to carry. Perhaps it gave Tanner a sense of security, or perhaps he only used it on expeditions to lonely country places where its size would have been an asset rather than an encumbrance. Dougal preferred not to admit it but he rather liked guns. Not as weapons, but as mechanical instruments which were small enough to understand.

He swung the cylinder open and emptied the cartridges on to the table. The six bullets were soft-nosed, with small slits at their points: homemade dum-dums. It was fortunate that Tanner had never had a chance to use them.

What else? There were two sets of keys. Lee also had a cheque book – from the Willesden Green branch of the National Westminster. There was a clump of paper handkerchiefs, which had come from Tanner's pockets; at least his cold was cured now.

The men had both worn chunky identification bracelets of eighteen-carat gold. Neither of the plaques had been engraved with the name of its owner, so perhaps they were merely bracelets. Hanbury should get one for himself and have ALIAS engraved on it.

Only the wallets were left. Tanner's contained a photograph of a tired-looking woman and a card, more dog-eared than the photograph: *Sonia. Private Modelling* and a London telephone number. Dougal pulled out the cash and tossed the wallet to one side.

Lee's was less revealing – much more cash, numerous credit cards, but nothing which was personal to the man.

Dougal put the empty wallets and the handkerchiefs in the stove and shovelled the rest back into the Harrods bag. The only exception he made was the cash – there must have been about 600 pounds – which he put with the money that Hanbury had sent him. He felt obscurely guilty, as if he had been reading someone's diary.

Boredom now threatened: Dougal could sense its approach before it arrived, like knowing that a harmless-looking cloud was not really drifting across the sky, but purposefully negotiating its way to a position which would block the sun's direct rays from the earth. His eyes followed the blue and aimless meanderings of the smoke from his cigarette. One wisp curled round his battered briefcase which stood on the chart table by the companionway.

On impulse, Dougal pulled the case over to the berth where he was sitting. He took out the photograph which had triggered off the whole affair. The print was crumpled and grubby by this time, but the clarity of that elegant, fluid script shone through the distortions of time and reproduction. Very pretty, he conceded, but not worth any more effort. The university and his thesis had retreated into the past at some unnoticed point during the last five days. The thought of going back to them was as unlikely as being seventeen again.

It was ironic that Caroline Minuscule had been the means of jolting him out of one era and into another. The future seemed crowded with potential novelties, whose outlines remained tantalizingly vague. Maybe he and Amanda would marry and live abroad for a while.

Where would spring be most enjoyable? Dougal toyed with a Tunisian villa for a moment, before rejecting it on the grounds that Amanda might find the Arab response to Western women rather irritating. Perhaps Greece would be better, despite the monotony of diet and the language barrier. And it would be pleasant to see what the country was like before the package holidays saturated it in summer.

It would be wise to think of the future as well . . . perhaps they could invest some of the money and become graciously cosmopolitan capitalists. Must ask Hanbury.

The dial of his watch flashed up at him as he stretched to slide the case back on the chart table. Midday. The others wouldn't be back for at least four hours. With the boredom had come its antidote: tiredness. He decided to take a nap. Even the coffee seemed to have made him sleepy. Kicking off his Wellingtons, Dougal slid fully dressed into the sleeping bag.

It smelt of Amanda.

★ ★ ★

If there were dreams floating through his mind, Dougal failed to notice them. He woke at half-past three, effort-lessly gliding back to consciousness. The siesta had done nothing but refresh him; there was no trace of the muzzi-ness which sleeping during the day usually produced.

For a second, he panicked: perhaps a shout from the shore had awakened him. He levered himself up on one elbow and peered through the grimy glass of the porthole. There was no one on the river bank, of course. Amanda and Hanbury wouldn't be back for at least half an hour.

He fought his way out of the sleeping bag, which had wound itself lovingly around his limbs, loath to let them go. His Wellingtons sprawled under the table like stranded amphibians. Even the rubber seemed dank as he pulled them on.

The stale taste of sleep clung in his mouth, so he ran a toothbrush quickly round his teeth. The heavily filled ones at the top right of his jaw responded with a twinge of pain. When had a dentist last seen them? He put a kettle on for some tea and stood watching it for a moment, scratching his head and wondering what to do while he waited.

Reading was the answer. Malcolm had a paperback copy of *Eminent Victorians*, whose pages he was system-atically using as lavatory paper because he disapproved of Lytton Strachey. Cardinal Manning and most of Florence Nightingale had been flushed away, but Dr Arnold and General Gordon had so far survived intact.

But Dr Arnold failed to absorb Dougal. He merely succeeded in reminding him of Rosington School, a line of thought which naturally enough led to the events of the last few days.

Just before four, a movement on the bank caught his eye. Dougal tossed Strachey on to the chart table and hurtled up the companionway to the cockpit. As he reached the open air, a voice from ashore bellowed, 'Ahoy!'

He swung round and stared towards the land. A sense of something wrong was crawling over him before he saw the squat figure gesticulating beside the stile, before he recognized who it was.

Philip Primrose.

Dougal rowed rapidly up the creek towards Pee-Pee. He had left his gloves behind and forgotten to fasten his jacket; he was dimly aware that the cold was cutting into him. What the hell was Philip doing here? Had Amanda and Hanbury been forced to alter their plans? Nothing, surely, could have gone really wrong. Underneath the questions, he felt deflated – expecting Amanda and getting Primrose was like finding two slices of cold Spam on your plate when your nostrils had been quivering to the smell of roasting beef for the past two hours. Maybe the others were up at the house . . . but why bring Madame Pee-Pee, for God's sake?

The bows of the dinghy grated on the mud. Dougal splashed into the shallow water, sending sludgy eddies perilously close to the top of his boots. He scrambled up the bank and found himself smiling at Primrose.

'Hullo, Bill.' Philip had swathed his college scarf around much of his neck and face and topped the assembly with a brand-new deerstalker hat. Between the two, his nose protruded pinkly, giving him the appearance of an invalid rabbit.

'Nice to see you, Philip,' replied Dougal with cautious politeness. How much did he know? 'D'you want to come on board? It's freezing out here.'

'Yes, that is, no . . . about the boat, I mean. As a matter of fact, I'm rather prone to seasickness. Do you mind?' Primrose sounded ashamed, as if he felt the failing was incompatible with his temporary character as a secret service agent.

'Shall we walk up and down?' suggested Dougal, smothering his impatience. Primrose nodded, and they began to pace self-consciously along the line of the water.

'Well,' murmured Pee-Pee (in case of hidden microphones?), 'congratulations, old man. I gather that between you you've pulled off a pretty startling coup, by any standards.'

'Not at all . . . and what we have done, we couldn't have managed without you.' Whatever it was that Primrose thought they'd done, Dougal tried to align his features into an expression of modest nobility.

'Amanda came to see me around lunchtime, with that chap from You Know Where. No introductions were made, of course – better that way. Though, oddly enough, he did let drop that he believed we shared an alma mater. Small world, eh?'

Dougal, recognizing the unmistakable Hanbury touch, said that he supposed it was.

'I didn't know they still bred that sort of mandarin type at Whitehall. Reassuring. Amanda said (when he was out of the room) that he reports directly to the minister, though that can't be news to you . . . it's a bit muddy here – shall we turn round?'

Primrose finally reached the reason for his presence. Something had come up, it seemed, which forced Amanda and Hanbury to go to London immediately. 'Nothing to worry about. They said you'd understand.' Amanda had asked him to deliver a small package as soon as possible. He, Pee-Pee, had only been too glad to oblige a lady . . .

It was a thick manilla envelope with Dougal's name on the front in Amanda's looping handwriting. It reminded him of that other envelope, the one Hanbury had sent him.

Dougal thanked Primrose and said he mustn't keep him. 'I'll have to attend to this at once, I'm afraid.' He waved the envelope. Perhaps the excuse would turn out to be true. Primrose opened his mouth, and then closed it as his compulsive curiosity about the envelope's contents was beaten back by his belief in the necessity to be discreet.

They walked back to the stable yard where Philip had left the Escort. Amanda, he said, had told him that he could have the use of the car for the rest of the fortnight it had been hired for. Wasn't that nice? The sky was darkening and he kept swivelling his eyes about, in the manner of an early Christian martyr, uncertain where the lions were.

Dougal tried to reassure him. 'I think the danger is over now.' Then, realizing that Primrose was probably enjoying the drama, he added, 'Mainly, that is. We can't be absolutely sure for a day or two.' That should keep him happy. It was possible, he thought, to argue that conning people could be an altruistic exercise, in some respects. Pee-Pee's memories of this business would certainly be happier than his own.

In the stable yard, they shook hands with becoming gravity.

'I'll be seeing you back at college, I hope?' Primrose's voice sounded hoarse with all the whispering he had been doing.

'Next week, probably.' Dougal's attention had wandered to his hand, which was feeling the envelope in his pocket. It could well contain a wad of money. But why? 'We must all have dinner together when this is over. I'll be in touch.' Could an ally of Lee's have appeared from the blue to threaten them at this stage? The police?

He waved as the Escort jerked towards the drive like a mechanized kangaroo. Primrose's departure, though desirable on all counts, felt like a desertion when it actually happened. Dougal found himself running through the dusk towards the creek, as if he was fleeing from the desolation of Havishall Place to the company of the almost human *Sally-Anne*.

By the time he reached the river bank, his heart was throbbing in his chest, generating a painful warmth throughout his body.

His mind, however, was blank and cold. He rowed across to the *Sally-Anne*, trying to fill the emptiness with little, harmless thoughts: it was blowing up again tonight – he must check that everything was secure on deck; he might have that can of pheasant soup soon – hadn't they bought some claret in Ipswich?

In the saloon, he tossed the envelope on the table and busied himself with lighting the lamp, straightening the sleeping bag and pouring himself some brandy and water. Well, why not?

Then he slit his way into the envelope and extracted its contents, making sure that he missed nothing.

There were two piles of banknotes, secured with thick elastic bands, and a sheet of foolscap paper, folded once. Dougal lit a cigarette with exaggerated deliberation, as if he faced an audience of millions. He pushed the money to one side and opened the letter.

Amanda's familiar scribble covered most of the paper. He had never had a letter from Amanda before. It was written in biro – the familiar green Bic which she always carried.

William darling,

There's been a change of plan – hope you don't mind. James & I are going straight to A'dam from here. Could you lose the Lancia in London, and wait there till we join you? J. says all 3 of us going abroad might be rather cumbersome – a slicker operation wd be better.

It's good timing for us, too. I've been trying to say

this for a while, but it's not been easy and then there was all this excitement, which put a sort of wrong perspective on us – made us seem closer than we are, or anyway more than I want to be with anyone at present. I mean, next thing you'll be wanting to marry me!! I just don't feel ready to settle down. Another thing: the last few days have changed everything somehow – & maybe we both need time to sort it out.

Don't feel bad about it, please. Better be honest about it now, & see what happens in the future, than grind on together. I need to be with someone like James, who doesn't make claims, for a while. Father complex, you'll think, but it's more than that. Actually, all that's happened so far is this weird biochemical click & that's quite enough to be going on with.

See you when we get back to London. Enjoy yrself. J. sends the enclosed to keep you solvent. He says it may take a while to arrange the sale, but not to worry.

Love (lots of it),

Amanda.

P.S. Cd you drop by Chiswick at some point & water the plants? If you want to write (please do) send it Poste Restante, A'dam.

Dougal read the letter once more. His mind understood its contents perfectly, but he still found it difficult to digest. *But this shouldn't happen to me.* So Hanbury had pulled one last surprise. Perhaps the man was addicted to the sensations which surprises caused, and continued to produce them out of habit, like a conjuror persisting in turning silk handkerchiefs into doves long after the audience had gone home.

But that ignored Amanda's part in it.

He gulped the rest of the brandy and poured some more into his cup. It dissolved, or at least weakened, the numbness inside. Tears pricked behind his eyelids, though he knew he wouldn't cry.

There was a terrible temptation, he thought, to wrap himself in a warm, smothering cloud of self-pity. Not only would it be easy, but it would also be the customary reaction for situations like this. The hard core of his mind refused to let him take the option. At least when he had found Gumper's body, he hadn't needed to bother about reactions – his body had decided that for him – he had been sick.

Dramatic solutions danced through his mind, attractive in their meretricious finality. He could take the *Sally-Anne* out into the North Sea and open her stop cocks. He could go after Hanbury and Amanda with Tanner's Smith and Wesson.

No, Dougal told himself, this was wrong: he was wondering what he should be feeling, rather than what he actually felt. But his true feelings were so difficult to catch that he suddenly doubted the value of pursuing them . . . why bother? Amanda had left him, just as certainly as he had killed Cedric (though perhaps less irrevocably).

A squall of rain hit the *Sally-Anne,* setting the boat

skipping at her moorings: the noise of the rain drowned the silence.

Tomorrow he would go to London, pay off his debts and get a flight to somewhere warm. He would write to Amanda later. He would take Philip out to dinner – the old-fashioned grandeurs of Simpson's in the Strand would be suitable, perhaps, provided there weren't too many American tourists – and tell him how pleased the minister was. In May, he would be back in England to meet Malcolm; maybe they would be able to work out a congenial way to make a living – he couldn't face going back to finish the university term.

He poured himself another three fingers of brandy. A flicker of tipsy excitement shot through him. Whether or not he got his share of Vernon-Jones's legacy, the search for it seemed to have increased his options immeasurably, by removing some of those strange taboos which hedge people in . . . he now had more unmentionable details for his curriculum vitae.

Swaying to his feet, Dougal crossed to the galley to put the kettle on. He'd had enough thinking for the time being. He would go to bed with a pot of tea, the rest of the bottle of brandy and Lytton Strachey.

And let things settle in their own way.

Amanda's letter on the table, her clothes strewn like discarded intimacies on the starboard berth, mocked him. But only if he chose to listen.

He wondered what Caroline Munns would do when *she* grew up.

'They say you always remember the first time, the first one. William Dougal was the hero of my first novel. He was my first character. At the time I thought he had quite a lot in common with his creator. As time went by, however, Dougal became a multi-murderer and a louche private investigator of low moral fibre; and I like to think that any resemblance has decreased to the point of invisibility.'

Andrew Taylor

Dougal returns in

Waiting for the End of the World
September 2007

Our Fathers' Lies
December 2007

An Old School Tie
March 2008